JOHN

KRIS MICHAELS

KMRW LLC

Copyright © 2020 by Kris Michaels

All rights reserved.

No part of this book may be reproduced in any form or by any electronic or mechanical means, including information storage and retrieval systems, without written permission from the author, except for the use of brief quotations in a book review.

❦ Created with Vellum

CHAPTER 1

John Smith leveled his M-4 and stared down the sights before he dropped it and slapped a clip of ammunition into the receiver. With practiced ease, he drew the charging handle back and chambered a 5.56-millimeter round. His thumb grazed the firing indicator to ensure it was on 'Safe' before he shouldered the weapon. He grabbed his backpack by the carrying handle.

"You ready for this?" Luke Wagner asked his question as he approached. He'd met the operative he knew as Tempest at the Rose when he'd installed machinery and trained Joseph on how to use the passport press. When he was there, he'd run the Rose's training courses with Luke. He'd never beaten the man, but there was a thin margin in his defeat.

He squared his shoulders. They'd done this dance four times before and they'd found nothing. The variables of combining the numbers as latitude and longitude were numerous. Thankfully, they'd eliminated several as nonplayers without sending a team. It was safe to say there was no enemy stronghold at the bottom of the Marianas Trench. They had one more location to search after this one. The reality that this could be another failed mission before it even started weighed on him, but he'd follow it through to the end. "I am."

Luke rolled his shoulders and cracked his neck before he spoke again. "Mind me asking a question?"

"Shoot." He'd answer what he could.

"Who is she to you?" Tempest dropped his snowshoes and took a seat on the log John had just vacated.

"My sister." Tempest raised his eyebrows, and John chuckled before he clarified, "We both worked for a certain agency doing certain things. The agency decided we were... liabilities. She was killed and they tried to do the same thing to me."

"So, what are you hoping to find?" Tempest talked to the ground as he attached the wide pad to his boot.

John sighed and shook his head, staring at the

frozen forest ahead of him. "Answers, I guess. Why? Who ordered it? I'm officially dead, so the inquires that were made by Guardian had to be subtle. I've moved on. Hell, I learned how to manage a ranch and I'd never seen a cow before I showed up in South Dakota."

Tempest laughed and tossed his other snowshoe down. "Amazing what we can become when we need to."

"Thing is, I like it. Maybe better than anything I've ever done."

"Done a lot?" Tempest retied his boot after snapping his snowshoe on, just like he'd done to the previous boot.

"More than you could possibly imagine." John snorted. As a child, he'd been a master grifter, grew up, got caught, and became a sniper for his country before he and Lori worked designing deep-cover identifications. His sister had introduced him to *that* career. Lori was also the reason he'd left the service. His father had been murdered and she needed him.

"I can imagine a lot. You're not the only one with a past, although with the protection orders we have from the very top of the agency, your past must be very interesting. Any wife or kids out there?" Luke stood up and grabbed his M-4 from where he'd propped it.

He appreciated the sudden change of subject. He wasn't going to talk about his past, and Luke had just informed him he wasn't going to press. He chuckled, "Nope. You?"

"Wife, or soon to be." Tempest smiled and winked at him.

"Well then, you watch your ass out there today."

"Damn straight, and right back at you. If I bring you home with so much as a scratch, I think the Kings would string me up."

John snorted. "Frank just wants his ranch manager back."

"If that's what you think, you don't know those people. They are all about family. Everyone who works for them is important, but those they've taken under their wing? Nah, son, your sister may be gone, but you've got more family now than you'll ever need."

"Huh." Well, that piece of the puzzle slid into place.

"What?" Tempest looked at him.

"Makes sense now."

"Again, what?"

John spoke the words he'd heard numerous times

but hadn't really assigned a meaning to. "Whatever it takes."

"Because we're family. Yeah, that's right. We'll do whatever it takes for as long as it takes." Luke turned and nodded to the team's leader. "Skipper, we're set."

Travis motioned and the men moved away from the vehicles. As they worked their way northeast from the dead-end road just past Keewtinohk Converter Station in Gillam, a small town in Manitoba, they followed the Nelson River. The cold had solidified the snow. Still, the snowshoes were a necessity due to the drifts. He fell into formation as they moved silently through the river valley. They moved at a steady but relaxed pace. Sweating in the bitter cold was a recipe for disaster and a rookie mistake the men of this squad wouldn't make. John settled into a shuffle and let his mind wander back to the event that had pulled him from the obscure safety where he'd been existing.

The mare's dark chestnut coat shivered under his fingers. He followed her swelling belly with his hand and talked to her to keep her calm. "You are going to be a good momma." A soft muzzle reached back, looking for the carrot she knew he had for her. He couldn't wait to see what kind of foal she'd throw. He'd bet anything the babe would be big and beautiful, just like her. Yeah, come June she'd be a fine mom. He chuckled and pulled the carrot pieces from his back pocket and held them in a flat hand for her to take. The loneliness he lived in was lessened by Dancer's affection. It had been a long road to get to this point. Not only for the horse but for him. He came to this ranch under the guise of assuming the role as ranch manager. Manager—hell, he'd never seen a horse, cow, or chicken in person. But he put on the cloak provided for him by Guardian and disappeared into the long, hard workdays where he battled the elements and thousand-pound beef critters. The animals, work, and protection given to him here on the South Dakota ranch had saved him, and because it had, he'd dedicated himself to learning everything he could about ranching. Frank Marshall was one hell of a teacher.

He grabbed the curry comb and gave Dancer some more attention. The mare's neck stretched out and her upper lip danced when the brush hit her spot.

"You're spoiling that mare."

Frank's voice from the stall door snapped his attention from his musings and the horse. "She's a survivor, she deserves it." He'd rescued the horse as a colt. She'd been caught up in barbed wire, the scars were still visible, and she was wild as hell, but when he'd seen her at the live-

stock auction, it was love at first sight. He recognized the fear in her eyes and her desire to escape. They were kindred spirits, both forced into a place they didn't understand, and they both needed to learn how to adapt in order to exist.

"Your plane only landed ten minutes ago." He gave the horse one last stroke with the comb and turned to his boss and friend. "What's wrong?"

Frank reached into his pocket and pulled out a piece of taffy. He extended his hand into the stall and John shook his head. He knew that gesture meant there were either words of wisdom or words of caution coming. Since he heard the plane bringing the crew back to the ranch land about ten minutes ago, it was safe to infer Frank was not here to check up on what he'd been doing for the last two weeks. "I'll take my straight talk without the sugar coating."

Frank pushed his ball cap back on his head and nodded. "Guardian has found something."

John stepped out of the stall and shut the door behind him. "Regarding?"

"Lori."

John's gut dropped to the hardpacked dirt beneath his feet. It took two attempts to draw a deep breath. He'd watched his sister die in a car bomb. A bomb planted by someone within the CIA. "What about her?"

"That's just it. They aren't sure. Her name and some numbers were found embedded in code. The numbers could be longitude and latitude."

"Where was the information embedded?"

"Programming code." Frank held up a hand. "Don't know much more than that."

"I've got to go." His gaze danced around the barn before it settled on Frank, although he saw nothing but the vision of that ball of flames as the car his sister had gotten into exploded.

"I know it. The aircraft is being refueled. Come back when you're ready. This is your home." Frank extended his hand. "It may well be nothing."

He nodded and took his friend's hand. "I know, but still, if there is any information on who killed Lori..."

"I understand. Get yourself packed. Jason said the same protocol is in effect."

John nodded. In Washington D.C., his plane would be taxied into a hanger, the doors would be closed and wouldn't open until he was sequestered inside a blacked-out SUV. No one would know he was in town. Which kept him alive. He glanced back at Dancer.

"Don't worry. I'll spoil her while you're gone," Frank chuckled when the horse stuck its head out of the stall and nudged his shoulder. "Although, she's going to miss you."

John turned and gave his horse one more pat on the

JOHN

neck. "I'll be back, girl." He zipped up his coat and grabbed his cap. Frank nodded toward the door. "My truck's outside. Take it and leave it at the airstrip. I'll have someone bring it back to this side of the ranch."

John nodded. "Thank you. For everything."

Frank grunted. "This ain't goodbye, son. Get your ass in gear."

John nodded and started walking to the door and then he jogged. Coordinates. Of what? Her killer? Something else? Only time would tell. Time and access. Thanks to Guardian, he had both.

His wool slacks, open-collar blue linen shirt, cashmere coat, and handmade Italian leather shoes comprised a uniform from years past. He'd worn camouflage for the USA for eight years, but two four-year stints in the Middle East and two purple hearts made getting out and getting on with his life an easy choice when Lori handed him an opportunity he couldn't resist.

He waited for the security team at Guardian Headquarters to process him through the many catchments and failsafes. No one except those thoroughly vetted by Guardian gained entrance to the facility. There was no public entrance, no pretense or apologies. Guardian's hierarchy and nerve centers were a fortress that couldn't be infiltrated.

A soft chime sounded, and the last door lock clicked open. "Mr. Smith, I'm Sonya. I was sent to escort you to CCS. Archangel and Alpha are waiting for you." A tiny woman in sky-high heels smiled at him and spun on the toe of one of those shoes, setting out at a quick clip. She tossed a quick, "Did you have a good trip?" over her shoulder as she deftly navigated the passages.

John allowed a distracted smile and out of pure ingrained politesse, he assumed words came out of his mouth. What he'd said? He'd never be able to recall. The fact that he was being escorted to Archangel and Alpha the second he entered the facility screamed urgency.

Had they found Lori's killers? Had they determined who'd ordered her death—and his? If they'd located the bastards, he'd be the one to take them out. He'd be the one to watch the life fade from them. By military training he was a sniper; his father and sister had taught him another talent. One the CIA had latched onto and exploited.

He followed the woman through the halls without further conversation. Sonya stopped at a door and swiped her ID card and then leaned forward and lifted on her toes for a retinal scan. The door opened and he held it for her as she passed through. He glanced at the corridor they were heading down. He hadn't been here before. There were chairs and benches to the left. To the right were what he assumed were operational theaters. He looked in the one door that remained open. Stadium seating, massive screens, and computer consoles equaled mission control centers in his mind. Three of the theaters had red warning lights illuminated outside, which he assumed meant there were active operations happening. Given what he knew about the size, structure, and scope of Guardian, it was probably a slow day.

Sonya stopped at a vault door, swiped her ID, and entered a code. A light on the camera activated above the door and the lens shifted, almost silently. A disembodied voice from the speaker commanded, "Stand by."

Sonya smiled up at him and then motioned to the side of the hall where she was standing. "You might want to stand over here."

John stepped across the hall a split second before the vault door opened and literally thirty people exited the confines. They were laughing and joking. Several had what appeared to be their lunch with them. Most acknowledged Sonya with a wave, nod, or a quiet 'hey.' When the flood of people waned, Sonya stepped into the room and he followed her. She turned and pointed up a steep stairway that led to at least ten levels of computer desks.

"The door at the top of the stairs. Sorry, but until they

install an elevator, I'm only making that trek in an emergency. Go straight up, you can't miss it."

"Thank you." He took the stairs two at a time and sent his gaze over the setup. The huge monitors at the front of the room were displaying screensavers, and blue lights at the end of each desk level indicating the stations had been sanitized held steady as he walked up the stairs. If he wasn't so damn anxious about his meeting, he would have loved to find out how the system worked.

The door at the top of the stairs opened. Jacob King waited for him. He jogged up the last fifteen or so steps and extended his hand. "Jacob."

"John, come on in."

John walked in and nodded at people he knew from the ranch. Zane, Jewell, Jason, Tori, and Jacob. A family affair.

"John." Jason motioned him over to a computer bank where Jewell was sitting. "I'm going to cut through all the bullshit. We don't know what we have, but as it could—and I do mean 'could'—involve your sister, we brought you in. Jewell, give him the short version of the story."

Jewell smiled at him. "Okay, we were involved in a case where a Russian hacker infiltrated our systems through a trusted operative. We have the hard drive with the information that he gleaned from our system. We recently had confirmation that some not-so-nice people had a copy or a clone of the hard drive, so I went through it again to make sure we were covered." She pulled a pencil from her messy bun and twirled it nervously. *"I couldn't find anything, so I went a step farther. I looked into the programming installed on the drive. That's when I found this."*

The monitor in front of her listed a host of letters and numbers. He stared at them and shook his head. "And this means what?"

Her head went up and down in a vigorous nod. "Yeah, that's exactly what I thought when I saw them. But, when I ran it through a program to put them into logical sense, this came up."

LORI BAKER ENGINEER

"And look, the numbers could be coordinates." Jewell tapped the keyboard. *"These are non-players. They don't land on anything but ocean. These we've eliminated because of various circumstances, but these are the ones we think have potential. They are remote, but there are structures around each of them."*

A sharp snap drove the entire team to their knees. He dropped and shouldered his M-4 as did every other man on the op. With hand signals, Travis sent Ricco and Scuba out on recon. The rest hunkered down and waited. Every nuance of sound was a cautionary study at this point. The satellite pictures of the coordinates they'd been able to obtain through Guardian showed two buildings about a klick further northeast at the river's edge. It was possible whoever resided in those buildings was making the trek out.

Ricco and Scuba sent a signal to indicate their return. Travis mimicked the low sound, letting them know they were secure and waiting. The two men appeared from the forest and made straight for their skipper.

"A branch broke about five hundred meters southwest. Heavy enough to break through the snow crust. That's the only thing we saw. No tracks anywhere." Ricco whispered the report, but they all heard him.

"All right. Harley, head out and get us eyes on those structures. Luke, you've got point. Scuba, Ricco, you're on our flanks. Coach, you've got our six. John, you're with me. Let's go."

John fell into step as they worked silently through the last mile of forest, snow, and bitter cold. Harley had ghosted into the trees ahead of them,

JOHN

silently working at a faster clip without the sound of the team to give away his location. Travis, as the team captain, had a responsibility to make sure he made it to the target and out alive. John's time in the service and training at the ranch—and sometimes at the Rose—made him less of a liability, but the dynamics of the team changed with each new member. From what he'd understood, Tempest had joined them recently. Trying to integrate two newbs into the fabric of the team would have been a mess, so John shadowed Travis. Which was smart, even if it was a bit... emasculating. He'd earned his patches, for fuck's sake. He was a sniper.

Was.

He pulled the reins on his attitude. He'd traded in his rifle for a computer and printer. It seemed like a good gig. Lori recruited him to work with her when his second hitch was up. She had a sweet job working for the alphabet agencies in D.C. Who knew his misspent youth could lead to a life of comfort behind a computer and a sophisticated printing system? His old man, a conman and world-class grifter, had trained Lori and him how to make fake IDs when they were eleven. As children, dear old Dad never directly used them in any of his schemes, but he used the IDs they made for him. The ones he didn't use they sold on the streets. They got damn good at copying state-issued identification, and out of sheer stupidity, they moved on to federal.

He got caught with multiple fake federal IDs and the judge gave him a choice, join the military or go to jail. He could laugh at his day in court now, but when it was happening, it seemed like a B-movie with no happy ending for him. He made a choice, one that he'd never regretted. He joined up and begged Lori to come with him as soon as he hit his first duty location. She refused. His sister was headstrong and determined to make money. She told him she'd take her chances playing it fast and loose. He fucking hated she wouldn't join him, and he never stopped asking.

Travis held up his hand, stilling the five men behind him. Harley jogged past Tempest and reported, "Just over the rise. There is smoke coming from one of the buildings. The other is dark. It looks like the second structure, the one with the stovepipe, has electricity. There is a light coming from under the door and I hear a generator. I found an array. It looks like a sat phone link-up. This is looking prime."

"Any indication of how many people?"

"A ton of footprints from the second structure to

the riverbank. It hasn't snowed enough to cover them, so the traffic has happened within the last day, no more than two days ago. Only one set of tracks to the small outbuilding. Big-ass footprints."

Travis lifted his hand high in the air, palm to the front, and made a large circular motion. The entire team rallied on him. After a quick recap of Harley's info, Travis bent down and drew on the snow. "Here is the outbuilding. Harley and Luke, you clear that as we set up around the other structure. Ricco, you take out the array but don't damage the equipment too badly, Guardian might learn something from it. When Harley and Luke rejoin, we are going to breach this structure. Ricco, you have entry. Scuba, you have his back. Harley is in third, break right. I'm in with John glued to my six, then Coach and Luke, you have our fallback and are responsible for backflush. I don't want anyone surprising us. We sweep right. When we've cleared a room, I'll give the order to move on. Nobody goes without my order."

All eyes shifted to Coach. The guy made a face and lifted his eyes toward the heavens. "One time, two years ago. Let it go, will you?"

A snicker broke from the rest of the team. Travis gave a quick smile. "Don't lose your edge. Just because the last targets have been a wash doesn't mean your ass won't get capped on this one. Be aware and be safe." Travis looked at each of his men, waiting for them to acknowledge his command, and then finally he stared at John. John looked him square in the eye and nodded.

Travis glanced at his team again. "Anyone in there has the potential to have information. Information we need. Lethal force is a last resort. Understand?" The team nodded again.

"Whatever it takes." Tempest's words carried quietly on the bitter-cold wind.

Travis stood up. "As long as it takes. Move out."

CHAPTER 2

Pain split her head in two and blasted Shae Diamant from blackness into a vivid hell in about a nanosecond. A wave of unsuppressible nausea pushed up her throat. She tried to roll to vomit, but she was tied and immobile. Bile burned along her throat when she swallowed it back down. It was either that or die from aspirating it. She turned her head and coughed, spitting out what she could. She still managed to pull some into her lungs and choked on her own gastric juices. The torment worsened when someone turned on a light. Nausea from the brilliance that sliced through her retinas returned with a vengeance. Shae tried to suppress the surge of bile but lost the fight. Someone grabbed her hair and twisted her head to the side again. "You aren't going to die on your own puke, bitch. We have plans for you, and right now, she needs you alive."

Shae struggled against the man's hold. A needle was jabbed into her shoulder, and whatever they injected into her burned along the muscle of her arm. She was released. The pain that catapulted her into consciousness forced a moan between spasmatic coughing fits. Shae tried to clear her throat from the acid that clung in her esophagus. She rasped, hacked, and coughed with every breath because of the stomach juices she'd breathed into her lungs. Shae recognized that she was laying in her own vomit. But she was alive, and if she was alive, she could fight.

She tried to piece together the events that led to her being here now. Her thoughts were muddled, and whatever they'd shot into her arm was pulling her back down to the dark abyss. Shae clung to words that were sneered at her moments ago. She wasn't supposed to die now. She'd wake up. She'd have to wake up…

A cold splash of water brought her out of her stupor, to a degree. Shae blinked against the water dripping into her eyes. Shards of white-hot pain lanced her skull. She tried to move her arms, but it was useless. Managing to open one eye, the bright lights catapulted another wave of nausea, and she puked. That was when she noticed she was tied in a standing position. Her hands high above her, her legs spread and ankles tied, preventing her from moving. Another hard spray of water battered against her chest and face. She coughed against the forceful blast of water that was forced up her nose, choking her.

"Enough!" Shae heard the woman's command a few seconds before the water ceased. She gasped for air, her lungs battling the water with coughing fits that splintered her skull with a searing pain.

Someone grabbed her hair and yanked her head back. She cried out against the violent stab of torment that rolled through her head. Her ears filled with a roar and she chased the darkness that crashed around her.

"I said wake up, bitch!"

Shae gasped. Under pressure, the water that hit

her face pushed up her nose and into her mouth. She turned her head and tried to take a breath. She kept her head turned until the force of the water moved from her face to her body. The pressure tore at her skin. She heard the compressor and knew she was being sprayed by a pressure washer. The concentrated stream burned her exposed skin. The thin rags she wore did little to protect her.

"That's enough."

Shae panted against the sensations burning across her body. The pain shattering her skull kept her eyes closed. She made fists of her hands, noticing for the first time it was rope that bound her. She cracked her eyelids open and reeled from a wave of nausea, but she could see her feet. She was attached to what looked like an old metal box spring.

"Hello, my dear. Are you awake?"

Shae lifted her head and blinked. Her eyes moved to those across the room. Some were seated, and some were standing on a raised dais. The one man who wasn't on the small stage wore heavy rubber boots. She rolled her eyes along the perimeter of the room. A car battery and jumper cables sat on a portable table. She turned her head and blinked back the surge of bile the movement caused. The wall on that side of the room contained a litany of torture implements—or a great night in a BDSM dungeon, but Shae had a feeling these guys weren't into safewords.

"Who is your superior within the Mossad? How did you find us?" The snarled question from a woman seated at the center of the raised area in front of her brought her attention back to the front of the room.

Shae concentrated on that face. She blinked to keep her in focus. "I'm not Mossad." She croaked out the words.

"Liar!" The woman yelled out at her. Shae blinked, focusing on the raised platform. The woman who shouted was one she *hadn't* seen before. As a matter of fact, she hadn't seen most of the people currently facing her. They must be the all-important and fucking invisible layers of Stratus. She tried to memorize the physical details of the woman who spoke, "I don't believe you."

"I don't know anything about the Mossad!" She wailed, hoping the bastards would hesitate in their assumptions. "Please, I beg you, let me go!" Shae bawled and kept repeating herself.

"Enough! Shut her up." A blast of high-pressure water painted her raw skin with a million needles of pain. She screamed against the force of the water.

When the water pulled off of her, she continued to weep, letting them see her as a victim, not an assailant.

"Your partner told us you were Mossad." The woman's voice floated from across the room. This time, the woman didn't yell. She didn't have to. The authority in her voice cut through the room.

Her partner? She hadn't seen Joshua since the night their car was broadsided. God, how long had she been held? She gathered the strength to deny the accusations. "I don't know what you're talking about."

"I want to know who you work for and what you've told them. You are an inferior and inconsequential thorn in an otherwise pristine operation. Your lies will not be tolerated."

"Please, I don't know what you're talking about!"

"We'll soon see, won't we? I'll leave you in Maurice hands for a day or two. That should put you in the mood to be truthful. If you are willing to confess before that, too bad. Consider it payment for wasting my time." Shae heard the steps of the people as they filtered out of the room. The man with the thigh-high rubber boots remained. She watched him closely as he went to the wall and pulled down a ball gag. Shae narrowed her eyes at the fucker. She wouldn't break. They'd have to kill her first.

Snot hung from her nose in a long, thin thread. For some reason, she focused on that string as it stretched. Her ragged breathing rasped in desperate pulls around the ball gag. She couldn't feel her hands or arms. Her legs no longer supported her. Two cycles with the car battery and she'd lost control of her bodily functions and defecated where she was tied. Maurice dutifully disconnected the battery, pulled out the pressure washer, and washed the filth down the drain in the floor. Her clothes were all but gone; shreds of cloth remained over her shoulders. She shivered uncontrollably. The concept of someday dying had become a concrete fact. She would breathe her last breath here in this cement pit. Maurice hadn't asked her a question. He'd just plodded through the sessions with the quiet and efficient intent to cause her the most pain he could without killing her. Shae concentrated on that fact rather than the man who once again had the heavy flogger in his hand. He hadn't pushed her over the line... yet.

She had lost track of time, of the number of times she'd passed out and then been brought back to consciousness by the sadistic bastard. Sometimes he'd remove the gag and she'd beg. He'd grunt or laugh and move to the next instrument of torture. Floggers, whips, spreaders, then there were the weighted gloves and brass knuckles. Shae thought she knew the concept of pain, but the bastard who tormented her had quickly changed her mind.

There was no light in the room where she was tied except for the bare bulbs that swung overhead. She didn't know if it was day or night. There was no concept of time, only pain and humiliation. Her determination to remain strong had been systematically stripped away. She trembled when Maurice looked at her. When he approached, she'd begged, cried, pleaded for mercy. She offered to tell him whatever he wanted to know. She would have given him anything to make him stop, but he didn't want her to talk. She was being broken for that woman's enjoyment. Shae blinked back the shroud of agony that encompassed her, although she didn't know why. It seemed it was the last of her coping mechanisms left because she had no hope, and she had no doubt she would die here in this cesspool. Strange, but that thought didn't scare her anymore. The pain just needed to stop. She watched through bruised and swollen eyelids as Maurice attached the negative ground of the jumper cables to the bed frame she was bound against.

A phone rang from the wall by a small work table at the side of the room. It saved her momentarily from the inevitability of Maurice the positive cable against the wire frame. Shae could no longer lift her head, but she was cognizant enough to hear him answer his phone. "Hello," and, "Yes, I understand," were all she heard. But it was enough. His tone held disappointment. That meant either the people witnessing her torture were coming back and he had to stop, or Maurice had been told to kill her. Shae heard his approach. His heavy rubber boots squeaked against the wet tiled floor. Wet. Fuck. She was soaked. The bastard was going to electrocute her in a pool of water. This was truly the end. She wanted to cry, to beg again for her life. She wanted to live, but the realization that these were her last moments denied her that dream.

Maurice reached out and lifted her head with a rubber glove-covered hand. "She said you must die now."

"I know." And she did know. Her prayers had

been said numerous times and she drew a painful breath. "Please..." She rasped out the request.

"I could make it quick, but I won't." Maurice dropped his hand and chuckled. She closed her eyes and waited. If there were a merciful God, her heart would give out and deny the sadistic bastard his fun. She heard him lift the cable and step toward her.

CHAPTER 3

As Luke and Harley rejoined the team, a thrum of adrenaline once again coursed through John's body. Ricco slipped into formation and nodded. The phone was disabled and the outbuilding cleared. He placed his hand on Travis' shoulder as Coach gripped his. They were going in tight. He'd watched the entry procedures countless times before he practiced them over and over with this team. If he made a misstep, it could cost lives. He'd be damned if he would be the one responsible for any harm coming to this team.

Ricco twisted the door handle and the damn thing swung open. Ricco, as the number one man, twisted in a balanced turn using an economy of motion to round the corner. His M-4 raised, he moved forward. Scuba entered the room immediately behind him. By the time Harley entered, Ricco had called the room clear.

"There's nothing here." Ricco spun and addressed Travis.

"Has to be something," Tempest spoke as he entered. "The generator is still running, and what about the sat phone array?"

John nodded to the wall of shelves. "Behind there." His father had had several safe houses, and each had places to hide from cops or people he'd fleeced. Fake walls were his favorite.

Scuba and Coach found the hinges first. "Skipper?"

Travis nodded, and as they opened the shelving, all guns trained on the opening. The sound of a phone ringing froze everyone. John could hear a man's voice. Travis nodded again and Harley headed down the stairs, followed by Ricco and Scuba. He was on Travis' ass with Coach and Tempest right behind them. At the bottom of the stairs, he heard a man and then... a woman?

Travis lifted three fingers and then pulled them down one at a time. On zero, Harley pulled the partially closed door open.

The sight that met them would be one John would never forget. A fat bastard dressed in rubber boots and apron held a jumper cable. His surprised expression morphed into understanding about two seconds too late. Tempest's knife embedded itself in the bastard's thigh, bringing him down. They both bolted toward the woman as the team cleared the large room. Her limp body hung forward. The tattered rags she wore were soaked with blood. Luke used John's knife to cut her bindings, and John lowered her to the floor.

John's fingers pressed against her throat. "I have a pulse."

"We need to get her airlifted out of here ASAP. Ricco, get us a line to Guardian." Travis barked out the order. "Luke, you know what you need to do."

John pulled a mylar blanket out of his pack and hazarded a glance toward Luke. His teammate had the big guy bound and was pushing him out of the door. Harley followed him out as an overwatch.

Coach tore open his medical kit and started to examine the woman. "Fuck, Skipper, I don't know where to start. She's breathing. If we move her I could make matters worse. I'm a medic, not a trauma doc, and she needs one desperately."

"Do what you can, Coach." Travis knelt down

with another blanket and helped cover her. "I'd like to skin that bastard. How is she still alive?"

"I don't know." John pushed the woman's hair away from her swollen, battered face. She'd been abused for a long time. *Strong.* The word popped into his mind. Damn it, she had to be one of the strongest people he'd ever met, the degree of pain that had been inflicted on the poor woman. Fuck, he agreed with the Skipper. He'd like to skin that fat bastard, too.

"Look at this shit," Scuba said, almost to himself. John glanced over at the array of implements that were precisely positioned on the wall. Sadistic bastard had everything he needed to torture a person.

Ricco jogged down the stairs and into the room. "Guardian was waiting for us to come on line. They have a GPS fix on us now and are sending in a doctor and EMT via helicopter. As soon as they get her stable, we are out on the same bird. They want any equipment, paperwork, notes, or phones."

Travis stood up. "How long for the helo?"

"Fifteen minutes."

"Coach, you and John stay with the woman. Ricco and Scuba, let's gut this place. Nothing is too small or insignificant. Bag and tag everything.

Channel Jared-fucking-King. If you find a dead gnat on the stairs it goes into evidence, let the laboratory crimefighters sort it out. I'll video the room with my phone. It will have to do, no time for pictures."

John watched as blue gloves and evidence bags were taken out of backpacks, but his attention migrated back to the woman. He picked up her hand and held it. She was so damn cold. He wasn't much on praying, but he'd been introduced to it when he started living around Frank and Amanda Marshall. Those people lived what they believed. He bowed his head and sent a word Heavenward. It couldn't hurt.

Coach slid a cuff around her arm and inflated the device. "Her heart rate and blood pressure are low. She has significant soft tissue damage, her nail beds are shot. Toes *and* fingers." John continued to hold her hand as Coach ran experienced fingers down each limb, careful to only expose the area he was examining.

When Coach sat back on his heels, John asked, "Will she make it?"

Coach slowly shook his head. "I don't know, man. Depends on internal injuries and her will to live. Right now, she's breathing and I'm going to do my best to keep her that way until the real doc gets here." Coach glanced at his watch and then back down at the woman. "You hear that, lady? You need to hang in there. Don't you dare quit on me now."

John let a sad smile spread across his face. "That's why they call you Coach, isn't it?"

"Yeah. Halftime pep talks. That's what the Skipper calls them. Sometimes it's the best first aid I can dispense, you know what I mean?" The younger man's stare met his eyes. "A person has to know they matter, that someone wants them to fight." He pointed to John's connection with the woman. "That hand-holding you got going on there, you keep that up, and talk to her, too. She needs to hear a kind voice."

At the unmistakable sound of a helicopter above, Coach jumped up. "I'm going to get them down here and brief the doc on her injuries so he can bring what he needs. You got her?"

"Yeah." John nodded. Coach hit the stairs at a run. The others didn't even look up from collecting evidence. John moved so he was sitting beside her. Hunks of her long brown hair had been hacked or sawed off and the vivid bruising and swelling prevented him from knowing anything else about her. She wore no rings on her damaged fingers. John leaned down and whispered, "You're safe now. Be strong just a bit longer. We'll make sure no one hurts you again."

He carefully stroked the back of her hand with his thumb. It was the only place he wouldn't encounter wounds. He glanced up when he heard a light step coming down the stairs. A woman with strawberry-blonde hair pulled back into a long ponytail jogged across the floor. "I'm Poet. I'll take over. Thank you for staying with her." The woman glanced at the men in the room. "You have three minutes to finish collecting evidence. I want you out so we can work on her."

Travis swung his head her way. "Roger that, we'll be done in two."

John stood up and backed away from the poor soul on the ground. He snapped himself out of the weird connection he felt with the woman. "Travis, what can I do to help?"

"All the bags over there in that box, take them up and get them on the helicopter. We'll have the last of it in a minute. Then go find Luke and Harley. They need to get that fucker into the helicopter and have him hog-tied so he won't cause her any more damage. I hate taking that bastard back in the same transport as his victim, but it can't be helped."

John grabbed the box and headed out but stalled

at the bottom of the stairs. A tall blond man and Coach were coming down the stairs carrying a stretcher that had a fuckton of equipment on it. The new man nodded at him but kept his rapid-fire questions of Coach going. John glanced back as Scuba and Ricco started to collect the team's equipment. He ran up the stairs and headed to the waiting helicopter. One of the pilots saw him and jogged over to help him. He shouted over the motor noise, "These can go in the exterior skid storage bins."

The man led the way and John followed. John shouted, "There's more coming."

The pilot gave him a thumbs-up, and he bolted to find Luke and Harley, passing Scuba and Ricco on the way back. He hustled to where the men were. Time was of the essence.

CHAPTER 4

John leaned against the fence and gazed at the herd that lingered near the fence line. He was physically exhausted and was damn glad about that fact. Since he'd joined the Marshalls, he'd worked from sunup to sunset and worked damn hard. When he first showed up, his body was soft from far too much time behind a computer, but the march of time and countless hours of hard work had honed his body into the tool he needed to perform the countless tasks of manual labor ranch life demanded. He glanced up at the sky and pulled his cowboy hat off to mop the sweat from his forehead.

He wiped the sweatband of his hat as he glanced up toward the ranch house. House? Hell, it was a mansion. He chuckled when he thought of Frank

Marshall's indignation when he told him he wouldn't stay at the main house, nor would he partake in meals with the family. John insulated himself from all contact. He'd occasionally play a hand of poker with the twins or Chief, but that was only when the isolation of his existence began to gnaw on his soul. When you grew up knowing how to double deal, stack the deck, and had an almost indistinguishable mechanic's grip on the deck, he could wipe out the friendly card game within a few hands. It was why he didn't play cards. Too many memories, most of them bad.

He glanced down to the leather strapped around his wrist. He'd lost his only remaining reason he had to be happy the day the CIA determined he and his sister were liabilities. There was no way to prove they'd killed Lori, but he didn't believe in coincidences. He was burned by someone inside the CIA, his identity outed to the world. Every faction of every intelligence-gathering agency in the world wanted to know what was stuffed inside his brain. The man he was died, and John Smith emerged.

He drew a deep breath and gazed over the rolling hills that were dotted with cattle. The low calls and swishing tails were now familiar and safe. He pictured his sister's face. The blonde hair and hazel eyes weren't as easy to recall these days. He didn't have many pictures of her, but he did have one he'd framed and put in his small office. All his belongings were blown to hell and back after he was 'killed' in a car bombing.

John's thumb tapped the rail where he leaned. If it hadn't been for Gabriel, he *would* have been in that car—and he *would* be dead. He glanced down to the weathered pole and picked at a loose piece of wood. The series of operations he'd participated in this past winter had led to nothing; well, except for the woman they'd rescued up in Canada. He last saw her in Winnipeg when they'd dropped the woman and the medical team off at the helipad on top of the medical center. He'd never heard if she'd made it or not. It was hard to imagine being able to come back from that type of trauma.

"Deep in thought." Frank Marshall's voice snapped his attention back to the present. He'd damn near jumped a foot at the sound of the man's voice.

"Ah, yeah." John shifted on the rail, giving Frank room to lean against the fence.

"Worried about anything in particular?"

"No, just doing some reflecting." A hobby in which he indulged far too much time.

Frank grunted and shifted his gaze over his property. "Need to ask you a favor." The older man took out a piece of taffy and offered one to John.

"Adding sugar on top of the favor? Must be something big." John chuckled at the glare Frank shot his way. The man might be able to fool the kids on the ranch, but he wasn't the callous old fart he pretended to be. The man had a heart the size of the Dakota skies and it was filled with love. Love of the land, love for his fellow man, but most of all, love for his wife and those people he claimed as family.

"Got a little problem. Guardian has a special case coming in tomorrow. Rehab." Frank unwrapped his candy and popped the confection into his mouth.

"How's that a problem for us?" John looked at the pink and white candy in his fingers and pulled the ends of the wax paper, unwrapping the peppermint-flavored fluff.

"Yeah, well, physically the Mossad agent is on the mend. I don't mean to spread Guardian business around, but she's been seeing a professional for the things that happened to her up in Canada. Her mind isn't healing as fast as her body. She's pretty messed up." Frank looked off into the distance.

The dots connected in his mind. It took him a

couple of minutes before he asked, "Is it the same woman? The one Sierra Team and I brought out?"

"Yeah. She's in a bad way. Guardian found out the Mossad had let her go. Too damaged to continue to work, but she was found on our op. We weren't going to do that. She's got a long road to walk. She's pretty much shut down, but we'll do everything we can to make sure she has a shot at a new normal." Frank looked down at the ground and dug at it with the toe of his boot.

John shook his head. Damn cold of the Mossad to drop an asset like that. "The mental and physical effects of the torture."

"Yeah. This undercover operation took a lot from her. Her partner's body washed up on a beach in Italy. Don't know how they managed to end up half a world apart, and that woman ain't talking. To anyone for any reason." Frank cleared his throat before he straightened and slapped the pole. "Anyway, she needs to heal. I offered the drover's cottage next to your house. She accepted, but she made it clear she wasn't ready to see anyone or talk about what happened."

"You know, she might never be ready to talk about it." John turned, leaning his back against the fencepost.

"Yeah. Heard that from her doctors. Anyway, they got her set up with Dr. Wheeler over in Hollister. He's an all right Doc." Frank nodded as if confirming his words in his own head.

"So, what is the favor?" John watched his boss. He knew it was hard for Frank to ask anyone for anything. It just wasn't the man's way.

"Could you on occasion look in on her? I know you don't cotton to the neighborly ways, but a word here or there. She's hurting and lost, and I don't want to force her away from the one chance she has at getting herself healed up."

John stood and put his fingers in his pockets, letting his arms go slack. He glanced down at the ground and gave the request some serious thought. He shrugged and averted his gaze toward the little drover's cottage that sat about three hundred feet from the house Frank had built for him. He'd lived in the cottage while the three-bedroom home he lived in now was being built. The cottage was snug and had everything he needed—a small bathroom with a shower and a tiny kitchen. The entire space was the size of his kitchen now. Frank cleared his throat again, snapping John back to the conversation. "I can do that. Not going to lie, it ain't in my comfort zone, but I'll speak when I see her or... something."

Frank chuckled and headed back toward the main house, clasping John's shoulder as he passed in acknowledgement. John turned back to the pasture and shook his head. If Frank Marshall had his way, the old cowboy would draw him into the people he considered family. That thought sent a chill down his spine. No. Never again would he get close enough to feel the depth of loss he felt when he lost his father and sister.

Never again.

CHAPTER 5

Shae shifted the pillow behind her back, padding the plush leather seat of the G6's seat. Her body was still healing. Months of hospitalization, treatments, and surgeries had knit together her body. Once her physical ailments had been corrected, the Mossad cut her loose. She had nothing until the man from Guardian had requested permission to speak with her. She shifted again and winced. She had no recollection of how she'd injured her leg, but she'd been dealing with the nagging injury since she regained consciousness. Shae jumped and grabbed the armrests of the chair when the landing gear engaged. She flinched when the Guardian doctor's eyes bounced to her as if the sudden sound was the event that would cause her to shatter.

Her anger and humiliation at the cat-on-a-hot-tin-roof reaction to the noise added one more brick to the wall she was building to keep everyone away. She couldn't stand the sympathetic looks or the solicitous manner of speech as if a stray word would break her. People didn't know how to relate to her anymore, and she sure as hell didn't know how to communicate what she needed from them. Because she didn't know. She didn't have the slightest clue what she needed from them... except space and time. Her mind was a battlefield on a good day and a graveyard on the bad ones. She was fighting a war that didn't have defined rules. Her own mind, her thoughts and feelings, were harbingers of doom and guilt. The physicians referred her to shrinks, the shrinks medicated her to 'manage' the physical reactions to the emotional turmoil, and nobody—absolutely nobody—could understand the demons that were screaming at her all day, every day. She closed her eyes, shutting out the concerned looks. She didn't have the energy or the desire to deal with their disappointment and concern. Waking up to face another day was struggle enough.

The plane landed and she somehow managed to

tear her death grip off the armrests. She took off her seatbelt and drew her legs up into the chair with her, adding to the mental distance with a physical shield. Not that it worked. Her medical team barged past her barriers, and *that* hurt almost as much as the distance she was trying to build.

"Do you want to have dinner with us?" the nurse who was traveling with them asked. It reminded her of the time her mom rescued a puppy from the side of the road. She'd nursed the little guy back to life using that same tone of voice. Shae hated that anyone thought they had to use that tone with her. She shook her head and looked out the window, waiting for the door to open so she could escape. Escape from her new agency and their well-meaning intentions. She shook her head. No, she didn't want to eat, not with them, not at all.

The doctor, Adam Cassidy, stood when the aircraft stopped. "We have a small cottage set up for you. I'll go down there with you and make sure you have everything you need." Her nurse placed a hand on her arm. Shae jerked her arm away; the action sent guilt careening through her. She didn't deserve or want their kindness. They had no idea what she was willing to do during those last moments, what she'd told Maurice, how she'd begged, bargained,

JOHN

and pleaded... She needed to be alone so she could breathe.

Shae folded her arms around her stomach and shook her head. "Just... please, get the door open. I need to get out. Now."

The doctor was moving toward the door before she finished her statement. He opened the hatch as the last engine was shutting down. The door to the cabin opened and the pilot, a huge man with strawberry blond hair, ducked through the opening. He glanced at the doctor in question before he cast her a look. Yeah, that was pity. Great, just great. Now she felt guilty for feeling the way she did. Why couldn't she just stop acting like this? But then again, she didn't know if she *wanted* to stop because her reactions were honest. At least, she thought they were, although she couldn't tell most times if she was reacting to the people around her or the past, and *that* confusion compounded the twenty tons of brain garbage that she shifted through every fucking day. She was so tired of trying to act the way everyone expected her to act. The more she tried, the more shit stacked on top of her already-overwhelmed ability to cope.

The nurse spoke in that soft don't-scare-the-rabid-dog voice again, "We'll get your bags down there for you. No need to worry about them right now."

Shae made rare eye contact with her nurse. She couldn't look anyone in the eye because for some reason she knew if she met their stares they would *know*. She dashed her eyes down and examined her nailbeds. A single nod of her head was the only movement she made. She heard the others deplane. Her nurse stood and walked over to the door and waited.

Shae stood and took a moment to get her balance. She still limped after she first stood up. The injury to her right ankle caused shooting pain at times. Shae clenched her teeth and waited for the sensation to pass. She used the chairs to make her way to the door because she couldn't stand anyone touching her.

The nurse made a move to grab her arm to help her out of the door and down the steps. Shae shook her head and grasped the thin railing. "No." Her word cut through the silence.

The nurse raised her hand and backed away. Shae gritted her teeth and hobbled down the stairs, aware of the nurse's presence directly behind her and Doctor Cassidy's to her side. The sound of a motor

JOHN

drew her attention when she finally made it to the cement tarmac.

A four-seat ATV pulled around the nose of the aircraft. It stopped directly in front of her. "Get in. We are not taking no for an answer. We'll take you to the cottage, get you inside and settled, and then we'll leave you alone. For the time being." Doctor Cassidy placed her suitcase into the rear seat next to him, leaving her the seat beside the driver, a man she didn't recognize. Shae stared at one and then the other. Finally, Doctor Cassidy spoke, "You're just wasting time on this beautiful April day. Get in or we'll stand here all day."

She carefully folded herself into the seat not a foot in front of her. She wrapped her arms around herself and tried to become small enough to disappear. She prayed the distance to the cottage wasn't far, but as they trundled over the field, she thanked God the Doctor had made her get in. She wouldn't have been able to walk the entire way and everyone but her seemed to understand that far better than she did. The crisp coolness of the April air swirled around her. The trip took longer than it should have because the man was driving like an old lady, but if he'd gone faster, she'd probably be in tears. Her shrink and physicians said some of her pain was from the depression she was suffering, but her body couldn't differentiate the physical from the mental pain. The tears in her eyes were real, caused by real pain from even the gentle jostling the ATV had caused.

Shae refused to look at either man and forced herself out of the vehicle and to the cottage door. The suitcase was taken inside and lifted onto a small table, and the doctor pulled the zipper and opened the case. He turned back to her and she averted her gaze. She wanted him gone so she could collapse.

"We will be here. You don't have to go through this alone." The doctor's soft voice sent daggers through her nerves. Of course, she had to go through this alone! They didn't understand what she'd been willing to expose that day and she could never tell them.

Shae rubbed her arms and stared at the ground, waiting for them to leave. The Doctor drew a deep breath and exhaled a sigh. "I know you are hurting, and we want to help. Doing nothing and giving you space you are demanding is hard. Every last one of us here at Guardian are the type to rush in and fix the world. I understand we can't fix what's broken in your world right now, but if you need us, no matter what time it is, you call us, and we are here." He placed a cell phone on the counter. "My number, the number to the main house, and the number for your new psychiatrist are programmed in here. I'll be back to check on you first thing in the morning."

Shae felt a tear fall and watched in utter despair as it splashed on the hardwood floor where her eyes were fixed. She rubbed her arms harder, hoping like hell he'd leave but not wanting him to go. Boots scraped against the wood floor as he departed the small space. Shae waited until she heard the door latch behind him and gave in to the emotion that she'd been holding back. She was free from the confines of the hospital, but she wasn't home, either. She had nothing back in Israel to return to. No job, no man… no reason to go back.

Shae walked slowly to the medicine kit in her luggage bag and took out the p.m. edition of her drug cocktail. She shook the required pills into her hand and stared at them. The assortment made the feelings go away, took the edge off her pain, and numbed the reality of her life to a dull hum. She went to the kitchen, pulled out a bottle of water from the small fridge, and took the drugs. She didn't want to face herself or anyone else.

John glanced out the window when the ATV pulled up to the cottage. The woman who carefully lifted herself out of the vehicle was the woman they'd found nearly dead months ago. He leaned against the sink and watched as Doc Cassidy took her into the small cottage, but he was inside only moments before he exited. That was unusual as he could talk the paint off a house. The guy was friendly. Obviously, the woman had sent him packing.

A nudge at his ankle brought his attention from the cottage door to his own world. John glanced down at his boot and chuckled at the antics of Drake's cat. The thing was uglier than sin, half its ear was gone, and it had a bobbed tail with a crook in it. Hell, even its damn purr was broken. It would get to rumbling and then a hitch in the procession would make the cat squeak before it would start the wind up all over again. He'd made the mistake of feeding it when it would stop by. Now, it made the rounds to his house on the regular. It and that puffball of a dog Joy kept were constant visitors. The animals came and went as they pleased. Whatever; he was a sucker for a sad story, and by the looks of Cat, it had the saddest of sad stories. John reached down and ruffled the mousy brown fur at Cat's neck and chuckled at the squeaky purr. "Let me get a shower then we'll split a can of tuna." Cat turned and trotted off toward his bedroom. The damn thing was uncannily smart. Either that or John was losing his shit because it sure seemed like the animal understood just about everything he'd ever said. That poofy dog, though? Not so much. Pretty thing, but no brains to be had.

He let the warm water wash his day away before he padded back to the kitchen in nothing but a pair of jeans. Cat sat on one of the chairs at the table and watched him putter around the kitchen. He opened a packet of food that he'd bought for the damn animal. He'd actually gone to town and bought it and Sasha treats and food. Stupid, but the animals were constant visitors so what the hell. It was the only time he'd gone off the ranch that *wasn't* absolutely necessary. But he'd be damned if he'd ask anyone to buy treats for Cat or Sasha. Nobody needed to know that he had an affinity for either animal. Not very manly and he wouldn't give any of the ranch hands ammunition to dole out a ration of shit. Nope, he'd made the trip, bought the food, and brought it back. So what if he unloaded it in the middle of the night? Not like it was anyone's business that he'd decided he liked the little animals.

John rinsed off the plate and startled when a light

in the cottage turned on. He glanced down at the sink and shook his head. That girl was having a rough time of it. He got that but denying herself the people who could help her wasn't smart. He bristled against the idea of talking to her. He didn't do small talk and he figured she didn't either. Not sure why the hell Frank thought she'd welcome any conversation period. He finished cleaning the sink and put his plate into the dishwasher. The small lamp by the window in the living room of the drover's cottage extinguished, leaving the cottage in darkness. He nodded. There had been many nights where he'd sat in the dark and prayed the demons that haunted him wouldn't be able to find him. He didn't know the particulars about the woman and didn't care to, but he'd make the effort. Somehow. John turned away from his window and waited for Cat to join him before he headed for the living room, the evening news, and a chapter or two in the latest Clancy book.

CHAPTER 6

Shae carefully opened the cottage door and hobbled outside. She'd started going out to sit in the sun. Not for long, just a couple moments between naps. She'd been using the sleeping pills she'd been prescribed. They worked to help her fall asleep, but the haunted memories that shrieked and awakened her at night prohibited more than an hour or two at a time. The only benefit she could find to the sleeping pills was that they ruined any appetite she had. Not that she'd cooked anything. The food in the kitchen sat untouched and spoiling. The nurse had stopped by with food twice. She'd eaten a few bites the nurse had brought with her and then ended up throwing away the remainder after the woman left.

The sun felt good against her skin. She was always cold now. The cottage was dark and cool, and she drifted from moment to moment on a haze of drugs. Shae closed her eyes and let the warmth soak through to her bones.

"You missed our appointment."

Shae tried to draw a deep pull of air into her lungs and peeked through her lashes at the man standing in front of her. He had long black hair, a snake tattoo on his neck, and full sleeves of ink showing out of the t-shirt he was wearing. He held a motorcycle helmet under his arm. The specter of fear seized her. She lifted off the seat and tried to reach the door. The pain in her ankle shot through her leg and she lost her balance. The man reached out for her and she screamed, tumbling back away from him.

Shae pulled into the fetal position and covered her head with her arms. She couldn't breathe, the terror lodged in her throat stealing her ability to beg. Her mind and body were back in that hole, and she was going to die. The roar that followed her to the ground consumed her and took her further down into the darkness.

JOHN

"Holy fuck, why didn't her doctors tell me she was this bad?" Jeremiah Wheeler paced in the small living room as he rifled through her medical files. He'd picked her up after she'd passed out and put her on her bed. The first call he made was to Adam Cassidy, the second was to the referring psychiatrist. "How the fuck did they release her?"

"Do you think she should be institutionalized?" Adam sat on the couch fuming about the lack of information flow, not only to Jeremiah but to him, too.

"What? No, I mean... Hell, I don't know, I haven't had the opportunity to assess her."

"Physically, she's doing well, they put her together and discharged her, which is usually best for a patient. But now that we know they pushed her out the door, let's start with the obvious." Adam pointed toward the kitchen counter and the array of medications lined up along the counter. Jeremiah nodded and flipped her medical records to the correct page. He glanced from the bottles on the counter to the list of antidepressants, pain killers, and mood stabilizers. Fuck, the woman was a walking cocktail of overpriced medication. Jeremiah held up a bottle of particularly nasty meds. The side effects had prevented him from prescribing it in his last practice at the maximum-security penitentiary in Lompoc, California. Adam lifted a bottle and handed it to him. Holy fuck, whoever prescribed the pain medication didn't consult with the doctor treating her mental issues. Those two drugs should never be taken in combination. Jeremiah threw the folder at the table and swung his gaze to the woman lying on the bed. He felt like a complete moron. Someone should have been overseeing the volatile cocktail that she had been taking. Switching her meds was a priority. He pulled out a chair and gestured toward the other seat at the small dinette. "Let's get to work, Adam. We need to redesign her treatment and get her off this combination."

Adam Cassidy pulled out the small chair and straddled it backward. "Right, first things first." Jeremiah nodded, and they started at the front of her recent, extensive medical history.

Shae woke on her bed. She blinked through the fog that was her constant companion. Her watch beeped again. It was time for her meds. She pushed herself off the mattress and pulled her hair out of her eyes. She froze, blinking back her shock and surprise.

"Why are you here?" She recognized Adam Cassidy but the other man... oh, fuck... he had... Shae's sense of humiliation and remorse had found a new depth. Not that it mattered because no one would ever understand that pain.

"I came by to find out why you weren't at the clinic. You were supposed to meet me for your initial appointment. I'm Jeremiah Wheeler, your new psychiatrist." Shae blinked as she tried to assimilate the information. Her mind stuck at the part that the long-haired, leather-clad, tattooed mountain of a man was a shrink. She peeked at Adam, who nodded his confirmation. "When you had your panic attack and passed out, we took a look at the medications you are on. Obviously, the right hand wasn't talking to the left when you were being treated. The medications you are on are fighting each other and could be causing some side effects that you shouldn't have to deal with."

Shae pushed back and leaned against the wall, pulling her legs up and wrapping her arms around them. She leaned her forehead against her knees.

"We have changed up your meds, Shae." That was from Adam. Shae shrugged her shoulder as a response. What did she care? She'd take whatever they gave her and force herself to make it through another day. Hell, she'd stopped thinking about days as a unit of measure. Now she pushed herself to make it from one dose of medication to another.

"You'll feel a lot better once some of that shit they gave you is out of your system. One of the drugs we have to gradually reduce, or you might suffer withdrawal symptoms." Adam stood and took the two steps it took to get to her kitchenette. "I'll deliver the doses every morning and I'll get someone to bring down your evening meds. You aren't eating, you aren't taking care of yourself, and if you try to fight me on this, Jeremiah and I will have you admitted to a private clinic in Denver." Adam grabbed a bottle of water and walked over to her, extending his hand with the medication in his palm.

Shae stared at his hand. She wasn't a child. She could take her own meds. *No, you're weak and worthless.* Shae closed her eyes at the searing accusations of her own mind.

"Shae, take the meds." Adam's voice brought her back to the small cottage.

She sent a furtive glance at his hand and shook her head. "Put them down." She flinched as he moved to put the pills on the blanket beside her. He set the water bottle down next to them and backed up. Shae waited until she was sure he wasn't coming close to her again and picked up the meds. She popped them into her mouth and swallowed them dry. She lifted the heavy water bottle and struggled with the cap. She finally got the perforated edges to release and took a small sip.

"When was the last time you ate?" That came from the tattooed man. Shae shrugged again. She didn't have a clue.

Adam sidestepped to her kitchen and pulled a can of soup from the small cabinet that served as her pantry. He opened the can and put it into a saucepan before he turned on the heat and started to warm the soup. Shae closed her eyes, trying to hide from the fear of both of the men being so close to her.

"Shae." Her eyes popped open at Adam's voice. A small mug of soup and a slice of toast were on a plate beside her on the bed.

She glanced from it to the two men sitting across the room. She turned away from the offering, her stomach revolting at the thought of eating.

"Eat, even if it is just a small amount." The biker doc's voice seemed to bounce off the walls of the small house.

Shae lifted the mug to her lips and took a sip. She grimaced and set it down again.

"We need to discuss who will be bringing you

your evening meds." Adam held up a hand when Shae physically flinched. "The foreman for this ranch, John Smith, lives in the house just down the drive. You can see his home from your front door. I'll have him stop by and bring you your meds. John was actually on the team that found you."

Shae closed her eyes. God, she just wanted them both to leave. She wanted to sleep and to get lost in the haze of the medications and forget... just forget.

"Shae, are you all right with John bringing your meds?" Adam's voice grated against her nerves.

"I don't care." She whispered the words, but she assumed they heard her when they both moved, their weight making the small chairs groan in protest.

"I'll be back tomorrow morning. I'll bring breakfast. My sister owns the diner in Hollister and makes some kick-ass cinnamon rolls and breakfast biscuits. Which would you prefer?" Biker Doc rose from his chair. He towered over her, and unlike Adam, who she knew, the man terrified her.

Shae pushed back further into the corner and shook her head. No, she did not want this man to come back.

"We will sit outside and visit. I understand that you aren't comfortable with me yet. I won't force

JOHN

you to be alone in a small space with me." Shae nodded if only to get the man to leave. Thankfully, he did. Adam, however, remained.

"I can vouch for him, Shae. He's a great doc. Eat some more of your soup." Adam leaned back and the chair moaned in protest.

Shae lifted the cup to her lips and took a sip. The warmth of the liquid down her throat was soothing. She took another sip and put the cup down.

Adam leaned forward. "Eat a couple bites of that toast for me." Shae picked up the bread and held it in her hand.

"Shae?"

She closed her eyes and lifted the bread to her mouth. It was easier to do what they wanted so they'd leave. She nibbled at the toast and put it down on the plate with the cup. She leaned to the left and let her body slide to the pillow while still tucked into a ball. The soup sloshed out of the cup and landed on the plate. Shae didn't care. She'd sleep around the wet spot if it spilled out of the plate. She closed her eyes and prayed Adam would leave.

"We'll get you feeling better. We have a plan in action now and you'll feel better soon. I'll check in on you later and then be back in the morning." Adam's voice was far too close and Shae jumped, tucking further into a fetal position. She heard him set the dishes on the counter and then rinse them out. Finally, the door opened and closed. Shae reached for the blanket and pulled it over her. She was so damn tired of fighting the darkness around her. Why wouldn't they just leave her alone? A tear trickled out of her closed eye, across the bridge of her nose, and landed on her hand. She didn't wipe it away. What was the sense when there would be so many more to follow?

CHAPTER 7

John headed up to his house. He was later than usual tonight, but he'd been down at the barn with the vet. One of the horses had gotten tangled up in a loose strand of barbed wire. The bottom strand of one of the old fence lines had snapped and Sugar had somehow gotten it wrapped around her hock. The cut wasn't too deep, but infection was a real concern. He and Frank had made plans to order new wire and fence posts for the lower pasture where the working horses were held this time of year. They'd move them over to the smaller pasture when it was time to start replacing the fencing. With all hands on deck, they could replace posts, concrete them in, and stretch barbed wire around the pasture in three or four days. It wasn't the best time to be repairing the fence line, but the animals' safety was paramount, and that old section of fence needed to be replaced. The patches had been patched. John chuckled at the thought. With an operation as big as the Marshall Ranch, you had to set priorities, and that fence had just became one of the top three. Sugar was Amanda's horse and Frank wasn't too pleased to have to tell her about her mare's injury. Miss Amanda was Frank's world. Well, her and his extended family.

John came around the corner of his house and stutter-stepped when he saw Adam Cassidy sitting on his porch. "Hey Doc, what's up?" John walked up the steps and dropped into one of the Adirondack chairs he'd built.

"Need to ask you a favor." The clipped tone of his voice told him Adam wasn't happy about asking him.

"Sure." This was getting to be a thing lately. First, Frank asking him to talk to the woman when or if he saw her, and now, Doc.

"Shae Diamant is the woman who you and Sierra Team rescued in Canada. She lives in the drover's cottage." Adam leaned forward and ran his hand down Cat's back as the feline headed to John. It catapulted into John's lap and put both its front paws on his chest and rubbed her cheek against John's jaw. The loud, rumbling purr-slash-squeak pulled a smile from Adam's somber presence.

"Her medication was fucked up and she hasn't been eating. I'll be able to give her the morning medications and Doctor Wheeler and I will probably be here daily to help her start to get a grip on everything that happened to her." Adam leaned back and stared at the sunset that was casting beautiful orange and gold hues across the valley in front of John's porch.

"Okay…" John had yet to figure out what this had to do with him.

"I can't give her the evening medications and be at home. Keelee will talk to Amanda and then things will tumble downhill. Frank and Amanda will be the wonderful people they are and they may press Shae to come to the main house to stay. Neither Jeremiah nor I believe that will be helpful. I'd like to leave her meds here every morning and have you take them over to her at night. It wouldn't hurt if you made her eat something, too."

John stroked Cat's mangy fur as she clawed his chest in a rhythmic fashion, the squeak of the hitch in her purr becoming a consistent sound in the silence that spread between the two men. John put the cat down. "You need to go home before Sasha comes looking for you." The cat meowed and rolled onto its back, still purring. John ran the scenarios through his mind before he nodded. "I'll agree under one condition."

"Whatever it is, you've got it." Adam didn't hesitate to agree.

John chuckled as he saw Sasha bounding over the field between the houses. "There will be nights I won't be able to be back in time. I'll need someone to call."

"Call me. Occasional absences I can deflect. Every night? Not so much." Adam stood and pointed toward the door. "Okay if I leave her meds here in the kitchen?"

John laughed and watched Cat slink down to try to pounce on Sasha as the dog pranced up the stairs. "Let me show you a safe place where this monster or that little poof of a mutt won't get into things."

"Never figured you for a cat or a poof person," Adam quipped as John almost tripped over Cat.

"I'm not. I can't get rid of either one of them." He nodded at Sasha as she trotted up the stairs.

JOHN

"Yeah, doesn't look like you're trying too damn hard." Adam followed him through the spacious front room of his home into the kitchen.

John turned on the light in the kitchen and laughed when Cat jumped up into her chair and sat down, eyeing him expectantly. Sasha sat down next to the chair and waited. Hell, he *didn't* try too damn hard to get rid of the animals.

"This cabinet is where I keep my Tylenol and vitamins. If you leave her meds here, I'll take them over. What time do I need to get them to her?"

"Right now, between six and seven." Adam leaned back against the counter and stared at the hardwood floor for a moment. "She's gone through hell. Unfortunately, I think she's stuck there. Physically, they were able to bring her through the trauma."

John leaned against the counter across from Adam and crossed his arms over his chest. "I get that. It took me a long time to work through what happened before I came here." He wasn't going to elaborate, but he still fell into the old grind of blaming himself for Lori's death. If he'd only acted faster. He shook his head to clear the swelling memories. "I'll do what I can."

Adam nodded and stood up, extending his hand.

"Thank you. She won't say it now, but eventually, she'll thank you, too."

"Not doing it for recognition. Frank and Amanda took me in when there was no other place in the world I would be safe. If I can help, I will. Frank asked me to visit with her if I saw her out and about, but I haven't seen her. Guess I should have just stopped by."

Adam shook his head and put his hands on his hips. "Nah, she wouldn't have responded well to that. Jeremiah will remind her that you are coming tomorrow night. The new scripts will help. I hope."

John walked the doctor to the door and shook his hand again when it was proffered. "Come play poker with us one Thursday evening." Adam's invite took him by surprise. He'd never been a regular at the game, never felt the need to be around people.

Cards. Not unless he couldn't avoid it. His past screamed up from the buried past at the mention of the game. He shrugged. "I'll consider it."

"No, you probably won't, but the offer is there nonetheless." Adam lifted his hand in a wave as he dropped off the porch and turned the corner heading back toward the main house.

Cat meowed loudly and wound around his boots while Sasha sat there, cocking her head like she was a bobblehead doll. John reached down and picked Cat up, starting the rumble-squeak symphony again. He headed back to the kitchen to get her and her mentally-challenged sidekick some food. He glanced at the darkened drover's cottage and sighed. He wasn't sure he was the right person for the job, but if it meant he could help out Frank and Amanda, he'd try.

Shae stared at her therapist. He held out a towel and soap. "Go take a shower. I'm not moving from this house until you do. You smell. I know that is not the gentlemanly thing to say, but woman, I'm being honest. Shower and I'll air out this place."

The dense fog of her past medications had been lifting slowly. She was perceiving more and more of her surroundings, and having Biker Doc here in her home without anyone else wasn't terrifying. It was almost as if the ever-present fear that thrummed through her body had been dialed back a notch or two. She still felt it and knew that the anxiety was boiling under the surface. Her eyes locked on the fluffy white towel and bottle of body wash.

"I made sure there was shampoo in the shower.

Please, for the love of my olfactory senses, get some water and soap going." The huge tattooed man extended the towel again. Shae reached for the towel and then looked at the small bathroom.

"I'm going to open the windows and doors then I'll sit outside under that big cottonwood tree. It is a beautiful spring morning. I'll give you thirty minutes and I'll knock and announce myself before I come back in." He immediately turned and started unlocking the windows and throwing the old sashes up. He headed to the back door and opened it, leaving the screen door in place. It took him four steps to reach the front door and open it. He turned and lifted his wrist, glancing at his watch. "Thirty minutes. Go." Jeremiah pointed to the bathroom and then turned to walk out of the house. Shae watched as he settled under the huge cottonwood tree that the cottage was nestled under.

"Bossy, isn't he?" Shae murmured to herself. The sound of her own voice bounced off the walls. She lifted her arm and sniffed her pits. Oh, fuck. She *did* stink. She couldn't remember the last time she showered… maybe… hell, no… there was no recollection of it. She padded into the small bathroom and shut the door before she stripped and turned on the water. She avoided the mirror and gathered a towel from one of the cabinets. She lifted the towel in front of her face and draped it over the damn thing. Shae stepped under the warm water and sighed at the blissful sensation. But the feeling was fleeting and replaced with a wave of dread. She closed her eyes and tried to block out the building swell of emotion. She grabbed the shampoo and made quick work of washing and then conditioning her hair. She scrubbed her skin with a washcloth, trying to remove the layers of filth that clung to her. Not the physical filth—no, it was the contaminated sensation she felt every time her mind reached back to that pit, every time the memories broke through the haze of the medication. She shut off the shower and wrapped her hair in a towel before she dried off. It was only then that she realized she hadn't brought any clothes in with her. She cracked open the bathroom door and peeked out to see if Biker Doc was in the house. He wasn't, so she headed to her suitcase that she still hadn't unpacked and grabbed some clothes.

By the time she exited the bathroom a second time with clothes on and her hair combed out, Biker Doc was back in the house. He had two breakfast sandwiches in front of him, another on a plate for her with a huge cinnamon roll in the middle of the table. Shae smelled the unmistakable aroma of cinnamon and coffee. Her stomach clenched at the smell and she felt a wave of nausea pass over her. She was hungry for the first time in forever and she *wanted* to eat.

"Good morning." Jeremiah poured a cup of coffee out for her and pointed to the seat. Shae padded across the tiny front room with a hesitant gait. She pulled out the chair and sat down, keeping her focus on the buttermilk biscuit.

"How are you feeling this morning?" His question took her by surprise. She shrugged and tore a small piece of fluffy bread away.

"Just FYI, shrugging isn't going to work for me. I require answers. You don't have to be verbose, but if we want to make progress you need to talk."

Shae put the biscuit in her mouth and almost swooned at the wonderful, soft, buttery goodness. She picked another piece off and glanced up at him. "I'm hungry."

Jeremiah lifted an eyebrow at her before she dropped her eyes. "I take it you weren't hungry before?"

Shae shook her head and peeked up at him. "No." Slowly, she nibbled on the food until she'd eaten a quarter of it and he'd devoured his. The food warmed her in ways the blankets she'd layered on her couldn't. It was better, but she still wasn't... right? Shae knew her emotions were stopped behind a wall of medicine. She understood they were there, but she was relieved that she didn't have to deal with the entirety of what—

"Have you ever thought about hurting yourself?" His question startled her. Shae jumped up and rubbed her hands over her arms. She moved back to her bed and sat down on it, only then noticing that the bedding had been changed.

"Shae?" Biker Doc's questioning voice was jarring and demanding, even though it wasn't loud. His presence was jarring. He needed to leave. She wanted to find oblivion in sleep again.

He turned in his chair and leaned his forearms on his knees. "It is all right to admit it if you have. I'm here to help you understand and deal with the thoughts that are running through your mind."

Shae dropped her head into her hands and admitted, "Sometimes I think it would be easier for everyone if I wasn't here."

"Do you feel that way now?"

His question forced her to think. She shook her head. "No, not right now."

"Okay. I want to make a deal with you. If you

ever get to that place where you feel that way, you will reach out to me, or Doctor Cassidy, or Mr. Smith. We will be here to help you if things ever get to that point. You are not alone, Shae."

She nodded. Logically she got that, but her mind sometimes shouted lies to her. Sometimes? Hell, almost constantly.

"Come on. We are going to go outside and take a short walk. We can talk or not, it is up to you, but you need to start regaining your strength. Sunshine is a wonderful form of medicine."

Shae looked up at the hand he offered. "I don't want to do it. I don't want to kill myself. But I'm scared. Sometimes it seems it would be easier."

Biker Doc dropped his hand and squatted down in front of her. She glanced up and met and held his eyes for a moment before she dropped them again. "That's real good to know. I understand what you're going through, and I can help you find your way out of the labyrinth you think you're lost in now. It will be hard work, but I know you can do it."

Would she? God, she hoped so. Today, she only knew she didn't want to die. She sniffed back tears at that thought.

"We will take it day by day, Shae. We will find a way for you to deal with the hand that was dealt to you." Jeremiah stood and offered his hand again. Shae couldn't deal with the thought of physical contact. She shook her head and pushed up. Biker Doc stepped back, seeming to understand she wouldn't take his hand.

Her unsteady gait made for a very slow stroll to the cottonwood tree. They took a break there where she leaned against the trunk of the tree and rested. She gazed over to the house across the driveway and down the road a bit. A dark-colored cat walked along the top rail of the house. Shae focused on the animal as it maneuvered around support beams as if it was doing an acrobatic act. They talked about plans, what to do if she felt one way or another. The doctor spoke and she listened. His words provided her a respite in the storm of emotions that seemed to swirl constantly.

The doctor glanced at his watch. "Sorry to keep you for so long today. I've been here nearly four hours, but I think we've made some solid plans. I'm available any time you want to talk. Adam said you were given a cell phone with all of our numbers programmed in it."

She nodded. It sat on the counter, untouched. Doctor Wheeler continued, "We've removed several of the medications that were not supposed to be prescribed together. You should be feeling better. I've kept you on an antidepressant and kept the dosage pretty high but lower than what was originally prescribed. We will taper that off as we progress. I need to know how you're feeling now so I can gauge whether or not to change the dosage."

Shae threw a quick look at him. She drew a deep breath. "I'm tired. I don't feel anything except fear. I'm afraid all the time. But even that seems… distant."

Biker Doc nodded. "Did you sleep well last night?"

Shae shook her head. The drugs didn't knock her out as they had previously, but she wasn't sure if that was a good thing or a bad thing.

"Dreams?"

Shae shook her head. "Images. Thoughts. Feelings. Nothing like a dream, just a mash-up of a host of things."

The man nodded again. He motioned toward the house. "Let's go back in. Today was a good start. We've agreed you won't hurt yourself today and if you ever get to a point where you think you might you'll call me, or Adam, or Mr. Smith."

Shae glanced back at the house down the way.

She nodded. She wasn't going to hurt herself today. She wouldn't do that, not today.

"Words, Shae," Biker Doc reminded her.

"I'm okay today and I'll call if I'm not."

Jeremiah nodded at her. "Good."

John shook his head for the fifth or sixth time since wrapping a plate in tinfoil and grabbing Shae's medicine. Cat had decided to play dog and the dog had decided to go home. Cat was trailing beside him as he made his way over to the drover's cottage. He'd fed the darn thing—again—so she wasn't trailing because she was hungry. He stopped at the door and knocked lightly. There was a shuffling from inside the darkened cottage before a light turned on in the living room. He waited for the door to open. The woman who opened the door in no way resembled the bruised and battered human they'd rescued from that bastard. The bruises had faded, and her eyes were… brown, beautiful, and filled with apprehension. She was rail-thin and hunched in on herself.

"Hi." John had never felt so damn awkward in his life. She peeked up at him with another split second of a glance and nodded. He figured that was all he was going to get out of her. "I brought you dinner and medicine." Cat darted into the cottage and wound herself around Shae's ankles. The woman jumped away from the contact. "Shit, I'm sorry." John let himself in the cottage and set her food on the table along with her meds. He bent down to pick up Cat and throw her out of the house.

"Don't." Shae's single word stopped him in mid-motion. "I like cats." John lifted Cat into his arms, which started the rumble-slash-squeak machine hiding somewhere within the little animal.

Shae reached a hesitant hand out, stopping shy of touching the animal. John didn't move and waited for her to continue. Her hand dropped away without stroking Cat's fur. "She's nice, but she can be a demanding taskmaster. If you don't give her enough attention, she'll start with the meowing. She knows I'll do almost anything to keep her from that yowling."

He motioned toward the table. "Go ahead and sit down. We've already eaten. I'll grab you some water so you can take your meds." He dropped Cat and headed into the kitchen. Hell, he was rambling on like a schoolgirl. He grabbed a glass and filled it from the tap. The well water on the ranch was pure and delicious. When he turned around, he paused. Shae was sitting on the floor with Cat in her lap. The damn animal was playing with a strand of her brown hair, which the woman was dangling over the furball. John stepped back to the table and sat down to watch the two of them. Shae glanced up at him, and he wasn't sure, but he thought maybe a small smile pulled at the side of her mouth.

Cat noticed John and rolled languidly from Shae's lap, stretching before she wandered over to him and rubbed up against his leg. Shae lifted up slowly. She limped forward and carefully sat down at the table. John pulled the tinfoil off the plate. He'd grilled a massive steak and cut some up for her before he demolished the rest of it. He had corn and a bit of fried potato alongside the meat and a generous portion of homemade bread that Aunt Betty delivered on a routine basis. Of course, he'd slathered the bread with ranch-made butter because the butter was the best thing for miles.

Shae picked at the food, barely eating, but she took a portion of each. She pulled pieces of the bread away and nibbled on it.

"What is her name?" The question snapped his attention away from the way she was eating back to the person in the room with him.

John laughed as he responded, "Her name is Cat.

She's not mine, just a royal pain in the ass that always shows up when there is likely to be food."

Shae's eyes darted up to him and a shocked expression flashed across her face before she lowered her eyes again. "Have you no imagination? She needs a better name."

The whispered words forced a bellow of bitter laughter from him. His life up to coming to the ranch had been nothing but his imagination. He'd built lives for operatives that included minute details such as a scar on their chin. He used his vivid imagination to engineer elaborate lives for deep-cover agents that were impossible to breach. Some of his covers were currently entrenched on Capitol Hill, the Kremlin, Tel Aviv, and various countries of the Middle East. That was the reason he was hunted, and why he was 'killed.' As the architect of the covers, he was the only one to know each agent from the diverse organizations that utilized his talent. He'd been outed. His sister and father had been murdered, and if anyone knew he was alive he would once again be a hunted man. Oh, he had an imagination, all right, and it was his imagination that had cost him everything.

"I didn't figure she'd hang out around me too much. Her owner spoils her and I guess I do, too.

Made the mistake of feeding her one night and then someone pushed fast forward and she's still hanging around."

Shae took a small piece of meat and lowered her hand toward the floor. It took Cat about a sixteenth of a second to make her way to the treat. She delicately pulled the small bite from Shae's fingers and marched away with her spoils. John shook his head. Damn animal now had three people wrapped around her broken bobbed tail.

"Here are your meds." John called Shae's attention back to the table. She drew a deep breath and carefully lifted each off the tabletop. He waited while she took them and then set down the water glass.

"Would you like to keep the leftovers?"

She shook her head.

"Okay, well, if it is okay with you, tomorrow night I'll bring over two plates so you don't have to eat alone."

Shae turned toward where Cat had disappeared and shrugged. John guessed that was as good as he was going to get. He stood and collected the almost-untouched meal. He pulled the tinfoil over the plate and opened the door. "See you tomorrow night." She didn't acknowledge him and that was all right. He wasn't there to make a friend. He was doing a favor for Frank and Doc. That was it. The woman had big issues to deal with and he wasn't part of that. Cat darted out of the door when he opened it, meowing at the plate as if she was going to get the scraps. John pulled the door closed behind him. Damn cat *was* spoiled because hell yeah he was going to give her the scraps.

CHAPTER 8

The evening sun cast growing shadows through the cottage window. Shae was huddled in the corner of her small couch, which had become her normal position. Her session with Jeremiah this morning, like every morning for the past month-and-a-half, had consisted of him talking about shit that had nothing to do with her or what had happened. He told her about his life in Hollister and before when he practiced in California. He went on about his gramma and the impact she had on his life. Shae walked when he asked her to and tried to care, but she didn't. He'd tweaked her medication and the drug-induced fog had cleared, yet her carefully banked emotions still floated just out of reach. The disjointed feeling of... not feeling was difficult to understand, let alone describe. It was as if she was holding a balloon carrying all her emotions and she could see where they were stored but really didn't care if they floated out there in front of her.

Human contact was still a trigger for her. She couldn't stand anyone touching her. Adam had been down and checked on her every morning. She liked Doctor Cassidy, yet she couldn't even tell *him* that she'd been willing to sell out each and every one of her coworkers. She would have screamed out where each of them lived, how to find their families, where to strike them to make the most violent impact. Her compatriots at Mossad would have been laid at the altar of that bastard just so the pain would stop. She had begged for Maurice to let her tell the woman. To give information on her superiors, on the Mossad organization, and any information she knew about any operation.

She didn't deserve anyone's concern. She loathed herself. If her agency knew what she'd been willing to do to stop the torture, they'd… Shae shook her head. She should be dead. Sometimes she wanted to be strong enough to end it all. The thought of living no longer held the same power over her thoughts as it once did. Everyone would be better off without her. She couldn't dispute the fact.

JOHN

A small sound brought her out of her mind and spiraling dark thoughts. Shae made a slow, careful sweep of the little cottage. A meow, and then another. She lifted off the couch and took a moment to ensure she was steady before she made the slow trek to her door. Shae opened the door and Cat strolled in, rubbing her body against Shae's leggings. She left the door open slightly so the animal could leave when she wanted and made her way back to the couch. As soon as she sat down, Cat was in her lap. The animal promptly curled into a ball and looked up at her. Of their own accord, her hands stroked the ugly animal's fur. The animal meowed at her and rolled onto her side, stretching so far she ended up draped over Shae's leg like a limp noodle.

A knock at the open door sent it into the cottage. Cat jumped down and ran over to John Smith, who was carrying two plates in his hand. "Hey, you spoiled thing. I wondered where you'd run off to." John talked to the cat and ignored Shae as he usually did. John didn't expect her to talk to him which was… comforting? There was no pressure during their evening moments together. No anticipation that she answer questions or engage in useless conversation. He put the food on the table and headed into the kitchen to get two glasses of water.

Shae forced herself out of the chair and over to the table.

John returned and pulled the tinfoil off two plates of chicken and cheesy pasta with a side of peas. The aroma punched through to her senses, making her mouth water and her stomach growl. Macaroni and cheese was one of her favorite dishes. Her mom made it a lot when she was growing up. Not unexpected when you were raising a daughter without the help of a father.

John sat down and placed her water and meds in front of her. Shae took them and lifted a forkful and enjoyed the warm, melty goodness.

"I'm early. The twins and Chief want me to fill in as a fourth for poker tonight. They'll be heading down to my place soon. Frank and Amanda are gone a couple days and Doc has his hands full with two new guys at the clinic. An operation in Venezuela went south."

Shae frowned down at her plate. "I don't know who any of those people are. You'll have to explain that statement."

John stopped his fork halfway to his mouth, obviously surprised she'd spoken, and Shae could understand his shock. She'd said maybe six words to him in the last week.

"Chief—actually, his real name is Mike—he runs the Guardian side of the ranch. Dixon and Drake—Drake owns that bundle of fur—are twins and work for Guardian. Doc usually joins as a fourth, but he's not going to be able to make it tonight. Frank and Amanda own this ranch. They went to New York to watch a play on Broadway, so instead of playing up at the main house, they are coming down to mine."

Shae put her fork down, no longer hungry. "This is all a Guardian facility, no?"

"Actually, no, it is a working ranch, and a damn big one, too. From what I've been told, the Guardian side of the property started out with a small concept. A place for injured Guardians to come and rehab. Frank was able to rent them a sizable portion of land and it grew exponentially. The other side of that row of hills is a small town run entirely off the grid. Guardian has more resources than any other agency in the world. Including the Mossad."

That pulled a small smile from her. "You were there? Jeremiah said you were on the team that rescued me."

"I was. I'm not part of the team, I was looking for something else, but I held your hand until help arrived." John glanced down at her hands. "I'm glad you were able to survive."

"Survive." The word echoed around her mind. *Survive.* Had she? Really? Her body was here, but should it be? What she'd been willing to do? To sacrifice everyone she worked with or knew to stop Maurice from hurting her anymore? He'd broken her in ways that she couldn't articulate. Humiliation, pain, and more pain. Maybe survival wasn't enough.

"Eat, please. Cat is getting way too fat. Look at the belly on that thing. She's going to waddle before long. Maybe I should tell Drake to change her name to Duck."

Shae looked over at Cat, who was sitting at John's feet and staring at him. Her golden eyes never flicked from him.

Shae stabbed some more pasta with no intentions of eating it. "Cat isn't fat." Shae's mind swirled around the whispered ideas she'd been coveting. The whispers grew louder.

John laughed and speared a bite of chicken. "She's a spoiled, entitled animal."

"*You* spoiled her." Shae surprised herself with her response. It was as if her mind knew she needed to divert attention from the course of action that was firming up in her mind.

"I'll deny it to the day I die. I don't like cats." John

pinched off a small piece of chicken and casually tossed it to the floor where Cat pounced on it.

Shae lifted her eyes from the bedraggled feline to her dinner partner. "I can tell." Shae felt a moment of lightheartedness that flickered warmly inside her and then was swallowed into guilt that quickly swirled to steal away the happy thought. She dropped her eyes and put down her fork. She didn't have the right to be happy. Not anymore. Waves of remorseful condemnation and an ocean of self-loathing pushed against her. The small voices in her thoughts that taunted her now spoke loud and clear. She'd been struggling with the idea since she'd come here. If she was going to do it, it should be now. She looked up at John and drew a deep breath in. She'd wait until he left and then she'd end the pain and the guilt. Once and for all.

Yesterday, she'd written out her apology to her superiors and colleagues and had poured out her pain onto the paper. Seeing her sins in writing only compounded her guilt and humiliation. She hated herself. The world would be a better place without her in it.

John didn't say anything for a long time. Finally, he cleared his throat and stood, gathering his plate and hers. "Are you all right?" He asked the question as he stood at the door.

Shae nodded and even sent him a small glance and a smile. "Actually, I'm much better now. Much better. You make sure she stays fat, all right?"

John didn't understand or particularly like the sudden change in Shae. Something was off, almost as if a switch had been thrown in her mind. He couldn't suppress the feeling that something was terribly wrong. He stood at his kitchen counter and chopped up the leftover chicken pieces for Cat.

He'd learned to follow his gut. He palmed his phone and pushed Jeremiah's contact. The phone rang twice before the doctor came online. "What's wrong?"

"I don't know, but I got this feeling."

"Explain that."

"We were eating, and she was her usual subdued self. But then… It was as if I was watching all the tumblers in her mind spin and lock into place. The only thing is I have no idea what the fuck opened."

There was a long silence on the other end of the phone. John gave the man time to process his comments. "What was said?" He recounted their brief exchange word for word.

"Son of a bitch. John, get your ass back over there, I'll call Adam. I'm on my way." John hit the door in a full-out run. It took him little time to clear the distance between his house and the cottage, but the realization of the warning signs he picked up on earlier slapped him across the face.

She could be suicidal.

Fuck him, he prayed he hadn't been gone long enough for her to do anything. He hit the front door of the cottage, slamming the wood into the plaster behind it, and swept the area for her. He saw her curled up on the bed and launched after her. John pulled her into his arms and cradled her, pushing her hair away from her face. "God, tell me you didn't take anything, did you?" He searched the area for any sign she'd ingested any more drugs.

Shae shook her head and shuddered against him before a torrential sob tore from her chest. She grabbed ahold of his neck with a strength her weakened body shouldn't have. Her sobs vibrated through both of them. John moved back and leaned his shoulders against the wall, tugging her body against his. She folded into him and... hell, she lost her shit. He held her and tried to understand what she was saying. The sobbed words started to link up in his mind. He cringed at the guilt the woman was carrying. He stroked her hair and rocked from side to side, not knowing what else to do.

When Lori had been upset, she only wanted him to listen, not to fix anything, but just to let her talk out her worries and concerns. It was the hardest fucking thing for him to do. His DNA was wired to fix problems, make things work, define the correct channels, and assign meaning and responsibility. The woman falling apart in his arms didn't need that. She was so fucking broken, and thank God he'd been here and smart enough to call Doc Wheeler when something seemed off.

John heard a truck skid to a stop beside his house and then the pounding of feet across the small area to the cottage. Adam Cassidy pulled up short and then made his way to the twin bed where he was holding Shae.

The doctor's eyes swept the room the same as his had. John watched him as he searched the house and pulled several prescription bottles off the counter. He dumped them out and counted. His shoulders relaxed and his head nodded as if he was confirming his own thoughts. He crossed over to the desk and grabbed a pen and paper. A heavy envelope slid to the ground, moved past the point of balancing on the edge when Adam turned back toward them. He held up a note that read 'NO OD. JUST DO WHAT YOU ARE DOING NOW.'

John nodded and continued to sway from side to side and stroke Shae's hair. Her sobbing had subsided, but she still clung to him as if he was the only flotation device available and she was trying to tread water in the middle of the Atlantic Ocean. Her whispered, "I'm so sorry, I didn't know how to stop him," seemed to be important to her. She repeated it over and over. John tucked her head under his chin and hummed a song he remembered his mother humming to him when he was young. He closed his eyes and let the tune rumble through his chest.

He heard Adam sifting through papers and cracked his eye open enough to see he'd picked up the envelope and was reading the contents. John closed his eyes and continued to hum while he stroked Shae's hair. Her body fell limp against him. The ravaging sobs and unbridled crying left her, yet she still clung to him. His shirt was wet beneath her cheek and her thin body seemed cold. He gathered her tighter against him and she willingly allowed herself to be wrapped in his arms. Her breath hitched, no doubt the reflexive actions of leftover tremors from her breakdown. John couldn't imagine the weight that bore down on the woman. She obviously felt she'd done something wrong as she had apologized over and over again while he held her.

John had no idea how long he had held her. Cat appeared on the bed and curled up in the corner, watching them. A truck pulled up in the driveway. John opened his eyes and Adam held up a hand before he ducked out the door with the envelope in his hand. He could hear the men talking. When he again heard footsteps on the wooden floor, he opened his eyes. Jeremiah Wheeler seemed to examine the sight of them with some type of awe. John had no idea why nor did he care to figure it out.

Jeremiah moved over and squatted down next to the bed. "Shae, are you awake?" Her head moved north and south, and she tensed in his arms. He tightened his arms around her and started the slow back and forth sway again. He hadn't realized he'd stopped.

"Can you tell me what happened tonight?" Jeremiah's voice held a calm that John knew he wouldn't be able to match anytime soon.

"I wanted to kill myself, but I couldn't do it." Shae's quiet, hollow admission gutted him. "I had more prescriptions in my luggage. I was going to take them, but I couldn't."

"Okay. Thank you for sharing that, Shae. What made you think you should kill yourself?"

Shae lifted her head from his chest and turned toward the doctor. "I deserve it. I begged that bastard to stop, I offered to tell them anything, to give them information on where to find my people. I couldn't stand the pain anymore. I tried. God, I tried. He kept hurting me!" The tears that had abated tore through her again. John didn't tighten his grip, not knowing what he should do. He looked at Jeremiah, but the man's focus was directly fixed on Shae.

"Shae, you didn't do anything wrong."

Shae pulled away from him and screamed at Jeremiah, "Fuck you!"

Cat scrambled off the bed in a whirlwind of claws and fur. The animal flew past Jeremiah and out the door like Satan's pitchfork was prodding her mangy ass.

Shae damn near vibrated on his lap as she continued her explosive outburst, completely ignoring Cat's hasty departure, "How can you say that? Do you have any idea what I did? You don't. *I* know what *I* did! *I know*! I didn't do anything wrong? How can you say that? You don't know. Fuck! I was going to turn over my entire organization to those people! My organization, my coworkers! I would have told them anything to get him to stop!"

Jeremiah's face remained passive at the spewing barrage of hate. He nodded and rubbed his chin before he asked, "Do you think anyone else would have done differently if they had been tortured nonstop for days?"

Jeremiah's calm words were the antithesis of Shae's impassioned explosion, and with that one quiet question, she deflated like a balloon.

She collapsed back against John and slowly shook her head as if she was talking to an imbecile. "How would I know? You're the one with a university degree in crazy people." John suppressed a chuckle. There was a spitfire under all that hurt.

"Right. Okay. John, I appreciate your assistance, but I need to talk with Shae in private." John hesitated when Shae's body tensed.

"Are you okay with that?" John whispered the words to her. He was going to give her the choice. It seemed like she needed to be able to make that decision for herself. Shae nodded and crawled off his lap, moving into the other corner, her thick fall of hair covering her face.

John lifted off the bed and headed toward the

door. He turned before he walked across the threshold. "If you need anything, I'm less than a hundred steps away." He didn't wait to see if she'd respond but tapped the wooden frame of the door twice and headed back to his house. Adam, Dixon, Drake, and Chief were seated in the chairs in front of his house. Adam must have stayed after Jeremiah arrived and the rest were at his house for the Thursday night game. Dixon stood as he approached. "How is she?"

John shook his head and dropped into a vacant chair. "Beats the fuck out of me." He accepted an ice-cold bottle of water that was pressed into his hand. John glanced over at Chief and raised the bottle in a salute. He downed the damn thing in one go. After he crunched the thin plastic and capped it so it remained flat, he shook his head. "Doc Wheeler is talking with her now."

"Did she actually…" Drake's question floated out there half-asked.

John glanced at Adam before he spoke. "No. She didn't." John knew what Drake was asking, and he knew the Doctor couldn't say a damn thing.

John started the chair rocking just to give his body something to do. Listening to her tonight, he understood that guilt was eating her alive. He got it.

He'd tasted a version of that hell. Lori would be alive now if he'd acted faster, been more alert.

He'd had to learn how to cope with what had happened. He learned to understand he wasn't responsible for the leak of his information or what happened to her as a result of their work. He wasn't the person that planted the bomb under Lori's car. He wasn't the one who'd killed his father and left him to rot in a dumpster. But their work *was* the reason both his father and Lori had been killed. There was a portion of that responsibility that would forever fall across his shoulders.

Shae wouldn't believe it right now, but she was lucky. Damn lucky. None of her coworkers or family had died from her actions. John drew a deep breath and sat quietly in the dark with the other four men. The silent agreement to hold vigil until Jeremiah was finished bound them to the quiet and retrospective mood. Cat jumped up into his lap then hopped up to the back of the chair and jumped over to Drake's chair to hunker down with her owner. The beast's squeak-slash-purr was the only sound that punctuated the gentle nighttime sounds of the ranch.

It was close to three hours later before the lights in the cottage extinguished and Jeremiah walked toward the porch. John knew the man couldn't talk about any of the things he and Shae had discussed, but he damn sure hoped he could provide some kind of reassurance that she would be all right.

"She's sleeping. It was a big night for her. I think we turned a corner. She has a long road ahead of her and a lot of work." He gave a glance at the men sitting with John. "Sorry for interrupting your Thursday night tradition."

"Just glad she's okay." His friends rose and said their goodbyes.

Jeremiah turned back to him. "I need you to understand that she needs to make this progress on her own. I know you want to help, but let her extend her hand to you, don't push yourselves on her. She is a resilient lady." Jeremiah waved off a bottle of water he was offered. "I have to head home. I'll be back tomorrow morning. Adam, can we talk a moment?" The doctor unfolded himself from the chair and followed Jeremiah to his truck. John stood and stretched, glancing back at Cat, who'd woken up at all the movement. She lifted and stretched, looking like a Halloween silhouette before she jumped down and jogged after Drake.

John leaned against the railing of his porch and waved to both doctors as they departed. He sent his gaze over toward the drover's cottage. He wasn't supposed to care. He was supposed to be doing a favor, but that woman had reached out and grabbed him by the throat tonight. Got his attention real quick, and he wasn't about to turn away from her. She'd laid her heart bare while he held her. Emotion so deep and so personal that he felt like a voyeur for having witnessed it. How could he not care? He glanced up at the millions of stars in the South Dakota sky and drew a deep breath. If anyone would have told him years ago he'd be in a place where he gave a fuck about anyone again, he'd have called them a liar.

CHAPTER 9

Shae watched Jeremiah's pickup back out of John's driveway. It had been over a week since her meltdown. Jeremiah called it a turning point. She called it hitting rock-fucking-bottom. She'd spent more time with Jeremiah in the last seven days than she'd ever spent with any one man. Well, outside her partner. The doctor was helping. She couldn't deny it. She wasn't going to paint a rosy picture of unicorns and glitter, because... just fuck no, her life had never been about that girly stuff, but she was feeling better. Not much stronger physically but... better mentally. She still couldn't stand anyone close to her and Jeremiah had told her that aversion was natural given the circumstances of her detention. Shae walked out to the cottonwood tree and sat down at the base of the massive trunk.

She looked out over the ranch, glad that she could see the cattle and horses from where she sat. She was happy to be on the ranch side of the property. She wasn't ready to face Guardian's facilities. She'd seen glimpses of the detachment when she was trundled over to her small cottage the day she landed. Guardian had placed no mandates or timelines on her, yet assumably, they needed answers to their questions. But... not yet.

Jeremiah had left her this morning with more questions than she had answers for. The sneaky man did it on purpose. Her mind churned through their conversations today and snagged on several key points. She had touch aversion, except she'd let John hold her. Hell, she'd clung to the man that night. Shae closed her eyes and leaned against the rough trunk of the old tree. She felt safe in his arms. Did she have any idea why? No.

She called up his image in her mind's eye. He was tall, broad in the shoulders, and lean. Dark hair with touches of silver at the temples, brown eyes... five o'clock shadow every night that he stopped by. He had a cat that hung around him and adored him, even though it wasn't his. Shae chuckled at the thought of the poor thing. It was a busted, used-up excuse of an animal, but the thing adored John. And if she was honest, she liked that cat, too. She was sweet and wasn't a mean thing like the one her mom had when she was growing up.

Shae's thoughts plummeted at the thought of her mother. She'd called her mom once to let her know she was alive. Her mother didn't answer her phone, so she left a message and a call-back number. She was in that hospital for months and her mother never returned her call. Her mom was very happy with her new husband and *she* wasn't needed in her mom's life any longer. Yeah, she knew she wasn't ready for the emotion that would come with facing her mother or anyone else back in Israel. A horrible cloak of guilt flew at her from her subconscious. Shae popped open her eyes and drew a deep breath in, counting to ten, focusing on the numbers, nothing but the numbers, and then let it out for a count of... well, eight because she couldn't exhale long enough. She went through the breathing exercise and willed away the darkness. Sometimes it worked, sometimes it didn't. She had other tricks that Jeremiah had given her, or she had the magic pill. But she didn't want to have to take any more medication. She was tired of the disassociated feeling the drugs gave her.

She heard the truck pull up but continued her breathing exercises. At the sound of footsteps heading her way, she opened her eyes. John ambled over the grass followed by Cat and a white, poofy… was that a dog? John sat down in the shade and removed his hat, wiping the band with a bandana from his back pocket.

He grabbed Cat and lifted her into his lap where she promptly tucked into a circle and began cleaning her scraggly coat. The poofy dog pranced over to her and barked.

"Meet Sasha. I'm not sure if she has a brain in her head, but she's fun to watch." The dog started spinning around in circles and barking before it promptly sat down and started panting.

"I see what you mean." She reached out to pet the little dog, but it bounded away at a full run.

"Ah, Joy must be calling her. Joy is the dog's owner."

"Do you always collect other people's animals?"

He laughed and glanced down at the cat in his lap. "It would seem I do. How's the day treating you?"

Shae shrugged. "Some good moments, some bad. How was yours?"

"Typical day. Never-ending list of chores."

"How did you come to work for Frank? I mean, you were with the men who rescued me, so this job on the ranch, is it a... cover?" She couldn't conceive the exact relationship of a man on a rescue operation and a ranch hand.

"Ah, not really. Let's just say he was looking for a ranch manager. I was looking for a ranch to manage." John didn't look at her when he spoke; instead, his attention was suddenly focused on Cat. Shae got the message loud and clear. He didn't want to talk about it. She could respect that. She watched the man's strong, calloused hands stroke the pitiful-looking feline with tenderness that his size and stature belayed.

"Are you feeling better?"

Shae's eyes snapped up to his at the question. She didn't see the slightest hint of judgement or sympathy. It was hard to figure out what was in his expression, especially since the lower dose of antidepressants still fucked with her ability to instantly grasp what emotion she was internalizing.

"I never did thank you, did I?" She watched as he

dropped his eyes back down to the cat and gave a shrug of his shoulder.

"Any one of the people at this ranch would have done the same thing. They all care about you."

"That may be true, but you were the one who was there. Jeremiah told me you called him because you were concerned."

John met her gaze. He swallowed hard and nodded before he added, "I lost someone I loved. I bear a portion of the responsibility of her death. I understand what you're going through—to a degree—because everyone's experience in life is different. It took me a long time to be able to close my eyes at night and not blame myself. But I was able to acknowledge what happened, accept what responsibility laid on my shoulders, and move on. It hasn't been easy."

Shae took a moment to look out over the pastures and absorb what the man had just told her. "Does Jeremiah know about your loss?"

"Nah. I wasn't really associated with Guardian when I came here. I wasn't part of the organization to begin with. They gave me refuge from a bad situation. They gave me a safe haven after my usefulness at the other agencies I worked for ran its course. I didn't get professional help for the situation that happened. I gutted it out and struggled with the insanity I was putting myself through. I'm sure that's why it took so long for me to come to terms with what happened." John pulled a long strand of wheatgrass and tickled Cat's ear with it. She rolled onto her back and swatted at the blade of grass.

Shae considered the man's words—or rather, lack of information—carefully. There was more to him and his past than he was telling. That was fine by her. Unfortunately, the man was front and center when her life exploded, and he had a damn good idea of what her secrets were and why they were haunting her.

"Anyway, the reason I asked if you were having a good day was that one of the horses had her colt. I have to go down to the barn and check on her and the little one. Some horses don't really have any maternal instinct. They had to hand-raise this particular horse's colt last year, and if she doesn't take to the little one we'll have to do that again this year. I thought I'd ask if you want to go see the little guy." John pulled the grass along his jean-clad thigh and Cat pounced on him, grabbing the strand with a curled paw and attacking it.

Shae glanced at the distance to the barn. She could probably walk there, but it would take every ounce of energy she had. It was at least a quarter-mile. John followed her gaze and shook his head. "I'm not asking you to walk it. I know that would be a tall order and you are still recuperating. We'll take the truck. We can drive there and then maybe take a drive around the area after. You probably need to see something different by now."

Shae averted her eyes. The man was so damn thoughtful. She did want to see a baby horse. She'd seen horses in pastures when her school went on trips but had never seen one up close. In Israel, the horses were bred by the rich. Arabians of the finest bloodlines. She viewed the world as an amazing place back then. Hers to conquer and nothing was going to stop her. She felt the darkness creeping toward her again and acted on impulse rather than in fear. "I'd like to see the pony."

John laughed and got to his feet, offering her a hand. "Foal or colt. A pony is a small, fully-grown horse."

"Okay. I want to see the baby horse." John laughed at her obstinance, but she only noticed that he towered over her. Shae stiffened and tried to quell the fear of reaching out toward his extended hand. She froze, unable to move.

He slowly lowered until he was right in front of

her. "You trusted me when you were at your lowest. I haven't changed. I would never hurt you. Take my hand. I won't pull you up and I won't grasp your hand. You are in control. Trust yourself and trust me. Take my hand, Shae."

Shae moved her gaze from his outstretched hand to his face. The kind sincerity in his eyes softened his sharp features. She closed her eyes and reached out slowly. The rough callouses of his palm scratched the pads of her fingers. She opened her eyes and focused on the place her fingers laid against his palm.

"There you go. Now, let's go see that baby horse." John stood, leaving his hand in the exact same place. Shae tightened her grip and used his hand as leverage. As promised, he didn't close his hand or try to do anything other than support her weight when she pushed down on him. He remained motionless when she finally stood upright, allowing her to gain her balance. The pain in her ankle forced her to pause and wait for a moment. Her body trembled, not from the effort but from the contact. She slowly pulled her hand away and took a step toward his truck.

They walked slowly toward the massive four-wheel-drive king cab. Shae stopped beside the behemoth. She turned toward John and then glanced back at the high step to the cab. "I don't..."

John smiled and held up a finger. He went to the back of the truck, dropped the tailgate, and pulled something from the bed. He lifted a plywood set of steps and brought them to her side of the truck, positioning it directly in front of the door. John reached over, lifted the handle, and opened the door. He moved to her side and extended his hand just like he'd done minutes before. She looked at the steps, up at the truck, and over toward him.

Take my hand. The phrase echoed in her mind. Shae made the visual sweep again, resting her gaze on his outstretched hand. She moved up to the step and reached out to him. She pushed against his palm, gripping it tightly when she lifted her bad leg up the small step. He remained completely still and steady underneath her grip. Shae drew a deep breath and took the next step and the next. She grabbed the handle inside the cab of the truck and released his hand, finally sliding onto the leather seat. Her body was covered in a sheen of sweat and her heart felt as if it would pound out of her chest. She closed her eyes and leaned forward.

"Breathe. You did a wonderful job. It isn't easy to trust or to take chances when the façade of our normality is stripped from our lives. Rebuilding takes small steps, tiny movements that can gain momentum. Starting is the hardest part."

Shae opened her eyes and turned toward him. Standing where he was, he was just above eye level with her. "Starting sucks." It was the truth, and she'd never been one to sugarcoat a fact.

His face split into a wide grin and then he laughed, "It does indeed." He picked up the stairs in one hand and shut her door with the other. Shae automatically moved to pull the seatbelt across her chest and froze when the sensation of being strapped in became too much. She unclenched her hand and let the belt retract back to its position. She couldn't bear that. Not yet.

John got into the truck and started it before backing out of the drive and almost idling the quarter of a mile to the barn where the horses were kept. The steps reappeared and his hand extended for her to use. It wasn't easy, and it took almost five minutes for her to get down from a height she'd normally jump down from with ease. When she reached the ground, her legs shook, and she was awash with sweat. She glanced toward the barn and the short distance morphed in her observation. She was exhausted.

John motioned to the sidestep of the truck. "Have a seat. I'm going to head over to the corral and check on the new bull we got in. It'll take five minutes or so. I'll be within your line of sight. If you need anything just give a shout. After that, we can go look at the foal." There was another man at the rail of the corral, and John turned heel and left before she could form the words to object to his obvious lie.

Shae stared at his retreating back and gladly collapsed on the truck's shining silver step and rested. She'd bet her last paycheck that bull didn't need his attention.

Sitting in the shade that the truck threw over her, she tried to recover from the effort. Adam had said her diet was the primary reason for her lack of strength, and now that her meds had been adjusted, she'd started eating more and at regular intervals. The protrusion of her hip bones and collarbone told her she'd lost a lot of weight. She used to pride herself on the firm muscle she'd worked hard to build and maintain. She drew a deep, shaky breath and leaned back against the maroon door of the truck she was resting on. Her eyes flitted over the barn and corrals that were either butted up against the structure or in the immediate area. The smell of animals was strong. Shae scrunched her nose and gave a half-hearted swat at a huge fly that had invaded her personal space. Her eyes cut to the men at the rail. John laughed and pointed out past the corral, drawing the other man's attention out beyond the pile of muscle and horns that lumbered past the men. Neither one of them paid the massive animal any attention. A bark of laughter from the men brought them back into focus.

John Smith was a handsome man. Rough around the edges, but there was no denying he was attractive. Shae let herself stare. Before her assignment, she would have propositioned the man in a heartbeat. She liked sex. A lot. Sex with a man who could dominate her? Well, fuck, that was all the hotter because she'd never submit to a man who wasn't strong enough to take what he wanted. She used to love the chase, especially when it was her doing the chasing. But holy hell, when she found a guy that wasn't put off by her forwardness, one that would chase her... and then catch her...

Fuck. Tears built behind her eyes at the thought of what she used to think was enjoyable. The idea of a man holding her down now was terrifying. A tear pushed over her lower lid. So many things in her life would never be the same. She and Jeremiah talked about finding a new normal. She sniffed back more tears and swiped at the ones that were falling. *Damn it, she needed to be stronger than this!*

"Hey. Do you want to go back?" John squatted down in front of her.

"No, I want to see the baby horse." Shae swiped at her face again. Damn it, she sounded like a pouting child.

"Well, all right then, let's not delay any longer." John held out his hand.

Shae hesitated again. The fear was still there, and it was strong enough to rise the bile in her stomach. She closed her eyes for several seconds, trying to gather the internal strength to reach out and place her hand in his.

"Take my hand, Shae. A small step. You're safe." His voice remained calm and soft. She nodded to herself, acknowledging his words. She opened her eyes and used his hand to lift off the step, moving away from the contact almost immediately upon gaining her balance.

John ambled beside her as she started toward the barn. "Danny just told me Cheeka has rejected this foal, too. We won't breed her again, even though she throws some beautiful babies. Dancer is due to deliver soon, and we'll see if we can get her to accept the little guy when she foals, but I won't hold my breath. We were able to get Cheeka to stand still long enough for the colt to get the colostrum he needed. He'll want to feed every hour or so. So, we'll build a schedule. There will be a rotation of people taking care of him until he can be weaned."

Shae nodded, glancing at the huge animals inside the stalls. John walked a little ahead of her, casually leading her to a smaller area where a cream-colored spindle of legs and huge brown eyes stood. John opened a people-sized gate and motioned for Shae to go in. She hobbled into the pen and stopped. The colt wasn't any steadier on its legs than Shae was on hers, and for that reason, she felt an instant affinity for the animal.

John produced a wooden box and set it behind her. "Sit down while I go get a bottle for him. He's harmless, although he may come over toward you."

Shae gave a half-hearted chuckle at the warning. She'd beaten the hell out of men three times her size. She should be able to handle a newborn horse. She heard John let himself out of the pen or whatever it was called in ranch talk. The little horse's ears flicked, and his head stretched out toward her. Shae lifted her hand and hummed some non-threatening sounds. She could be nice to a baby. The little guy moved forward a step at a time, his spindly legs reminding her of her first attempt at walking after...

Shae pushed the thought back as she talked in a low, soft voice to the precious animal. His mane was short and sprung up from his neck. It was a little darker than his cream color as was his little tail that twitched almost as much as his ears. She continued to speak to him, encouraging him to come closer. Finally, his little head stretched as far as its neck would allow. Shae felt his warm breath on her hand seconds before a soft brush of his nose.

John held still behind Shae as the colt ventured closer. He was proud of both of them—Shae for reaching out to the animal, and the colt for being the beautiful, sensitive animal that he had been bred to be. He was going to be a beautiful line-backed dun color when he grew up. His mom might not be a good nurturer, but she did throw a beautiful and well-conformed colt.

"He likes you," he whispered, not wanting his words to startle either of the nervous entities in front of him. Shae wiggled her fingers and the colt stepped forward again, allowing her to touch him.

"Oh, he's so soft. Like velvet." Shae stopped moving when the colt's head came up and he whinnied. John laughed and entered the birthing stall with the colt's meal.

"If you would like to feed him, you'll need to stand." John extended his hand and noted how quickly she was able to reach out and use him for support. It was probably due to the fact that the colt held her attention. He handed her the quart bottle with the rubber nipple on it and showed her how to hold it. "He's been fed twice before, but we may have to help him get on the nipple."

Shae held the bottle and John gently gripped the colt's chin, guiding him to the formula the vet had left with them earlier in the day. He'd sent a hand down to Rapid City to get more. It wasn't something they tended to carry up here and John wouldn't want to try to 'create' his own. The colt deserved a fighting chance since his mother had rejected him. Frank had agreed when they spoke this morning, and God knew the man didn't give a shit about the cost—it was all about the animals at the Marshall Ranch, and that was yet another reason why John loved working here.

"Oh, he's hungry!" Shae whispered as the colt sucked greedily at the meal.

"He's going to be spoiled. The hands all have signed up to feed him. I've got this feeding and the one first thing in the morning. It fit well with my other responsibilities. If you like, you can come down with me again tomorrow night. I could make us dinner after. I think the little guy really likes you." John hoped the incentive of the colt would break Shae out of the self-contained shell that she'd been trying desperately to shed.

"I'd like that." Shae held the now-lighter bottle with one hand and stroked the neck of the foal lightly. "What's his name?"

John shrugged and put his hand on the animal's withers. The animal's muscles twitched under his palm, but he didn't shy away. The more the colt was touched, the easier it would be to gentle him. "Haven't really come up with anything yet. You have any suggestions?"

Shae glanced back at him and smiled. "I'd call him Velvet. He's so soft."

John nodded. He'd have let her name the colt Ichabod if it put a smile on the woman's face. "Velvet it is."

CHAPTER 10

John threw a fifty-pound sack onto the bed of the truck and turned to grab the next one as his ranch hand sent it sailing from the dock outside the feed store. They were in Hollister on the monthly run. He rarely came to town, preferring to send two hands, but he wanted to pick up a few things, and he needed more cat food and dog treats.

"That's it, boss. Want to grab a bite at the diner?" Monty jumped down from the loading dock as he spoke.

"Nah, you go ahead. I need to get a few things. I'll meet you back here in an hour."

Monty nodded and spun on his heel toward the small diner that every one of his ranch hands loved to visit, probably because of the woman who ran it.

Seemed she was one of those beautiful women who attracted men like flies. Genevieve was her name if he recalled correctly.

John headed back into the feed store to the far corner. He wanted to get a halter and a lead rope for Velvet. The colt was exceedingly gentle. They were going to halter-train and gentle him so Shae would be able to amble about with the animal after she finished feeding him—not that it would be much of a problem. Velvet was a sweet colt and loved everyone, but there was a special affinity between Shae and the little guy.

He took in the array of colors. His choice was immediate. There was a nice dark brown leather halter and lead that reminded him of Shae's eyes. They were mesmerizing, especially when she smiled. He glanced at his watch. She had come so far in the last week. Today she was meeting with Amanda to get her hair trimmed. Jeremiah was hanging out at his house while Shae and Amanda visited at the cottage. He wanted to be there to assess Shae's mental state. Sharp implements like scissors shouldn't trip Shae's emotions, but they could, so... John hoped all would go well, but he'd be there for her tonight if there were problems. He snorted to himself, *Yeah, like you're a doctor.*

JOHN

"I'm sorry, did our tack offend you?" A woman's voice spun him around.

"Ah… no, sorry, I was lost in thought." John felt the woman's eyes roam up and down him like he was a side of beef, and *that* set him on his heels. He was a normal, red-blooded man, and the woman in front of him was the definition of blonde bombshell. He cleared his throat and turned back to the leather halter and lead, lifting them off the display hooks. "I'll take this."

"Nice. Do you have a filly you're looking to halter?" The woman's eyes traveled over his chest and shoulders. "You work out at the Marshall ranch, right?"

John felt himself blush and hated it. He motioned toward the cash register and the woman moved, albeit reluctantly. "The halter is a present for a special woman. She'll use it on a colt." He ignored the second question and the innuendo in the first. The less people knew about him, the better.

"Oh." The blonde's use of the term conveyed one hell of a lot more than the single syllable. John hated using Shae as a shield, but he had no desire to start anything with anyone. One death on his conscience was enough. Besides, what woman in her right mind would want to live a life on a ranch without the prospect of leaving?

"Cash, or do you want me to charge this to the ranch?" She looked up at him from under her lashes.

"Cash." John pulled out a roll of bills from his front pocket and peeled off five twenties. He picked up the lead and halter and walked out.

"Hey, do you want your change?" the blonde called after him. John lifted the halter and lead rope in a wave and left the store with the distinct impression the woman was digging for a date.

He made quick work of stocking up for Cat and Sasha and dropped his purchases in the toolboxes behind the cab of his truck. He didn't need to get shit about Cat or Sasha from Monty. John moved the truck in front of the diner and rolled down both windows, letting the early-summer breeze waft against his skin.

He glanced at his watch again, wondering how Shae was doing. She'd mentioned the trim to even up her hair while they were feeding Velvet last night. They'd fallen into a slow and predictable routine, one to which Doctor Wheeler had given his approval. Not that John had done anything. He knew that caring for the animals had made a difference to him when he arrived. It gave him somewhere to focus rather than inward. While he figured Shae had a ton of crap to deal with, she needed time outside her own head, too.

He could see Monty inside the diner tucking into his meal and was tempted to go inside and have a bite. The food was supposed to be something special.

"John. I didn't know you were coming in today." Chief appeared at his elbow. He barely prevented himself from jumping. Damn it, he'd lost all his situational awareness. He had the same training as the Guardian operatives who flowed through the training facility and that was something nobody needed to know.

"Yep. Needed the monthly feed run and wanted to pick up a halter for the new colt."

"That the one that Shae has fallen in love with?"

John nodded. He wasn't surprised Chief knew that. The ranch hands were worse gossips than the joint Catholic and Presbyterian Church Circle that met every week here in Hollister. Amanda King had been to one meeting and only one. She refused to be a part of the mudslinging, as she called it.

"How's she doing?" Mike leaned against the door of John's truck.

"Seems to be improving. Miss Amanda and her are talking today."

Mike's head swiveled toward him quickly. "That so?"

John nodded. "Not sure she's ready, but…"

"Not up to us, is it? She'll move as she sees fit, I guess."

"True. Her fears… to her… they're real, and they're painful." John vividly recalled the woman's sobs the night she decided life would be better for her family without her in it.

"Don't doubt that. She's special. Takes a strong person to adapt to a new environment when everything they knew was stripped away from them."

John glanced at Mike. That last comment sounded one hell of a lot like the man knew a thing or two about that road. "Yeah. I figured." He kept the response neutral.

"Just thought you should know, all of us on the other side of the ranch are hoping she gets better. I know there are a lot of questions that Guardian would like answered." Mike's words crashed through the veneer of normalcy he'd been smearing over what he and Shae were doing.

"I've been in her shoes, or as close to her shoes as anyone could be. I understand what she is going through. When she's ready, I'm sure she'll answer those questions." John leaned forward and grabbed a package of gum. He thumbed out a stick and offered it to Mike. The man took it and unwrapped it slowly.

"Once she's back healthy, she'll be leaving. Don't forget that, John. Keeping you tucked away is important to us. *You* are important to us, and I wouldn't want your past to find a way to catch up with you." Mike tapped the side of the truck and turned on his heel, leaving John feeling sucker-punched. Lori's face floated through his mind and then the picture of that fucking explosion burst into his head.

His fingers curled around the steering wheel. His grip tightened until his knuckles turned white. Mike was right because John had made a huge mistake. He'd gotten involved—personally. While he enjoyed the time he spent with Shae, he'd been burying his head in the sand. She *was* getting stronger. Soon, he'd need to start creating a distance. He'd talk to Jeremiah and try to figure out how to do that.

CHAPTER 11

Shae watched Amanda walk toward her small cottage. The guilt of what she'd been willing to do—no, what Maurice had reduced her to—still suffocated her. But Jeremiah had encouraged her to open up to meet another person on the ranch.

Shae stood back from the window out of the woman's sight. She was beautiful. Tall, like herself, but her dark hair held a sprinkling of gray. She paused, dropped a small bag she had with her on the ground, closed her eyes, and took a deep breath before she rapped on the side of the screen door.

"Come in."

Amanda came in and the fake smile morphed into a real one. Shae braced herself instinctively. Amanda stuttered to a stop in an awkward moment, her hand outstretched. She dropped it to her side, but the smile remained. "Hi. My name's Amanda. My husband Frank and I wanted to come down to welcome you to our home, but we understand you've had a very rough time. Most of my children work for Guardian, so I have a good idea of some of the things that can happen on missions."

Shae blinked back tears. The woman's kind words were straightforward and didn't hold any pity, just understanding. "Hi, I'm Shae."

Amanda glanced over at the small couch. "Can we sit down?"

"Yeah. I'd like that." Shae didn't move and Amanda hesitated again, finally moving away from her. Shae pulled in a huge lungful of air when the space between her and the door was once again open.

She waited for Amanda to sit down, walked over to the kitchenette, and dragged a chair over so she could face her. Shae dropped her eyes to the floor. Even though she'd practiced this conversation a thousand times in her head, at this moment, she had no idea how to begin.

The moment stretched and Amanda finally spoke, "Doctor Wheeler is a nice man."

Shae's head popped up at the comment. "I guess? He's persistent."

Amanda's smile flashed across her face. "I'm imagining that is a good thing."

"Probably," Shae admitted. She cleared her throat and closed her eyes. "I'm sorry—"

"You don't have anything to be sorry about. I can come back as many times as it takes for you to be comfortable with me in your space. I was a hairdresser for years. I don't really keep up with the latest trends anymore, but I'm sure I can manage a nice cut and style for you, just to even out the, uh… layers you have going. We can go outside if that would be better for you."

"Thank you. I haven't looked in the mirror lately, I'm sure it's awful."

"No, more like extremely modern." Amanda tried to hold back a smile and a laugh. "But I can fix it. Do you want me to try?"

"Actually, yes, I'd like that and yes, please, if we can go outside? It is hard to be in small spaces with people. When they had me…" The tears she'd been trying desperately to hold at bay crested and trailed down her cheeks unabated. Shae sniffed, her hands shaking from the emotional effort of the moment. "I think outside would be best."

Amanda smiled and nodded to the door. "You go first. I'll bring out a chair and a towel so you don't get hair down your shirt. I have my scissors and a spray bottle to dampen your hair so I can cut it, but we don't have to do anything today. I'm able to come back as often as you'd like."

"You came prepared."

"Well, that doctor of yours may have suggested a few things."

"Thank you." Shae smiled at the older woman and made a hasty exit from her small home. She drew a deep breath and held the door open for Amanda as she brought out one of the small kitchen chairs.

"Oh, let's go over there, under the tree. The shade is heavenly. It is getting hot early this year."

Shae bent over and picked up the small bag, walking with Amanda. Her strength was returning as was the mobility in her ankle. The more she walked, the more her ankle strengthened.

"I heard you adopted a colt." Amanda smiled at her. "They are adorable. My horse is a sweetheart. Someday, when that little guy is big enough, we should go for a ride."

Shae blinked and stopped walking. "I don't know how to ride." And she wouldn't be here then. Sooner or later, she'd have to figure out what to do and where to go.

Amanda chuckled, "Not to worry, we have several slow, older horses that love to teach new riders how not to be nervous. One is actually named Charmin because she's soft on the tush."

Shae chuckled, "As in the toilet paper? Well, that is where I would need to start. But not now. I need a bit more time, I think." Shae glanced into the small bag and saw a small pair of scissors and a spray bottle. She fought a shiver of apprehension. "I want my hair to look nice. I can tell it doesn't." She reached for the shorter portions that Maurice had cut away with a knife. Humiliation and degradation. He excelled in his job. She stopped. What had happened to him? Why hadn't she asked before this? Her eyes darted around her. Was he still alive? Had he escaped?

"So, tell me what you like to do in your free time. Do you bake?" Amanda asked as she sat the chair down.

"Bake? No." Her mother didn't have the time to waste teaching her anything. "I went to school, then into the Army for my two years. Then from there, I was recruited into the Mossad. I've never *not* had a job, so there is little free time."

"Oh, well, we have bake days up at the main house on Tuesdays and Thursdays. You are welcome to come up and help or learn, or heck, just have a cup of coffee and visit. Sky and Keelee are usually there. Joy, Jillian, and Taty are employed with Guardian, so we don't usually see them." Amanda motioned to the chair and Shae sat down. The woman went on about baking and then talked about the ranch. Shae knew the woman's dialogue was to keep her from feeling anxious. She learned about Amanda's sons and daughters, about the ranch, and about everything and nothing. She held the edge of the seat of the chair tightly when the sound of the scissors cutting her hair became too close to the sounds she remembered of Maurice hacking off her hair. Amanda's constant chatter helped, it really did, but she was getting close to losing it. Amanda must have sensed it. She stopped with the scissors and pulled a brush through her hair with long, soft strokes. "My girls used to love it when I brushed their hair. You have such beautiful hair. Thick and that natural wave, it must be a breeze to style."

She drew a deep breath. "I usually pull it back and pin it up."

"Oh, would you like me to give you a shorter cut? Something that you can just wash and let go?"

Shae turned around. "That would be nice, but maybe not today. Today just even it out?"

"I already have." Amanda smiled at her and continued to pull the brush through her hair.

"You have?" Shae forced her hands off the sides of the chair.

"Yes ma'am. We're done for today, but I'm being selfish and getting some quasi-mom time in."

"Mom time?"

"Oh, heavens, yes. Doting on my children and my grandchildren is my joy, only most of them live in D.C. Keelee is independent as her dad and the others on the ranch can only put up with so much mothering," Amanda laughed; it was a joyous sound. "Jasmine and her husband live on the next ranch over. Have you gone on a drive around the area? Have you been to the hills?"

Shae shook her head slightly, enjoying the soothing repetition of her hair being brushed. "No. John has offered, but I'm not ready yet."

Amanda sighed the man's name. "John. He has been such a help to my husband. The man works all day every day. He doesn't socialize much, keeps to himself, rather a loner if you know what I mean, but we appreciate everything he does for us."

Well, wasn't that something? John was a loner?

He didn't strike her that way. He wasn't overly gregarious, but he came over every night to get her to take her down to the barn and they visited about things that happened on the ranch. Safe topics that kept her focus away from the past... Although recently, she'd been talking to him about the questions Jeremiah had been asking her. She used him as a sounding board because... *Because she trusted him.* She blinked at the realization.

She trusted John.

Amanda left about a half-hour later. Shae thanked the woman and ran her hands through her hair, which felt lighter. She watched Amanda walk up to the big house and Jeremiah stop her to speak with her. Shae had refused to give him permission to speak to anyone about her treatment. She trusted him, too, so she assumed they were visiting as friends.

Jeremiah pulled the chair she had been sitting on around and straddled it, resting his forearms on the back of the chair. Shae leaned against the tree.

"What?" Shae threw the question at him, knowing he had something to say. He always did.

"I think it's about time we start addressing exactly what happened to you." Jeremiah dropped his chin to his forearms and tipped his head slightly to the side as he regarded her.

Her gut clenched so tight she couldn't breathe. "What?"

"You're doing great, Shae, but we both know there are questions that need to be answered about your time after you were taken. I think if we go slowly, we can work through it and answer questions in the process."

Shae jerked her head up, locking gazes with him. Shae's eyes bounced around the landscape as she tried to find a reason to rebuff his assertion. "You can't let me have a few days of peace?"

Jeremiah chuckled, "No, but in my defense, I'm all about making you better. I knew Amanda was here today and that talking to a completely unfamiliar person was a big step, but it wasn't, was it?"

"No, not really, but I'm so fucked up." Shae ran her hands through her hair and gripped it tight when her hands reached the base by her skull.

"We're all fucked up." Jeremiah's comment floated toward where she sat.

Shae released her hair and lifted her head. "Job security for you."

"I never looked at it that way." Jeremiah smiled at

her. "You made progress today. What's going through your mind?"

"Right, how about what isn't?" Shae leaned back against the heavy bark of the cottonwood tree.

"Fair enough. Let's shave away all the small things. What is the long pole in the tent for you? The one thing that is worrying you the most right now?"

"I don't know how to get from where I'm stuck to where I was."

"That is a simple answer, Shae. Trust yourself and take one small step at a time." Jeremiah's words echoed the phrase John had used on so many occasions during the last weeks.

Shae closed her eyes and whispered, "Take my hand."

"What was that?" Jeremiah asked, although his voice was almost a whisper, too.

"It is what John says when I get stuck. 'Trust yourself and trust me. Take my hand.'" Shae pushed her hair away from her face and glanced out at the pastures. The shadows were lengthening, which meant he would be coming back to get her soon. The trip to see Velvet every night was an escape from the lingering darkness in her mind.

"Does that work?"

"Hmmm?" Shae blinked back from her mental

trip to the barn and the comfort she felt when she was with Velvet and John.

"When John asks you to take his hand, do you?"

Shae nodded. "He doesn't try to hold onto me. I use him as a brace. I control the contact. He didn't know me before, doesn't expect me to be who I was, what I was. I don't have to figure out how to make it right with him. He's... safe?" She cocked her head at the doctor.

She heard John's truck pull up the short drive and watched him move about his vehicle and listened to the sounds of him unloading whatever he had in the boxes installed in the bed of the truck.

"Before I go, I want you to think about something."

"What's that?"

"I want you to think about the fact that you were compromised beyond what most humans could endure. You are holding yourself back from people because of what transpired. The information Guardian provided to me indicated you said the bastards didn't necessarily want information from you. They were hurting you with one goal in mind, and that goal was to break you."

"Goal achieved." Shae caught movement and pulled her attention from the conversation with the doctor to the sight of John walking across the small clearing to the cottage. She was beyond exhausted. The thought of the soft, sweet colt barely stirred through the miasma of lethargy that consumed her.

Jeremiah followed her gaze. "Going to see Velveeta?"

Shae chuffed out a huff and shook her head. "His name is Velvet, and maybe. I'm so tired right now."

"It was an emotional afternoon. How about I head him off and let him know you need to rest?" Jeremiah stood and lifted the small chair as if it weighed nothing, twirling it around.

"No, I'll talk to him." Shae was fading; the emotional toll of the afternoon was pressing on her harder than she'd care to admit.

"Roger that. You have my number. Use it if you need to." Jeremiah gave her a two-finger salute and headed back up to the Guardian side of the ranch where she assumed he'd parked his truck. Shae watched as he met John a few feet from the door and shook the man's hand. The exchange took seconds and John was beside her moments later.

"Hi." Shae reached for the chair.

"Hey. You ready to go to the barn?" John's soft, deep voice sent the question toward her.

"I'm not going to go tonight. I had…" Shae

searched for a word to describe the emotional upheaval this afternoon had actually been. "It was a long day." She didn't know how else to describe it.

"Ah, the visit with Miss Amanda." He nodded and handed her a brown paper bag. "For when you go tomorrow. Let me put this in the cottage for you."

Shae reached for the bag. John was mindful not to put his hand in a position where she would have to touch his. The contents weren't necessarily heavy, but whatever was inside contained more weight than she'd imagined. Shae pulled it back to her and unfolded the top to separate the sides of the bag. A twist of brown leather, some flat and weaved and some round and softer-looking, lay in a heap at the bottom. She reached in and pulled out a long rope with a huge industrial-sized snap on one end. The flat-weaved material she withdrew with absolutely no concept of what the hell it was. There were several silver hoops and longer and shorter lengths with one that had a collar-like closure. She held it up and glanced at him.

John laughed and took the blob of leather and shaped it, holding it out to her. "It is a halter for Velvet. His nose goes here." His fingers moved at the smaller end of the opening. "And this goes up the side of his face and behind his ears."

Shae suddenly saw the concept. "Oh! Like a collar?"

"Almost. It will allow you to walk with him. In the corral first and then later outside. I figured as you got better you could take longer walks together."

Shae reached for the halter and caught it when he tossed it to her. She lifted it the way he had. "Thank you."

"No problem. I'll get out of your hair and let you rest. Do you want to skip dinner?"

Shae watched him closely. She got the feeling something was off, but she wasn't sure what. It was almost as if he was relieved that she wasn't going with him tonight. She couldn't deal with subtext. Her life was so totally fucked as it was, she didn't have room for guessing games. "What's wrong?"

John snapped his eyes toward her and averted them just as quickly. "Nothing. Just realized I've been monopolizing your time. Should be working toward getting back to your old self and not spending the evenings with me." He swallowed hard and shifted on his feet before shoving his fingers into the front pocket of his jeans.

"What? *You* are the reason I'm out of this house at all. You and Velvet. The meeting I had with Amanda this afternoon was… exhausting. At least for me, it was. I don't understand. Did I do something wrong?"

John dropped his hands. His jaw was clenched, and he shook his head. "You've done nothing wrong. I was reminded today that I'm not the best person to be hanging around. I have enemies and a past."

Shae leaned against the tree. "Who doesn't?"

John chuckled, "Truth." He reached out and put the halter and rope back in the sack. "Come on, you're about to fall asleep standing up."

She couldn't argue that fact. Her eyes were so damn heavy. She closed them and dragged them open again.

His expression was warm, and he smiled at her. He walked with her to the door of her cottage. "Go to sleep. We'll visit Velvet tomorrow."

She turned to watch him cross the small field between them. "Tomorrow." She turned and headed straight for the bed. Emotional exhaustion was every bit as consuming as physical exhaustion and she let it win tonight. She'd fight harder tomorrow.

CHAPTER 12

He wasn't going to lie—the sight of Jacob and Jason pulled forth an internal groan. There wasn't any reason for them to be heading toward the stock pond he was working on this time of day. Unless it had to do with Lori. He stabbed the dirt with his shovel with too much force. Did he want to go on another wild goose chase? Yeah, he'd walk through the Sahara without water if it meant he'd be able to find out the why of what happened. Besides, Frank would have given him a heads-up if their visit pertained to his late sister, and he hadn't. That meant they wanted to talk about Shae.

He'd sent Monty and Danny back to the machine shed for the backhoe. The dam had weakened and was starting to erode. They needed to shore up the south side. The pond, or rather small lake, was an ecological glory hole and he needed to make sure the ducks, geese, small critters, and yes, his cattle had access to the fresh water the pond provided.

He glanced up as he threw another shovelful of dirt onto the cement barrier that had been exposed by the weather. The backhoe wouldn't be able to maneuver into this area because of the wet soil, so it was all mud and muck and manual labor. He'd never shied away from getting his hands dirty and he'd like to think it gained him some respect from the hands that worked beside him.

"Hey."

He wasn't sure which one of the men spoke, but John glanced up from his work and nodded toward the two shovels Monty and Danny had left.

"Hey yourself. If you're down here, you're working." John stuck the shovel into the heavy, wet earth and pushed down, filling the spade. He braced and lifted, following through with a toss to the area needing shoring up in one smooth motion.

He heard the men move and saw dirt starting to fly. "What brings you down here?" John didn't have time to play games and he was pretty damn sure Shae was the topic. His protective instincts fired like the bullets out of an M-60 machine gun—fast and searing. He drew a deep breath and worked through the irritating sensation. They weren't his enemy. They wanted their answers and, damn it, he couldn't blame them. Shae was making great progress. She'd met with Amanda twice more and from what she told him, the meetings were getting somewhat easier for her.

"We've caught a break in several cases but are limited in our knowledge, which is impeding the progress of mopping up Stratus. We need to know what Shae knows. Doctor Wheeler has indicated she could handle answering questions but has declined repeatedly," Jacob spoke as he sent mud flying.

John stopped and leaned on the handle of his shovel. "And why are you telling me this?" John watched as dirt flew to the face of the dam.

"You are the only one besides Doc Wheeler that interacts consistently with her. Doc won't say anything to break her patient confidentiality, and we get that, but you can talk to her, get her to see we need her to sit down with us and take us through her operation. We have a release from the Mossad, we're cleared to ask questions."

John huffed and shook his head, diving back into the work. He threw three large loads of wet dirt before he stopped. He'd needed the time to douse his irritations. He got that the men had questions that Shae had yet to answer, but… John wasn't about to talk about Shae with anyone. It wasn't fair to her. The woman had enough to deal with. She didn't need to be pushed in a direction where she didn't feel comfortable.

"While I appreciate where you are coming from, I'm not going to talk to her just so you can try to swoop in and start asking questions she may not ever be able to answer. You have no idea what she is dealing with."

"Granted, but we need to talk to her about what she learned about Stratus. It is imperative that we learn everything we can about the organization and Shae may have information she doesn't realize she has." Jason jammed his shovel into the ground and heaved a huge spade of dirt onto the area John was filling.

"And that makes it okay to push?" John flung his own pile of dirt and immediately jabbed the earth for another.

"No, it doesn't, but we wouldn't be here if it wasn't imperative. She's going to have to talk to us. Tomorrow," Jason spoke as he viciously shoved his spade into the quickly disappearing mound of dirt.

John stopped shoveling at that. He might not

have been Guardian, but he'd proved his loyalty to the organization by training Joseph and fucking taking out the bastard that was going to kill Keelee. It was his shot that brought the motherfucker to his grave. He may have been a social architect, but he hadn't always been one. "Don't push her." John growled the words. He wouldn't win a fight between the two of them, but he'd be damned if he'd back down.

Jason looked up. Concern and confusion laced his expression. "Why? Tell us what's going on here, John. Jeremiah thinks she's ready to start answering questions."

John scraped the now-level earth with his shovel and dusted the last of the dirt onto the now-solidly covered portion of embankment as he spoke.

"Look, I get that you two are trying to do what is best for her, but you don't have a clue what she's been through. Can't you just leave her alone?"

"Fuck, we'd love to, but what she knows is *important* to us, to our operations. We aren't going to hurt her, we'd never do that." Jacob stressed the word in a way that made John take another look at the man.

"Good to know." He grabbed his shovel and headed toward the ATV and small trailer they had used to pull the tools down to the pond.

"John, we've been trying to be polite here, but this is the bottom line. Get her to talk to us."

John spun on his heels with his shovel in both hands. "And if I don't?"

"I think that is about enough." Frank Marshall's voice rang out, drawing all three sets of eyes toward where he sat on horseback.

"Boys, you get back to the house. I'll be speaking with you tonight after dinner." John watched as the men in front of him physically bristled at Frank's comment. Neither moved.

"John, that girl is strong. Stronger than you give her credit for. Talk to her and ask her if she's ready, let her know it is important."

John nodded at Frank's comment.

The rattle of a diesel engine coming from the worn path that led to the ranch was the final straw to shift and ease the tense situation. Frank walked his horse down and looked at the manual effort to cover the exposed dam material. "Came down to help with that. Looks like the three of you handled it well enough."

John threw his shovel into the trailer and took off his cowboy hat, wiping the sweatband with his handkerchief. He watched the brothers as they headed back up to the ranch.

Frank leaned on his saddle horn and looked down. The shade his horse threw was a welcome relief. "You knew it was coming. Being a little overprotective with her, aren't you?"

"I have no fucking clue what you're talking about." John shoved his hat back on his head and stewed at the audacity of these men.

"Well, that's a load of cattle dung."

John glanced at the backhoe and the truck lumbering behind it. "Frank, I'm in a fucking no-win situation. Shae trusts me and you know how she's responding to Velvet. I've seen you watching us."

Frank nodded.

"Doc Wheeler told me pushing her from my perspective could be bad and that I need to tread carefully and segregate myself from anything Guardian. I care for her. I see glimpses of what she must have been and then those moments are snuffed out by the demons that haunt her. She has good moments and they are getting longer. She's eating, exercising, and she looks forward to seeing that colt. He's got her wrapped around his hoof and he's working it."

Frank chuckled, "Yeah, saw that the other night. I was in the tack room working before dinner. I heard the two of you. You're good for her."

"Tell that to them, would yah?" John muttered almost to himself.

"They are between a rock and a hard place. I'm probably talking out of turn, but lives are on the line and they need to talk to her. What's the real issue here, son?"

"Shit. I guess I've been trying to run from the inevitability of her getting better. Chief reminded me I'm not the safest bet for her going forward." John glanced up at Frank. "I get that. I can't offer her a future, but I can give her a little peace right now."

The backhoe lumbered around the back end of the stock pond, effectively ceasing all conversation. John lifted a hand at Frank, who turned his mount and headed off. John whistled sharply, catching Monty's attention in the cab of the machine. He motioned toward the area that needed shoring up first. Monty nodded and spun the massive hoe. John glanced back at where the men had disappeared. It seemed his and Shae's attempt at grabbing a piece of normal was done.

CHAPTER 13

Shae pulled the comb through her hair and shook her head in disbelief. When she'd asked Amanda to come down to cut her hair again this morning, it had surprised them both, but the result was freeing. The new style was a short bob that brushed the nape of her neck and angled longer toward the front. It was sleek and she really liked the result. Jeremiah had wandered toward the cottage from the Guardian side of the ranch as the women visited. The normalcy of the afternoon was rejuvenating.

Shae slid her sock-covered feet into her cowboy boots and stood, stomping into them. She grabbed a shirt to put over her tank top and smiled at the sound of John's truck pulling into the drive by his house. She left the cottage and walked over toward his. He must have gone inside the house because Cat ambled out the front door and meowed when she saw Shae. The little piece of ragged fur was round now. With Cat on the raised porch, she stood and looked straight into the animal's eyes. "You, my dear, have found a softy and are milking him for everything you can get."

Cat's eyes closed slowly as her squeaky purr started to roll out of her. Shae tickled the little beast under her chin for a couple minutes. Shae made her way to the front door and knocked. She heard a thump from the back of the house and a mumbled comment. "I'll take that as a come in." Cat meowed her approval from the shade where she laid.

She'd never been in John's house before and was pleasantly surprised at the warm colors and deep, rich textures of the leather. They blended into a comfortable environment but nothing that screamed 'man cave.' "Hello?" Shae heard the same noise toward the back of the house and headed that way. "Hello?" She sing-songed the word as she turned the corner.

Holy shit! John stood in the middle of a massive bedroom, still wet from the shower, wearing only a small, dark blue towel. She froze, her greeting stilled abruptly. She'd never been shy, and she used to like sex. A lot of sex. And the body that man had hidden beneath the work shirts and loose-fitting jeans was fucking mouthwatering. Her gaze dipped down to his towel and the wet outline of his…

Shae jerked her eyes back up, wide and apologetic. "I, ah…" She pointed back toward the front of the house and did her best Olympic speed-walking imitation out of the house. She put her hand over her mouth and sat down abruptly on the porch steps. Shae stared out at the expansive view but saw nothing except hard, cut muscle, a deeply defined Adonis belt, and oh, my God… that cock. She dropped her head into her hands and rubbed her face. *Wow.* She couldn't unsee that. Not that she'd want to because he was a fine specimen of a man. But how in the hell could she look at him now without seeing all of him? She chuckled at her thoughts and then stopped short.

Cat meowed and ambled over. Shae reached out and stroked the attention monger. She stared off into the distance. Oh man, would she have something to talk to Jeremiah about tomorrow. Not about seeing John naked, but about suddenly seeing John as someone she was attracted to. That was a good thing. Right? It should be? *Holy hell.*

A cowboy boot and a jean-covered leg appeared beside her. Shae glanced up and couldn't help taking in the bulge in his jeans that she'd somehow never noticed before. She dropped her eyes and shook her head. "I'm so sorry." If she were the type of person to be embarrassed, she'd be blushing.

"Yeah, me too."

Shae's head whipped around toward him. "Why? *You* didn't walk in on *me* practically naked."

The blush that flourished across the man's cheeks was adorable. He nodded and looked out over the ranch. "I was covered in mud. We were working on the dam and Monty caught a cement block in the hoe, it pulled out, and we had a breach. He was able to plug it quickly, but I was ass-deep in mud. I lost my right boot, my hat, and ruined a damn good pair of jeans. I ahh… needed to shower before we headed back down to the barn."

Shae nodded, trying not to laugh at the picture he painted. "I heard you moving around in there and I just didn't think."

"No problem. We can just agree to forget about the entire situation."

"Yeah, *that* will never happen." Shae swiveled her head toward him and noted the deep crimson that had overtaken his normal skin tone. She smiled and felt lighter than she had in... well, one hell of a long time. John was safe, sweet, and yes, very attractive. A glimmer of her former self lifted from the shadows. She looked down at her boots. Perhaps she'd allow herself to flirt—just a bit—and enjoy the small victory of acting almost normal.

He caught her attention when he moved and motioned toward the truck. "Do you want to drive or walk?"

Shae stood with him and started down the porch steps. She'd been making huge strides physically. Eating regularly and exercising was making an impact, but she still had off-days where she felt tired. Today was turning out to be a good day... on a lot of fronts. "Walking is fine." She waited for him and fell into step beside him.

"I ahh... like the... haircut." He glanced over at her and away quickly.

"Thank you. I had Amanda cut it. I didn't want to deal with it anymore and it was time for a change." She'd talked to Jeremiah about that, too, after Amanda left. She was trying to find a new 'normal' and he'd encouraged her to take positive steps toward that goal. Maybe that new normal included allowing herself to feel feminine. Maybe even to feel wanted. Oh, man, that would be something.

She'd never really felt wanted or needed. She was a 'responsibility' for her mother and as soon as she finished school, her mother expected her to make her own way. Her mom wasn't abusive. She had food and clothes, but that persistent longing to be valued or needed was one that had never been filled. Jeremiah's ever-present questions chased the thoughts around in her mind. She *did* want to feel needed. She stared at the distance, and yes, she wanted to feel needed by the man next to her. How had that happened? Would he return the feelings? Her mother never had, no matter how hard she tried.

"How was the visit?" She snapped her head up and blinked back from her musings. John's question wasn't unexpected. They generally talked about her day and how she was feeling, but she'd been lost in thought.

"Really good. I was actually thinking of calling my mother. She still lives in Israel." Shae shoved her hands in her pockets. "She didn't return my call from the hospital. It was really hard to realize that she might not care."

"Don't do that, Shae. Focus on how far you've come. Who you are now and what you need now." John stopped and faced her.

"How did you know?" Shae blinked back the

tears that inevitably started when she fell into the cycle of self-condemnation.

"I've spent enough time around you to know when your thoughts turn dark."

John chucked her under her chin and waited for her to lift her face to him. "One day at a time. Trust yourself."

Shae nodded and lifted her palm. "Take my hand?"

John's eyebrows rose in surprise. He cocked his head and extended his hand to hers, allowing her to hold his hand. Shae smiled at the feeling of safety and comfort that simple gesture provided. She held onto his hand and started toward the barn. "Did you know that several of your employers are here? The big guys." Her step faltered at his words. She made a sweep with her eyes back toward the big ranch house.

"I... no. I didn't."

They walked in silence for a moment before John spoke again. "I was thinking about going down to Orman Dam this weekend. Monty has offered to let me use his ski boat. I thought I'd take it out and have some fun. There are a couple of Airbnb's down there where I can hole up without seeing much of anyone. You'd be welcome if you think you'd enjoy it."

Shae dropped his hand as he reached for the gate to Velvet's pen. The little colt lifted his head, his ears twitched forward, and he chuffed out a breath of air at her. Shae stepped in and extended her hand. Her little boy walked directly to her. She reached out and started scratching his neck. He extended his head past her shoulder and lifted his lip into the air, wiggling it in delight when she found his spot. She cooed at him and spoke softly all the time she moved her hands over him.

John leaned against the rail. He'd go get Velvet's feeding set up in a minute. He needed to see this, to watch her interact with the young colt. He'd had a bitch of a day. The damn visit he'd had from Jacob and Jason had been replaying in his mind when he'd taken a shower. The more he thought about it, the more he realized they were actually asking for him to step in because Shae had told Jeremiah she didn't want to answer questions.

"You don't have to rescue me from them." Her words caught his attention. She was talking in the same smooth soft voice that she spoke to Velvet with, but the content was for him.

"I had a visit from them today." She glanced over her shoulder at him. The puzzled look on her face pushed some of his concern away. "Seems they think

JOHN

I could convince you to talk to them…" He tried to play it off with humor when he really wanted to throat punch something. She didn't respond. Instead, using a soft curry brush, she smoothed the colt in small, short strokes to get him used to being handled just like he'd shown her. "Am I stopping your healing by spending time with you?" Why he needed to know the answer to that question wasn't something he was willing to delve into, but he'd asked it all the same.

Shae turned, her newly-cut hair swinging along her neck. She walked over to the gate he was leaning on and stared at him for several moments. He took the time to examine the depths of her brown eyes. She tipped her head to the left and smiled. "I need to answer the questions about what happened sooner rather than later. You aren't stopping me, you're helping me. I'll talk to Jeremiah in the morning. But…"

"Yes?" He wanted to reach out and brush that blunt fall of hair along her chin.

"When I talk to them, I want you there. I need to do this, but I need to know I have you there if it becomes overwhelming." Shae placed her hand on his. He dropped his gaze down to their hands and locked it on her long, slim fingers. She drew a breath before she spoke, "I'm working on me. They mean well and they have responsibilities, I'm sure, but I'll never be the woman who can work an operation again. I'll never be her again. I'm slowly coming to terms with that fact. I'll answer their questions and make arrangements to pay for the care they've provided. But I won't be working for any agency again."

John turned his hand up and cupped her hand in his. "I like the companionship we have. I've missed having someone to talk to since… Anyway, I didn't know who you were before we found you. I don't have any expectations, but the woman you are now? I like the part of her that you let me see." He'd admit that much to her. His favor for Frank and Doc Wheeler had turned into a friendship that he truly cherished. She allowed him to care for her. They would never be intimate or have that complication. He was good with that. It was a solid fact she was a gorgeous woman. The new haircut framed her face, and her beautiful brown eyes, high cheekbones, and fine features were the classic example of timeless beauty. The frailness she had when she first arrived had for the most part vanished. She still had bad days, but the good days now outweighed the bad, at least as far as he'd witnessed.

JOHN

"Are you really going to the lake or were you just offering to get me out of here?" Shae traced her finger down his palm and tapped his wrist with it, putting an accent on her question.

"I had no plans to leave the ranch. Never do." He admitted the truth because if there was one thing he did not want it was to drive outside the property lines of the ranch.

"Thought so. No, I don't need you to take me away. But if one or more of my current employers can't abide by my boundaries, I do reserve the right to invade your privacy again and hide inside your house." John popped his eyes up to her at the taunt.

"I promise to shut my bedroom door when I take a shower." His embarrassment at being caught in a small-ass towel while dripping wet and fuming mad would not abate. Well, not anytime soon.

Shae pulled back and sighed, "Well, now, that would be a shame." She turned back to the colt, who was nibbling on her shirt, her voice once again soft and lyrical as she moved around the stall.

John spun on his heel and headed toward the back of the barn to prepare the colt's meal. His cheeks were hot and his mind spun at her teasing remark. He stopped and went back to the stall. "Are you flirting?"

She glanced at him and chuckled, "It has been so long, I'm not sure, but I was attempting to do so, yes."

Pole-axed, he blinked and then muttered, "Oh."

She continued to brush Velvet but looked at him. "Is that all right with you?"

There was a hesitancy in her voice that smacked him upside the head. He was such a fool. It had been so long… "Yes, but…"

She cocked her head and lifted an eyebrow. "But?"

"I'll never take advantage of you." He wanted that out there and upfront. "You lead. In flirting, and ahh… in anything else… that… that happens between us."

She smiled at him and then laughed. The beautiful, melodic sound filled the stall. "I believe Jeremiah would say the reason I'm flirting with you is that I know you are safe and I'm comfortable around you. Your warnings weren't needed, but I appreciate the graciousness." Velvet nickered and tossed his head. "I believe this baby is ready for his milk."

John felt his face heat again. Damn fair skin. He spun on his heel. Lori had loved teasing him until he was as red as a lobster. His dad told him he could never be a true grifter because he wore his emotions on his sleeve, unlike Lori. He did prefer to be behind a keyboard or detailing a cover. As a matter of fact, toward the end of his time in Washington, he'd been the one creating all the covers. Lori had started working with their father on something before he'd been murdered and continued whatever it was after the police had found his body. She'd abandoned all of the cover work to him. Not that he minded. He filled his hours with work, and when he needed it, he struck out and found some female company. But he'd never been in a serious relationship before.

He measured out the powdered milk into the bottle before he damn near dropped it. Was he in a relationship? His head snapped toward the stall where Shae was talking to the colt. *No. Maybe? Shit.* He was, wasn't he? He pulled out his phone and tapped a text out to Jeremiah.

John: >*Need to talk to you, non-emergency. Can you call in the morning?*

The text from Jeremiah hit him back immediately.

. . .

Jeremiah: >*You got it.*

Good. That was... good. He finished mixing the formula for the colt and capped the bottle with the nipple. All in all, the fucking shitty day he'd been having had turned around, hadn't it?

CHAPTER 14

John heard a truck pull up outside but didn't pull his head out from under the hay baler he was working on. The damn thing needed all the belts replaced. Sitting over the long, cold winter had cracked the rubber and he would be damned if he'd change a belt out in direct sun on a hot-as-fuck July day when he could do it inside before they got started.

"I need my oil changed." Jeremiah Wheeler's scuffed-up combat boots appeared beside him.

"You are out of luck. Oil changes are on Tuesday. Hold on a minute." He grunted the last part as he pried the new belt over the pulley system with a small crowbar. It settled into the groove with a satisfying snap and he blew out a lungful of air while he released the tension from his shoulders. With a twist, he slithered his way out from under the baler and looked up at Wheeler. "Thought you were going to call?"

"I'm here, sorry. Do you want me to go over to the other side of the ranch and call you?" Jeremiah laughed at him when he flipped the doctor off.

"No, but it probably would have been easier to talk to you on the phone about this." John stood up and grabbed a rag to wipe the grease off his hands.

"Oh, a personal topic then?" The doc crossed his arms over his chest and leaned back against the baler.

"Yeah. Look, I don't really know how to ask this, so I'm just going to put it out there. Shae was flirting with me last night. What should I do about it?"

The doctor blinked at him and brought his hand to his face, stroking the scruff he obviously didn't shave this morning. "Well, I guess that depends on what you want to do about it."

John rolled his eyes. "Typical shrink answer."

Jeremiah snorted. "Typical defensive behavior with a healthy helping of deflection thrown in. Do you want Shae to flirt with you or not?"

"Yes?" John clasped his hands behind his head

and walked away only to spin around and stare at the doctor, who looked like he wanted to laugh.

"John, was that an answer or a question?"

He groaned, "Both."

"Right, well, here's the scoop. If Shae trusts you enough to flirt with you, and you and she both want that to happen, then by all means, proceed."

John put his hands on his hips and glared at the man in front of him. *That was so not the point here...* "But what if it leads to other things?"

"Like?"

"Sex!" John threw up his hands and started pacing.

This time the doctor did laugh. "Do you need me to have the birds and bees talk with you? Is that what you're saying?"

"Oh, fuck you, you know it's not!" John pivoted and marched down the other way only to turn again and walk back. The activity was necessary, or he might knock that smirk off the doctor's face.

"All right, all right, settle down. Look, if Shae wants things to progress to that point and you are comfortable with it too, what the hell is the problem?"

"She has been through so damn much." John

stopped and stared at the toe of his boot. "I don't want to hurt her."

"Ah." The doctor lifted away from the baler. "Life isn't that easy, John. You can't protect her from getting hurt. It's going to happen in one way or another. If this between you proceeds and works out, you'll need to be there for her when shit turns south, just like she'll need to be there for you."

"Have you talked to her about us?"

"Nope. Not going there. I don't talk about our sessions with anyone but her." Wheeler cocked his head. "Just like I won't tell her you're freaking out."

"I'm not." John shook his head. "I just need to make sure I'm not going to hurt her."

"With an attitude like that, I'm sure you won't. At least not intentionally, but even the best intentions don't always work out. My advice? Communication. Dialogue between the two of you will go one hell of a long way to clear up these feelings you're having."

John nodded. "Just talk to her?"

"Yep. Be honest about your fears and concerns. Ask her what hers are. Have an open, honest conversation about things before they become an issue."

"Okay. Thanks, Doc." John extended his hand.

The doctor grabbed his and shook it. "No problem. My bill will be in the mail."

"I'd rather give you that oil change." John fell into step as they walked out of the barn.

"Oh, damn, that's a deal," Jeremiah laughed and slapped him on the back. "I'll see you on Tuesday."

John chuckled and watched the doctor climb into his truck. *Just talk to her. I can do that.*

"So, I hear the big bosses are here." Shae handed Jeremiah a tall glass of lemonade. It wasn't from scratch, but the mix was good and tart. He accepted it and she sat down under the shade tree with him. She could be in the cottage with him, John, Doctor Cassidy, or Amanda now, but the shade tree was where she and Jeremiah usually had their talks.

The doctor took a sip of his drink and nodded. "Yep. Saw them this morning. Are you going to answer questions for them?"

She could tell he was staring at her, looking for a reaction. She lifted her eyes and stared at John's house. "I'll talk to them and tell them what I can remember if the Mossad has signed a release."

"I'm told they have." Jeremiah took a sip of his drink and leaned back against the tree. "Do you want me there with you when you answer their questions?"

"No. I asked John to come with me."

"You're developing feelings for him, aren't you?"

The quiet question swung her attention away from the house and to her therapist. She drew a deep breath and nodded. "I think I am."

"To what end?"

Her surprised huff of laughter came out of nowhere. She shook her head. "Are you my mother now?"

"Nope. Don't want that role or responsibility. I'm just curious if you are using John as a crutch or perhaps making unwise attachments." Jeremiah took another sip of his drink.

"Unwise? No, I trust him as much as I trust you. He's my friend. The interest in him past that is natural, I think. I find him attractive. Is that wrong?" She met his eyes and stared at him while she took a drink of her lemonade.

"It is if you just want sex."

Shae inhaled sharply and aspirated some of the liquid into her lungs. She wheezed and coughed for about a minute before she was able to breathe and talk. "Better?" Jeremiah asked when she drew her third full lungful of air.

"Yeah," she managed as she wiped the tears from her eyes.

"As I was saying, if that is all you're going after John for, you need to talk with him and let him know what your intentions are. You wouldn't want to hurt him."

"Hurt *him*?" Her voice squeaked at the end of the question. John was the most stoic person she'd ever met. How in the hell could *she* hurt *him*?

"Yes, he is a solitary man who doesn't let too many people into his tight circle of friends. Those he does let in, he forms relationships with…" He stared directly at her.

Relationships. Her mouth fell open as understanding soaked in. She snapped it shut and squared her shoulders. "I like John as a friend and I'm willing to see if I like John as a lover. He's already told me he's willing to let me take the lead and to control what happens. I will not scare him away by telling him I want a committed relationship."

"Let's look at that from another angle. Will he scare you away if he tells you that he does?" Jeremiah cocked his head and waited.

Shae's eyes migrated back to John's house. She thought hard about that question before she answered, "No. Very little scares me anymore. A relationship isn't something that would upset me—*if* it were to happen."

"Excellent. Now, why don't we go over some of your coping techniques for the interview and have a mental line in the sand established? The point you'll talk to but not about. It will keep you in control of the conversation tomorrow."

Shae closed her eyes. "The chamber, after the people left. I won't talk about that. Nothing happened except what he did to me and… her phone call telling Maurice to kill me."

"Her?" The doctor leaned forward.

"Yes."

"Did you hear the conversation?"

Shae furrowed her brow and concentrated on her memories. "No, but he said… 'She told me to kill you.'"

"So, we know the person who ordered your execution was a woman. How do you feel about that?"

She turned to Jeremiah and narrowed her eyes. "I'm fucking pissed."

Shae leaned back against the cottonwood tree beside him and thought hard about each question he lobbed at her throughout their session. Her thoughts and memories were still laced with fear and humiliation, but those emotions no longer consumed her. She was able to discuss what she felt and examine why she felt that way. Jeremiah was a good doctor and there was little doubt in her mind that she would have given up if it wasn't for the support she found on this ranch. Yes, she *could* talk with Guardian now, and it *was* time.

CHAPTER 15

The Guardian side of the Marshall ranch had changed since John had moved onto the property years ago. Homes for the full-time workers who for one reason or another couldn't live in the small town of Hollister had sprung up down a small valley. The hospital had grown and the people who transitioned through the training classes were housed in a small apartment building that was located next to the cafeteria. There were other structures, but he had no idea what they were used for.

He steered Shae toward the office where Mike, Dixon, and Drake worked. He'd worked with Joseph when the man had questions about the machinery or software he'd installed at the Rose and had used the secure communications in the building numerous times.

Shae slowed as she approached the door. He stopped and turned her toward him. "You don't have to do this."

She shook her head. "No, I want to. It's time."

"Then what's the problem?"

She sighed heavily and wrapped her arms around her stomach. "After I tell them what I know, I'm going to tell them I can't work for them."

His inner caveman stood up and banged on his chest. He didn't want Shae to go out on missions any longer. "Why does that have you worried?"

She flicked a glance at him. "Because I won't have a place to stay and I don't want to go back to Israel. How am I going to leave here? I'll have to leave Doctor Wheeler and we've made so much progress. Besides, who is going to take care of Velvet?" Her eyes dropped to the pea-sized gravel they were standing on. She sniffed and looked away at the horizon.

"Well, damn."

She didn't look at him but spoke quietly, "What?"

"I wanted to be on your list of reasons not to leave." He threw it out there. *Communication, right?*

She slowly turned toward him. "What?"

"I would have preferred to be the only reason, but I can share the list. For a while."

Shae laughed and wiped at her eyes. "I didn't want to presume."

"Ah, well, let's settle this here and now. You can stay with me in my house if Frank and Amanda kick you out of the drover's cottage. I have two extra rooms. I doubt they will want you to leave—those two would build you a house if you needed a place to stay. Second, Jeremiah won't let you go anywhere if he doesn't feel you are ready. If you need help paying for his care, I have money." Loads and loads of offshore money that he could access with a few strokes of a keyboard. "Velvet is spoiled. You're responsible for him, nobody else wants to deal with him, so I guess you're stuck here for the foreseeable future."

"You forgot something." She put her hands in her back pockets and stared up at him. Her bright brown eyes filled with laughter, which was so much better than the anxiety-filled expression a moment ago.

He raised his eyebrows. "Really? What did I forget?" He was teasing her, and her laugh told him she knew it, too.

"You." She tipped her head back and smiled widely.

"Oh, well, you're stuck with me, too."

"Yeah?" She stepped closer to him and smiled.

"Yeah." He reached out and placed his hands on her hips. "Most definitely." He leaned down and placed a soft kiss against her lips. The sound of a stifled cough drew them apart, but their eyes remained locked for several seconds before once again a smile spread across her face. Damn, the combination of her taste and that smile were hypnotizing

"Most definitely." She echoed his words before she turned to look at the person who'd interrupted.

"Sorry, we're on a tight timeline and have to catch a flight back to D.C. Are you ready?"

"Mr. King. It's been a long time." Shae reached out her hand.

"Indeed. I'm sorry for pressuring you into this interview, but we are at a crossroads and we need as much information as we can get to make an informed decision… and lives could very well be at stake."

"I understand. I will have to see the release the Mossad has sent." Shae glanced over at him. "And

John will be present with me in the interview. That is non-negotiable."

"That won't be a problem. My brother Jared arrived this morning and he will be conducting the interview."

"Just how many brothers do you have, Mr. King? I met the other one, Jason, I believe. He introduced himself when you came to see me at the hospital in Winnipeg."

Jacob opened the door and ushered them both in as he spoke, "There are five brothers and three sisters."

"A big family." Shae reached back and grabbed John's hand. He took her hand in his and felt thirty feet tall, fire retardant, and bulletproof. Yeah, that inner caveman of his was howling at the moon he was so happy. The woman trusted him, and fuck—the sizzling jolt of chemistry that shot through his body at that little kiss? Well, it was still ripping through his cells with a gusto that he'd never felt before. There was no doubt in his mind that he and Shae were a good match. Their cautious friendship had morphed into a solid companionship which was changing yet again. He couldn't wait to see where they'd end up. But first, they needed to get through today.

JOHN

Jacob and Shae visited about a lot of nothing as they walked through the building. He waved at Mike and then at Drake as they walked by office after office. Finally, they came to a small room where Jared and Jason King waited.

Shae stopped in the doorway. "No. There are too many people." Her words were a whisper, but he'd heard them.

"Jacob, we'll need to do something about the overcrowding in this room." He took the lead, making sure everyone knew the number of people in the room would be a deal-breaker.

"Jacob and I aren't staying. I just wanted to say thank you again for talking to us. I know it is difficult to relive past traumas. We've all lived through things that were meant to kill us, so we do understand where you are coming from and I wanted to personally acknowledge your sacrifice in trying to run Stratus to the ground." Jason King stood up and moved to the door. He extended his hand to Shae. "Thank you."

She shook her head but took Jason's hand anyway. "I was unsuccessful in my mission."

"Due in part to the fact that we'd lobbed the serpent's head off when you were undercover." Jason nodded.

"What?" Shae's head snapped up. "The Fates? You found them?"

"We found and eliminated all three of them. Unfortunately, that has caused all the layers of Stratus to strike out or go into hiding. That's why we need you to tell us what you know. If we can patchwork threads of intel together, we may be able to make surgical strikes against the organization before it rises again."

John had no idea who the Fates were, but he'd heard enough about Stratus to know the organization was bad news. If Shae had been hunting the bastards that comprised that organization, she'd been swimming in shark-infested waters.

"Anyway, this is my brother, Jared. He's the investigator of the family and he is in charge of Domestic Operations, which this case isn't—strictly speaking—but he is one of the best we have, so we asked him to fly out and talk to you." Shae nodded and smiled at Jared King but didn't enter the room. Jason turned his attention to him. "John, I'm sorry we couldn't find the answers you were looking for earlier this year."

"Some things remain unanswered. Perhaps that's for a reason." He shrugged. The truth in that answer came easier than he believed it would. Perhaps both he and Shae were making progress.

"Regardless, it feels like we failed you."

"No sir. You gave me a home and a reason to keep going." He shifted his gaze to Shae. "Things worked out just the way they should."

"Well, I'm glad to hear that. Jacob, let's go." He squeezed John's shoulder again and the two men exited the small room. He could see Shae's shoulders relax. She drew a deep breath and walked into the room.

Jared reached across the table as if he knew the barrier would help. "Shae, it is a pleasure to meet you. Would you prefer the door to remain open?" Jared nodded to the door behind them.

"No, but I do need to sit by the door." She pointed to the chair she wanted to sit in. Jared nodded his head and moved down the table to sit closer.

"May I record this interview?" He nodded to a small, handheld recording device.

"Of course, but first I'd like to see the Mossad's release?"

"Absolutely. Here it is." Jared slid a folder across the table to her. She opened the folder and read the document before setting it to the side. John did a double-take. Shae chuckled, "Hebrew, not English. English is my third language."

"What's your second?" He glanced over to Jared. "Sorry."

"No need. Is everything in order?"

"It is." She answered Jared and then leaned over and whispered, "Arabic."

"All right. I'm with Shae Diamant and her witness, Mr. John Smith. We have an official release from Mossad which allows Shae to discuss her previous mission. Shae, would you please give me the background of your mission?"

"Certainly. My partner and I were assigned to track down leads the Mossad had generated in regard to Stratus."

"Do you know where the leads came from?" Jared didn't look up as he wrote.

"I do, but I am not at liberty to discuss anything except what happened from the date of my assignment forward." She nodded to the piece of paper on the table.

"Integrity." Jared glanced up and smiled at her.

"A small trap for me? Really, Mr. King, do you think I'd reveal more than my previous agency has allowed?"

"Actually, I was hoping you wouldn't. I like to

know the character of the person I'm talking with." Jared placed his pen on the tablet of paper and leaned back. "Please, continue."

"Approximately two and a half years ago, my partner Joshua Kadosh and I were assigned a case in which my superiors believed a person tied to Stratus had utilized connections to a nightclub in Tel Aviv to distribute drugs. When my organization did the initial background, it was also noted that five women had gone missing from the club. There was no tie between the women."

Jared looked up. "You believe the club was involved in drug and human trafficking?"

"It was our belief, yes. The local authorities were called off the case and I was put into the club as a waitress. I made friends within management over the next five months. After all that time I only had suspicions, hints from people, and rumors that the owner's lover was really running the club and all the activities. So, the plan was developed to have me start dating a local police officer who was brought into the operation. The next month, I warned the manager of a raid that was going to happen. It earned me his confidence and an introduction to the person people thought was his lover."

"She was his boss," Jared stated.

"She was. Amira Raz. She was less trusting. It took an additional six months before she approached me. She was moving and wanted a core of people to go with her. I was selected in part because I also speak French. I flew with her to Quebec. She arrived with five of us from the Tel Aviv club. Every night we were told what type of woman to watch for. The description changed. Sometimes every night, sometimes, when the looks were unique, we could look for weeks. Finally, six months after we arrived, one of the people who traveled with us from Tel Aviv found a woman who met all the requirements Amira required. I was told to serve her table drinks. Her drink was drugged. When she got sick, I followed her into the bathroom. The rest was a precision operation. Within minutes, an ambulance crew entered through the back of the establishment, they put her on a stretcher, one gave her a shot that knocked her out, and they left. They weren't in the club for more than three minutes. I was pulled from the floor to the offices upstairs. We watched as the women she was with looked through the club for her. They just left without her. Amira was the Cheshire Cat. All smiles."

"Do you know what happened to the woman?" Jared asked.

"My partner Joshua got to her. I had a burner telephone in a waterproof case in the bathroom and stored more in several other areas of the club. Places where there were no cameras. After they left, I was supposed to make sure there were no traces of them in the bathroom or the hallway. I sent a text to Joshua, my partner. He faked being drunk and swerved into the ambulance. The Sûreté du Québec were on scene almost immediately and they took the woman, and the Mossad, who operate in Quebec, were able to divert the ambulance carrying the two fake ambulance drivers. They were questioned and detained out of the country."

"And Amira?"

"She was livid. Life for those of us who worked for her was rough for a while. She was paranoid and had us watched. I didn't risk making contact with Joshua for almost three months."

"How long did you work for her?"

"I didn't stop. The information we received from the ambulance drivers confirmed her ties to Stratus. I was told to continue to make myself valuable."

"How many women were taken from the club when you were working there?"

"Five that I am aware of, but I didn't work every night. The nights I did, I tried to let Joshua know what was happening. We were able to liberate three women through different ruses. The first was the accident. The second was a traffic stop. The third was a drug raid on the location where the drivers left the woman."

"And all this caused more suspicion?" Jared asked.

"Yes."

"And eventually, they connected you to Joshua," Jared stated, nodding his head.

"That is what I hypothesize." Shae drew a shaking hand through her hair.

"Do you know what happened to Joshua?"

Jared nodded. His eyes darted from Shae to John and then back again. "He was tortured and killed. His body was found on the shores of a beach in Italy."

"She said he'd admitted we were Mossad. I can understand that. I know exactly why he broke." Shae drew a ragged breath and extended her hand under the table and John took it in his.

"So, what happened next?"

"I woke up in the pit."

"Go on," Jared prompted.

Shae cleared her throat. "No, I will not answer that. That's where I draw the line."

JOHN

Jared King glanced up from his almost completely-used pad of paper. "I'm sorry, what?"

"What happened to me in that pit is not relevant to the interview. I've talked with Doctor Wheeler about my boundaries. I will tell you about the people who came after I was taken. I will tell you what my captor said to me, but I will not revisit what happened to me during that time." Shae glanced down at her lap.

"I have no problem with that boundary. Did you ever get Amira's supervisor's name? Any information as to who she reported to?"

"No. After the first night, when we rescued the woman from the ambulance drivers, I was held at arm's length. Everyone was. Amira was important, but I got the feeling she was a smaller cog. But I know who worked for her." Shae closed her eyes and rattled off a list of names, physical descriptions, and small nuggets of information on each of the people she worked with during her time in Quebec.

"How did you get to the location we found you?" Jared's question sent another full-body shudder through her.

"Do you need a break?" John uttered his first words since the interview started.

She shook her head. "No, I need to finish." She

stared at Jared King. "I don't have any recollection. Other than glimpses of being broadsided by a car when I was driving home... When they brought me back to consciousness, I was in the pit and there were—" She closed her eyes and he could swear she was counting. "—eight people there besides Maurice. *She* was sitting in the middle. The woman in the middle was in charge. She was the one who asked me what the Mossad knew. I didn't break, not for her. I kept my cover, even when they told me that my partner had broken and given them information. I didn't say a word except to beg them to stop. I kept telling them they made a mistake."

"But that didn't work," Jared stated.

"No. She was extremely upset, but then that rage settled into a cold, quiet... evil. Her accent was American, not southern or like the people here on the ranch. Clipped, precise English, more like... more like a businesswoman. She turned me over to Maurice. They left."

"Can you describe her?"

"I can. I was in pain, but her? Yes, I can describe her to you. I will never forget her face. Ever."

"I'll have a forensic artist flown out." He tapped his pen against his pad. "You said she was the boss. How did you know?"

"The authority in her voice. She was the one speaking, no one else said a word. It was obvious she controlled everything. Also, she called, she ordered Maurice to kill me. He said so. It was the only thing that bastard said to me. That and he told me he wouldn't make it fast."

Jared nodded. "He was captured when you were rescued and he's corroborated exactly what you've said today in regard to the events in the pit, as you call it."

Shae wrapped her arms around her stomach and closed her eyes. "He told you what he did to me."

"In fine detail," Jared acknowledged.

She shivered. "He's a sadist."

"And a psychopath," Jared added.

"Is that all you need?" John nodded to Shae. Her eyes were closed, and she was shivering, even though it was stuffy in the room.

"It is. Thank you, Shae. I believe you've given us a considerable amount of information that we didn't have before."

She leaned back and opened her eyes. "I would like you to take your brothers a message."

"I can do that. What is it?" Jared stopped clearing his space and gave her his undivided attention.

"I cannot work for Guardian. I realize that I may

owe the company for my treatment and rent for my domicile. If you would please send John the bill, I will make sure you are paid. It may take some time, but I'm good for it." Shae stood as she spoke.

John rose and cracked the door open. Fresh, cooler air flooded the small room. She glanced over at him. A flicker of a smile crossed her lips.

Jared stood also and shook his head. "You don't need to repay Guardian for anything. We will call the information you provided today payment in full. As for the cottage, well, that is my stepfather's house. You are staying there because he said it was happening and nobody bucks what Frank Marshall says. Not on *this* side of the ranch and definitely not on *that side* of the ranch." The man chuckled, "None of us are that brave."

"I have met him and his wife Amanda. They are good people. If you don't have anything else?"

"No, we're done here. I'll send the artist to you as soon as we can get them a flight."

"Thank you, I will be here for the foreseeable future. Should that change, I will let you know."

"Thank you again, Shae. You helped advance our investigation. My husband is a survivor, you remind me a lot of him. You're tough."

"Surviving is the easy part, Mr. King. Living

after… that is cripplingly difficult. I'm glad your husband was strong enough to go on. I almost wasn't." Shae made for the door and took John's hand on the way out, damn near tugging him out of the door with her. He glanced back at Jared, gave the man a quick nod, and hustled out of the building, linked with Shae, who had a death grip on him.

CHAPTER 16

Shae sat on one of the chairs on John's porch. They'd fed Velvet and she'd spent a long time brushing him. The colt loved the attention and she needed to focus on something outside of herself. Velvet gave her that option. He was growing tall and pranced around the enclosure with his tail held high, making her laugh at his superior attitude. That façade crumbled as soon as she opened the gate to his smaller pen. He'd trot in and nuzzle against her. The utter trust and dependency the colt displayed was refreshing and rejuvenating. She lapped up his attention as much as he enjoyed hers.

John came outside with two glasses of iced tea. "Dinner will be about a half-hour." He handed one of the drinks to her.

"Thank you. For everything." Shae moved so she was sitting sideways, looking at him.

"No thanks are necessary." A light blush of red spread across his cheeks.

She smiled and shook her head. "They may not be necessary, but they are warranted. I felt exposed and vulnerable. My experiences on that mission changed who I am."

John took a drink of his tea and set it down on the boards that comprised the wrap-around porch. "I can imagine. Do you know why I'm here on the ranch?"

Shae closed one eye and squinted at him. "Frank Marshall was looking for a ranch manager and you were looking for a ranch to manage."

John threw back his head and laughed, "Damn near word for word what I told you, but no. My sister and I worked for an agency that decided we were liabilities. She was murdered and I ran to the only agency I knew that had integrity and the resources to get me out of D.C. without raising suspicions."

Shae put her drink down and lifted her feet up into the chair, wrapping her arms around her knees. "Guardian." He nodded and stared out over the pastures. "Did you have other family?" She had her mother, but they weren't close. Not any longer.

"My father was killed about four months before my sister was murdered. The police didn't have any suspects or leads, but my sister told me he was working a con against a connected family, so maybe his luck finally ran out."

Shae cocked her head at the term. "Connected?"

"Ties to the mafia. Lori said he bragged to her that the con would net him fifteen million dollars."

"Wait, your father was a conman?"

John grimaced. "There is a lot about my past that I can't talk about. It's dangerous."

"Why?"

"Because it could get you killed." He turned and stared at her.

She cocked her head and narrowed her eyes at him. "I think I've proven that I am pretty hard to kill."

He blinked and then snorted. "Yes, you are one tough cookie."

"Then tell me." She shrugged. "Who am I going to tell? You know my darkest secrets and I trust you to keep them. Maybe letting someone you trust in could be cathartic."

"I couldn't tell you specifics."

"Then keep it general. I understand, you know I do."

John nodded. "My old man was a grifter. I was picking pockets by the time I was six. He used both Lori and me in cons and I could run my own scheme by the time I was fourteen. Hell, we were expected to make money, to pay him back for everything he invested in us. We didn't know any other way."

"So, you went from working with your father to...?" She left the question open.

"Ah, well... Lori and I were very proficient at making false identifications. We were damn good, actually. We went from state-issued identification to federal," he laughed and rubbed the back of his neck. "The Feds didn't like it and they were a hell of a lot more tenacious than the state authorities. They caught me with a pocket full of IDs. This was after Nine-Eleven and I was caught up in the Homeland sweep. After they cleared me of any terrorist activities, I was shoved in front of a judge who told me I could fight for my country or I could rot in a cell. I went into the service. It was... liberating."

Shae blinked and shook her head. "Military service was *liberating*?" She'd served in the Israeli

Army for two years; the forced discipline was anything *but* liberating.

"Oh, God, yes. My father was a master manipulator. He used us. When I joined the military, his power over me was gone. I loved the regimented lifestyle. I thrived on it, actually. I was damn good with a rifle and became a sniper." He sighed. "I guess that's probably why I love the ranch so much. I know exactly what needs to be done and when it needs to be done. It feeds something in me that I didn't have when I was growing up."

"Your sister stayed with your father?"

He nodded. "I took the rap for everything with the IDs and I served two enlistments doing exactly what the judge demanded. I fought for this country. I asked Lori to come with me, told her I'd take care of her, but she was making money hand over fist. Lori loved money, probably more than our father did. She was so damned focused on her future, on gaining more and more money. I could care less. I didn't want to leave the military."

"Then why did you?" Shae leaned back against the chair and stared at his profile.

"She called out of the blue about the time I was considering whether or not to re-enlist and told me she had an opportunity I shouldn't pass up. The... entity she was working for wanted us both. She'd told them about the cons we'd developed, the things we'd done. They recruited me and threw a lot of money in our direction. So, I got out and went to work in D.C."

"Then you weren't needed?" She was trying to understand any rationale for an entity to eliminate a valuable resource that they'd recruited.

John stared out over the pastureland, but she doubted he saw anything but his memories. "When a person knows too much there comes a time when their value becomes a potential liability."

"You knew too much..." Shae stared at him while he stared out across the horizon. "You knew too much." Reality dawned on her. "About things or people they didn't want discovered. They killed your sister and wanted to kill you to make sure those secrets were never divulged."

John nodded. "Exactly."

She slid off the chair and knee-walked the small distance to where he sat. She rested her hands on his thighs. The warmth and hardness of his flesh under the material were difficult not to notice, but she wanted an answer to a question he hadn't answered yet. "You said you never leave the ranch. Why were you in Canada?"

He opened his legs and she moved between them. He covered her hands and gazed at her a second or two before speaking. "Guardian had uncovered an obscure message about my sister. We were running down hunches."

"Thank God you did." Shae leaned forward and rested her head against his chest. He held her loosely in his arms. The warmth of his body leached into her and she let her muscles relax against him. If he hadn't chased that hunch, she'd be dead. A shiver ran through her at the thought. "Did you uncover anything?"

"Besides you? No. All the coordinates were a wash. All except yours. I've resigned myself to never knowing who in the organization ordered Lori's death and my assassination. Not knowing will always haunt me and keep me here. Not that I mind. I'd be perfectly happy here. Now."

Another shudder of sensation raced through her, but this one wasn't initiated by fear. No, the thought of living here, with John…

"Are you cold? We can go inside."

The vibration of his deep voice rumbled under her ear. "I'm not cold, but I think we should go inside." She lifted away from the light embrace and stared at him. She could see the hesitation in his eyes. "I need to feel something good, John. With you."

"Are you sure?"

"Very." She leaned forward and kissed him. It took a second or two for him to catch up as the tentative kiss continued. He shifted on the chair, moving closer to her, and gently enfolded her into an embrace. The kiss they shared this morning wasn't a fluke. Was it? Not the actual contact, that was definitely intentional, but her reaction to his touch... She'd played it over and over in her head as she cared for Velvet and John did his nightly chores in the barn. Had the extreme emotion of revisiting her past caused her to misjudge the chemistry between them? Did he feel the same connection as she did?

Shae leaned away. He chased her lips and moaned just a bit when she extended the kiss. No, she wasn't imagining this morning. The reaction that buzzed through her body now had affected him, too. She leaned away, smiled as she stood up, and offered him her hand. "Let's make some good memories."

He stood and wrapped his arms around her again. "All the memories I have of you are good."

"Then let's make even better ones." She lifted on her toes and he lowered to her for a kiss.

John dipped his head to taste Shae's sweet lips. His sex life had been dormant since he'd taken up residence in South Dakota. But all of his past, the hiding, and yes, the healing, had brought him to this place and this woman. He reached down and cupped her ass in his hands, lifting her up. She wrapped her legs around his waist, and he walked—or rather, shuffled—forward, trying to walk, kiss her, and keep his balance at the same time. He broke the kiss. "This isn't getting us to the bedroom."

She dropped her legs from his waist and grabbed his hand. "I know the way." She tugged on his hand and he moved. Damn, did he move, just as quickly as she did. She laughed when he jogged the last few feet and turned on the overhead light. "Turn it off." She slid past him, brushed up against him, and purred the words.

He did as he was bid and cut the switch he'd just flicked on. He could see her in the shadows of his

JOHN

room. The drapes cut out most of the lingering evening light. He kicked off his boots as he watched her remove her clothes. There was no hesitation in her moves, thank God. He wanted her desperately, but there was no way he'd take events past what she could handle. He didn't know what was done to her in that damn pit, but he'd seen the aftermath.

Shae shimmied out of her jeans as he pulled off his. He left his boxers on, giving them a small layer and another conscious act of permission for Shae. She extended her hand. "Trust me to know what I want."

He slid his fingers over hers and let her lead him to the bed. He waited for her to lie down on the center of the bed and carefully positioned himself on his hands and knees above her, taking in the glow of her exposed body. "My God, you are beautiful."

"I'm not. Too many scars, too many battles." She pushed her hand through his hair as she spoke.

He shook his head but held eye contact. "Don't you understand? The scars, the battles, the things you don't want me to see and cover with the dark? I'll never be able to see them. I only see the beauty inside you, the strength and strong will that pulled you out of a hell you didn't deserve. To me, you are beautiful for reasons that have nothing to do with the perfection of your skin."

"What did I do to deserve you?" Tears glistened in her eyes as she trailed her fingers across his cheek. He captured her hand and kissed her palm, then trailed kisses to her wrist, down her arm, and to her shoulder. He didn't care what cosmic collision occurred to push them into each other's orbit, he was caught in her gravitational pull. She was impossible to resist.

He mapped her body with his lips, trailed the small ridges of scars with his fingers before he worshipped them with kisses. This night was about Shae, about showing her that she was beautiful and that he was the lucky one.

He mouthed the swell of her breast and clamped around the tight nub. Shae arched under him and grabbed two handfuls of hair, keeping him from moving. He smiled against her skin and doubled his efforts. His body ached to be inside hers, but there wasn't anything that would keep him from making their first time perfect.

He trailed a hand down her side to her hip. He followed the juncture and found her core. She was hot and wet, slick with desire. He groaned as his fingers slid through her folds, finding the hardened knot at the apex of her cleft. He smoothed his thumb over it and applied pressure as he moved it back and forth. Shae arched and gasped his name. Oh fuck, that was something he wanted to hear again and again. He teased her breast, one then the other, while stimulating her with his fingers. She grabbed at his shoulders and then his chin, bringing him away from her swollen nipples. "I want you inside me. Don't make me beg."

He lifted up and put all his weight on his elbows. Her eyes were burning with desire. He knew his reflected the same need, but he had to check one last time. Panting and his cock screaming in revolt, he asked, "Are you sure?"

Shae grabbed him and stared at him. "Fuck me."

He shook his head. "Never, but I'll make love to you."

A smile spread across her face. "Then do that."

"Do I need a condom?"

"No, I've taken care of that."

He lifted her leg and centered himself to push in. If it was physically possible, his eyes had to have rolled back in his head when he entered her, but since he was staring at her the entire time, he doubted if the feat actually happened. Still, her heat encased him like their two bodies were tailor-made for each other. He dropped his head to her shoulder when he finally filled her. "Dear God, so good. I'm not going to last long."

"I'm so close." Shae panted the words under him. He nodded against her shoulder and swiveled his hips, grinding into her clit. Shae mewled her pleasure under him so as he seated deep in her again, he rotated his hips and withdrew. Lifting above her, he cupped her head with his hands and found a rhythm that catapulted both of them toward ecstasy. Shae shattered first; her fingernails dug into his skin as her body seized around him. The sensation swallowed him whole. No longer could he recognize anything other than pure pleasure. Carnality, sensuality, and an undeniable thrill careened through him as he lost himself inside her. He managed to stay on his elbows long enough to recover his vision and drop beside her instead of on top of her.

"Wow." Shae panted the word between labored pulls of air.

"Yeah." He agreed with one word because fuck, what they'd just done was so far out of the ballpark from any other hookup he'd had. Only this wasn't a hookup, was it? This was something more. He closed his eyes and pulled her closer to him.

She rolled onto her side and tipped her head. He

glanced down at her and smiled at the expression on her face. A cross between cat-meets-cream and exhaustion. Her brows scrunched together. Well, that expression shouldn't be anywhere within a 30-mile radius based on the existential experience they'd just had. "What?"

"I... well..." She looked at him and narrowed her eyes even further. "I'm not sure what I should do now. Usually, this is where I get my clothes on and leave."

His eyebrows lifted in understanding. "Well, in full disclosure, I'm not on any firmer ground."

"No long-term relationships for you?" She lifted on her elbow and stared down at him.

"Yes and no. There were a couple ladies while I was in the military, but with deployments and overseas tours, they didn't last. Then, when I was working with Lori, the job took priority. If I felt the need, I'd go out." He shrugged. She'd get the inference that he'd pick up someone to get laid. He wasn't proud of it, but he wasn't going to deny it either. "I take it you haven't had a long relationship either?"

Shae's eyes went wide and she blew a puff of air making her cheeks pop out. "Not even one lasting a couple months. There were a few men who I'd visit when I was in their area, but I was married to my career, which has recently divorced me, so like I said… I'm not sure what to do now."

"Well, I guess the question is what do you *want* to do?" He reached up and pushed her hair behind her ear so he could see her face better.

She cocked her head at him. "I want to stay here at the ranch. I want to see what happens between us, but I have no resources. I have a small nest egg. I guess I need to ask Mr. Marshall if he'd rent the cottage to me and how much rent will be."

He shook his head and laughed. Frank would be offended. Frank Marshall was all about taking care of people, but he could see where Shae was coming from. She didn't want to be a burden and was obviously used to making her own way in life. "He probably won't take a cent."

"Then I need to get a job. A visa first, then a job. How do I apply for a visa? I've never done that. The Mossad always took care of the process. What kind of jobs are around here?" She tugged her bottom lip between her teeth and worried it as she focused over his shoulder. "I don't know what I'd do though. I can't see much need for an ex-Mossad operative around here."

"Come here." He tugged her down on top of his

chest. "You don't have to worry about anything tonight."

"I think we both need to worry. You've attached yourself to a woman who is damaged, is probably in the country illegally, has no way to support herself, and from what you've told me, people want to kill you for what you know."

John ran his hand through her hair. "I didn't lie, Shae, I *am* a wanted man, although I'm only guilty of doing my job. I didn't tell you specifics, but you're damn smart, you can get the inference. I can't leave the ranch. Ever. This is my life. My destiny. All my cards are on the table."

Shae closed her eyes. "We both got a bad deal."

"But we know what cards we're working with."

She opened her eyes again and stared into his. "A level playing field."

"A dangerous playing field," he added.

"I don't know any other kind of game." She closed her eyes and fell asleep wondering if life ever got easier.

John's hands moving across her skin woke her sometime during the night. Shae ignited at the dance of their touches and the warmth of John's embrace. His fingers trailing down her back and past her hip left spires of electricity, white-hot and burning through her sexual need. She rotated her hips and was rewarded with the feel of his sizable shaft, hard and hot beneath her core. She shifted her attention from his mouth to his neck. His hands cupped the sides of her breasts as she pressed against his chest. His thumbs pressed through their connection and found the hard buds of her nipples and stimulated them with an almost-too-slow sweep. She ground down on top of him as she lifted up. Reaching behind herself, she lifted his cock under her. John's hands found her hips as she lifted and balanced her weight on her knees. As she lowered, she closed her eyes and reveled in the warm pressure entering her. She lifted and lowered, sinking lower each time. When she finally consumed him, they were both panting. She leaned forward and braced herself on his shoulders. With a twist of her hips, she lowered and then lifted. Her pace quickened by a compulsion of her need and want. The glorious fullness at the bottom of the drop was magnified when she moved faster. And faster. Dear God, the jolt of his cock buried deep in her was glorious. The fullness ignited sparks that illuminated the darkness behind her eyelids. She wanted more—no, she *needed* more.

Her world rolled and John was on top of her. She grabbed the bedding and hung on as he gave her what she needed. His hips set up a quick, deep penetration. Her body became a bowstring pulled back and ready to catapult forward. John shifted slightly; his angle allowed him that perfect reach. Every muscle in her body tightened and then detonated in a flood of electric, pulsing sensation. She felt him drop to his elbows and wrapped her arms around him, holding him while he chased his release. The intimacy of the moment surpassed anything she'd ever known. She held the man who in no small part was responsible for her being here today. The rescue, the friendship, the trust that built into the relationship they were starting... John was the single common denominator in all of the major events in her life since she'd been found in that pit. She slammed her eyelids shut. No, those memories weren't welcome here between them. Never.

John dropped to his side and pulled her with him, still warm inside her.

Shae mindlessly ran her fingers through the hair on his chest. "John?"

"Hmmm?" His sleepy response put a smile on her face.

"Thank you."

He pulled away and opened one eye. "For what exactly? Putting you in danger?"

"For asking me to take your hand."

He smiled and kissed her nose before resuming their previous position. "Thank you for taking the risk of trusting me."

She smiled and closed her eyes. There was no one she trusted more.

CHAPTER 17

"What do you mean?" Shae stared at Jared King. The man shrugged and took a sip of his coffee. Her stare went to John and then back to Jared. "Is this legitimate?"

"Yes. We contacted the Mossad as a courtesy to inform them we were going to extend you a job opportunity, one that wouldn't require you to be in the field. Two hours later, we received that email." Jared nodded to the email in her hand.

Shae read the email again. "They want me back." But not in any position of responsibility. It was a way for the agency to save face. Having Guardian offer her employment after they'd determined she was finished was egg on the Mossad's corporate face, so to speak. "I believe this offer isn't one they would give if you had not mentioned you were going to offer me a job." She glanced from the email and lifted an eyebrow.

"I one hundred percent agree. I was asked to offer you a position." Jared stretched his long, jean-clad legs out.

"Within Guardian? Where would I be working and in what capacity?"

"This complex was originally conceived as a rehab facility for wounded operatives. It has since morphed into a well-organized mishmash of entities. Mike White Cloud is in charge of the entire operation and he has put in a request for an assistant. His wife, Taty, works linguistics in the training facility and she has no desire to move laterally, and quite frankly, we like where she's at, so there is an opening and we always try to promote from within."

"I'm not one of you." She ping-ponged her eyes from Jared to John and back again. This opportunity was too good to be true, especially since she'd just vented her concerns to John last night. Not even twenty-four hours later, one of the Kings of Guardian was sitting in her little cottage and offering her a position that would allow her to stay here in South Dakota.

"Technically, you still are. Jason asked that I offer you the position prior to processing your resignation."

"But what about my clearance?"

"We've vetted you and matriculated the Mossad's clearance pending our own agency's investigation. We are only a few steps away from providing the documentation to the Office of Personnel Management. They usually fast track our candidates. You should be ready to work in full capacity in a month or less." Jared took another sip of his coffee.

She turned her gaze to John. He shrugged. "It gives you financial stability and a purpose other than spoiling Velvet."

She nodded and pulled her bottom lip between her teeth. A thought popped into her head. "Where would I stay?"

"Well, there are a few options. There is a series of rooms that we utilize for the rehab patients when they don't need to be hospitalized but still need care. You can stay there as part of your compensation package. Rent-free. There are very few rentals in Hollister. Most of the rest of the staff has taken what there is, but Frank wants you to stay in the cottage."

"He does?"

Jared nodded. "He'd rather have someone in it than let it sit fallow, his words, not mine."

"I'd have to pay rent." She wouldn't take no for an answer.

Jared cleared his throat. "Then he's going to pay you for the time you spend working with Velvet."

"What?"

She sent a furtive glance at John, who shook his head and held up his hands in surrender. "That was not my doing."

"That's Frank. He's going to get what he wants. I've learned just to let him have his way. And I will deny it if you tell him this, but his way is usually right. Okay, always right, but again, *I* didn't say that," Jared chuckled and downed the remainder of his coffee. "Sleep on it. Talk it over and let us know by the end of this week."

She stood when Jared did. "I don't need to think about it. If this Mike thinks I'm qualified as his assistant, I'll take the position."

"And the cottage?" Jared cocked his head and smiled at her.

Shae rolled her eyes but couldn't prevent the huge smile on her face. "Yes, and the cottage. I'll thank Mr. Marshall for that the next time I see him."

"Good. I'll put a push on the clearance issue with OPM. Glad to have you on board with us."

"Thank you." She shoved her hands into the back pockets of her jeans, thankful that Jared didn't offer to shake her hand. She was growing stronger but still had issues from the hours she spent in the pit.

She stood beside John as they watched Jared walk up to the Marshall ranch house. "You had nothing to do with this?"

"I swear on my sister's grave. The organization and that family are the absolute best. They take care of their people and if they've claimed you as part of the family, you're lucky." John put his arm over her shoulder. "Looks like you're going to be staying."

She turned to him and wrapped her arms around his waist. "How do you feel about that?"

He bent down and kissed her lips softly. "How about I take you inside and show you just how happy I am with your new job?"

A roll of electricity tumbled through her just under her skin. "Oh, yes, please do."

The session with the forensic artist was taxing and Shae was exhausted. The woman had appeared this morning without any warning. John was out replacing fencing with the other hands, so she'd worked with the lady alone. For three hours they refined the drawing until the woman she remembered stared back at her.

She needed her time with Velvet and came down to the barn early. She was careful and knew how to handle the colt, so John wouldn't be upset with her coming down. Velvet was her stress relief.

She felt a tug and turned around. "What do you think you're doing?" Shae laughed at Velvet, who'd taken her leather glove from her back pocket and held it in his mouth. The colt's wide eyes and still stiff-legged shock mimicked a *'I have it and now I don't know what to do with it'* expression. She reached for the glove and the colt jerked his head back.

"Oh, no, you don't," she laughed and slid her hand through his halter, halting his retreat, and grabbed her glove.

"Even the little ones are devils."

Shae spun in surprise. Two women sat on the top rail of the small corral where Velvet now stayed when he wasn't out with the other foals.

The blonde chuckled, "Pay no attention to this one. She is all hard edges and no tact. I am Tatyana

White Cloud. You will be working with my husband, soon. Yes?"

Shae held Velvet's halter and smiled. "Yes, if everything goes well with my paperwork. Your accent, Russian, perhaps?"

The woman nodded. "Yours is Israeli?"

"It is. I'm Shae Diamant, but of course, you knew that." Shae shifted her eyes to the woman who was all hard edges. She had beautiful long black hair and was just as petite as the blonde but with the exact opposite coloring and—it would appear—attitude. Shae stared at the woman. "And you are?"

The woman sighed dramatically. "Bored. My close-quarters defense class was canceled. Taty here was heading down here, so I came along." The woman pointed at Velvet. "That thing is only going to get bigger."

"Well, I should hope so, he's only a baby horse now." Shae attached his lead rope to the halter. "Should I call you Bored, or do you have an abbreviated form of that name that you prefer?" Shae stared at the woman and waited.

The woman stared right back at her. Shae mentally calculated what weapons were within her reach and the dark-haired woman's. She wasn't one hundred percent—hell, she wasn't even sixty percent—but she wouldn't back down if the woman pushed her attitude into the corral.

Tatyana snorted and spoke to the dark-haired woman. "Oh, I like her."

"My name is Joy."

Shae's head kicked back. "Sasha's owner?"

The woman smiled hugely. "She's my baby. Dumber than a box of rocks, but she's always loved me for me."

"Well, there is something to be said for loyalty." Shae picked up the curry comb and started her work on Velvet's coat.

"Damn straight. Speaking of which, we like John." Joy crossed her arms and fell back into the pissed-off staring mode.

Shae snorted. "Here to warn me not to hurt him?"

Taty laughed, "She might be, but I'm here because I was curious who my husband was going to be working with and to invite you to Winchester Wednesday."

Shae stopped brushing Velvet and stared at the women over his back. "You have rifle Wednesdays?"

Joy threw back her head and laughed, "Right? Exactly what I said, too. No, they watch this television show and drink wine." If the woman could have held the word 'wine' out in front of her and dropped it like a dirty rag it couldn't have been clearer she didn't approve of wine as a drink.

Shae chuckled, "I assume you bring your own..." She cocked her head and took a stab at what the woman would drink. "Vodka."

Taty laughed and nodded. "Oh, damn, you're good. She doesn't drink lady drinks. Usually, it's bourbon, but she's been known to do damage to a bottle of vodka."

"I suppose you drink wine." The petulance in Joy's voice bordered on comical.

"I don't care for it unless it accompanies food. I prefer Scotch. Single malt. But I must admit it has been a very long time since I've had any." She hadn't wanted to chance it with the meds that she'd been on, but as of last week, she was no longer on antidepressants, and physically, she'd been cleared months ago.

"I can find a bottle of good hooch. Come up to the big house tonight at seven. We can get shitfaced while they watch two dudes beat up some demons."

"Demons?" Shae blinked and slowly turned her head toward Tatyana. "What is this show you're watching?"

"It's called Supernatural. Awesome show, good

looking men, and unlike the real world, the good guys always win. Will we see you tonight?"

"I'd like that, but I don't think I'll get... what did you say... shitfaced." The expression was one she hadn't heard before, and in reality, she thought it was rather vulgar.

Joy retorted, "Whatever. At least I'll have a drinking partner." Taty carefully stepped down from the rail. She noticed the woman favored one arm. *Shoulder injury, perhaps?* The other woman jumped from the top rail and landed on her toes in a fighting position. Shae saw the smirk and slight nod from Joy. Shae recognized the acknowledgement and tipped her head in the same way. Female warriors, both of them. It was good to know she wasn't the only one on the ranch.

John sat on the rocking chair. Cat and Sasha had wandered over when Dixon and Drake headed to Adam's house for poker. He lifted a hand in acknowledgement when he saw them pass by. The distance was enough to prevent conversation, which is the way he liked it. Most of the time. Tonight, especially.

He watched Shae bounce off the walls with anxious excitement. She was animated in a way he hadn't seen her before. The prospect of a new job and the invitation from Taty and Joy had put air beneath her wings.

Cat cuddled up next to Sasha at his feet. He rocked gently as he stared at the multitude of stars that illuminated the heavens. He was home. He had no doubt he'd live out his days on this ranch or at least as long as the Marshalls or their descendants would tolerate him taking up space. He glanced up toward the main house. He couldn't see it from here, but just over the hill, Shae was meeting the rest of the women who lived on the ranch full time. *Would it be enough for her?* He closed his eyes. *Would he be enough for her?*

His eyes popped open. He turned his head toward the darkness between his house and Shae's. "Trying to sneak up on me?"

"Hell, no." Frank moved from the shadows. "All the women in the house were making it impossible to find a quiet place to relax. Figured I could find that here."

"Cat's noisy." The animal lifted its head and meowed before it started its motorboat purr, stretched its front legs, and kneaded Sasha's thick, white coat of fur.

"I can live with it." Frank dropped down into the chair next to him. "Fall is coming on quick. According to the Farmer's Almanac, it will be damn cold this winter, more snow than usual. Winter coming on sooner rather than later."

He nodded. "Fencing is done. Gregg and I finished the last section this afternoon. We are in good shape. We'll be ready."

Frank grunted. "Need to bring the herd closer the first part of October. Don't need anyone caught in a freak storm. We have enough feed stored to bring them closer earlier."

"Yup. I have it scheduled for the second week of October. Asked Dixon and Drake to take the helicopter up after we bring them down to check for strays."

Frank snorted. "Ah, hell. They'll give the cows a heart attack."

"Maybe, but last year they found six head that probably wouldn't have made it through the winter."

Frank grunted an acknowledgement but continued, "Saw Shae at the house. She looked happy."

"Joy and Taty invited her up."

John waited for the man's grunt and smiled in the

JOHN

dark when Frank acknowledged his words with it. Frank spoke again. "She's opening up. Blooming. Think you did that."

"She did it. She's put in hard work with Doctor Wheeler. Thank you, by the way, for letting her stay in the cottage. I think she needs that sense of independence."

Frank rolled his head and pinned him with a stare. "Not fit for an extended stay."

"I'm aware." He smiled at his friend. "Things need to progress at her pace, not mine."

Frank pushed his chair and rocked for a long while before he spoke again. "Glad she was able to give the artist a description. May help them track down that woman. I'd like to see one of you two get some closure."

"I'm afraid I'll never know who ordered Lori's murder."

"Someone in that agency." The vehemence in Frank's voice was expected. He had a particular grudge against the CIA. He'd never explained why, but John would hate to be on Frank's bad side and prayed the CIA never bumped up against Frank Marshall. They'd lose in a big way.

John shook his head and thought once again about his demise from favor and sighed. "I've gone over it a million times. The only question I have is—why. Why take *her* out? I'd been the only one working on covers for... hell, for almost two years. Even when she was there, she wasn't working on the particulars." Lori was too busy climbing the agency's ladder to be bothered with formulating the deep covers he was constantly building. It was tedious, detail-oriented work and Lori wasn't interested in putting in the effort, time, or mental energy. He loved it, though. Loved putting together a puzzle, making sure all the pieces fit exactly as they should, and carving a person with a detailed history out of his imagination. Hell, when he rode fence, he'd work up a history or make up a profile to keep his mind occupied.

"Protecting assets."

He huffed, "As if I'd release that type of information." Frank pulled out a piece of taffy and offered it to him. "No thanks."

The man pulled on the wax paper and popped the candy into his mouth, tucking it into his cheek. "Ever think that maybe they were more concerned about Lori?"

He sighed. "More than once. She had a lot of Dad in her. Did she say or do something that would lead someone to believe they couldn't trust her? Maybe. I have no delusions about my sister. I loved her; she was my only friend growing up. We moved in the middle of the night, skipping out on rent or leaving because my father's scams were imploding. He'd leave us for weeks at a time and we fended for ourselves. Was she perfect? No. But no matter what she said or did, she didn't deserve…"

"Never said she deserved it. Just worrying the problem with you, son. Trying to figure out the why of it." Frank rocked slowly with him as they stared out into the night.

"Did they get any information from Shae that they could use?" John asked the question as they continued to enjoy the quiet of the night.

"Don't know. If there was anything, they'd be working it now. Takes time." Frank pulled out another candy and slowly opened the wrapper.

John turned and stared at his friend. "How long were you a Guardian?"

Frank paused unwrapping his candy for a second before he continued. After he popped it into his mouth and carefully folded the wax paper and pocketed it, he stood. "Not long."

"Miss it?" John stood and stretched.

"Nah. My life is here. I'll leave it to the kids. They

have what it takes. Me, I was just a cowboy out of water... or in water, as it turned out."

"Navy?"

"SEAL."

"Impressive."

"It was what it was. You still practice with that long iron?"

"Every chance I get. The range is usually busy."

"Asp will be back eventually. You two need to go up and get some practice in. Tell Chief to work the schedule to make that happen."

"Yes, sir." John appreciated Frank's determination to keep his skills sharp. The ranch was tucked away and protected, but if anyone were to ever find out about what was happening behind that hill on Guardian's side of the ranch, everyone would be needed to defend the innocents that lived on Marshall land. Hell, within weeks of coming to the ranch, he'd used his skill to take out a madman at a church in Hollister. Yeah, he and Asp had a certain skill in common. They spoke the same language. Death at a vast distance.

"Night." Frank nodded and walked off the porch.

"Night," John echoed and leaned against a porch post. He looked up at the stars. This wasn't just a ranch. This land was a haven to broken and battered souls. Maybe the land would continue to be a balm for Shae as it was for him. God, he hoped it would be. He'd fallen headfirst into love with the woman. Inch by inch, conversation by conversation, and kiss by kiss, his heart had jumped ship and landed in her hands. What she did with it was up to her. He'd just continue to show her love the only way he knew.

CHAPTER 18

Shae shivered as she jogged up the steps to the training complex's administrative offices. She scurried into the building and quickly shut the door behind her. Her trajectory was the breakroom and the coffee pot. As soon as she saw the twins, she asked, "What the heck happened to autumn? This place went from summer to winter in one night."

Both Dixon and Drake laughed from in front of the coffee pot. "Don't worry, it will warm up again. Autumn in South Dakota is a fickle beast." Dixon handed her the mug she'd claimed and filled her cup.

She wrapped her hands around the ceramic mug and shivered while she waited her turn for the sugar and creamer. Drake passed her the cream first and then the sugar. "Why didn't you wear a coat?"

"I don't have one." She dumped a generous amount of sugar into her coffee and stirred it.

"You need to order some cold-weather gear. Boots, gloves, coats, and such. John should be able to help you do that." Drake took a sip of his coffee but continued before she could speak, "I'm so damn glad we have an indoor gym this year. Running in the snow was fun when we were younger, but it is not my idea of a good time any longer."

"Hey! We never got our night!" Dixon slapped his brother.

"What in the hell are you talking about?" Drake moved out of striking distance.

"The Skipper promised us a night out on the town when we won…"

"Holy shit, dude, that was *years* ago." Drake snorted and nodded in his brother's direction. "You'll have to excuse him. Brain damage."

Shae laughed when Dixon choked on his coffee. "Don't worry, I understand. He said the same about you yesterday." She dropped that bomb and slipped out of the room when Drake turned on his brother.

"You said what?"

"No, I didn't, Shae… Hey, Shae, you can't start shit and then leave," Dixon yelled down the hall.

"Watch me!" she laughed and ducked into Mike's office, shutting the door behind her.

"You know, you really don't need to start anything between them, they are more than capable of amusing each other," Mike chuckled as she sat down at her desk.

"I know, but it is so easy to spin them up." Shae pulled her keyboard toward her and entered her password, pulling up their calendar. "You have a meeting with Kaeden at nine, a teleconference with Joseph at ten thirty, and then we have utilization and budget meetings this afternoon."

Mike nodded and looked at the printout of the calendar she'd placed on his desk yesterday after he'd left for the day. "Do you have the information for—"

"The proposed budget is in the shared folder, the allocations from Guardian need to be tweaked, and we have a deficit we need to address in logistics, and also in structures. The storm that blew through here three weeks ago is going to put us into the red. The contractors' bids are due in by noon today. I'll compile them in time for the meeting. The twins submitted the proposed training schedule for the next quarter, and there are new classes that are going to need to be funded." Shae stared at her computer for a moment before she spun and asked, "How do I order clothes?"

Mike's head snapped up. "What? Clothes? For whom?"

"Me. The twins said I could order clothes. I need warmer clothes for winter."

"Ah, hasn't John told you how to do that?"

"No, he hasn't because I haven't asked him. I don't need him to take care of me. I am a capable person. Wouldn't you be offended if everyone told you to ask Taty every time you had a question?"

"Do we do that?"

"More than you realize." She'd had about enough of people thinking John was running her life. It was true they were in a relationship, a damn good one, but she was an independent person, she always had been. People assuming she was dependent on John needed to stop. Now.

"Damn, I didn't realize we were misogynistic, at least not to that degree." Mike shook his head.

Shae cocked her head at him. Perhaps they didn't see it as well as she did. She wasn't the same person who'd first come to this ranch. She was reverting to the woman she used to know. Not by leaps and bounds, but with steady steps, she was regaining her confidence. "Well, now you do. Perhaps just knowing will help, yes? How do I order clothes?"

Mike stared at her for a moment and then nodded. "I will ensure that everyone is aware of what we've been doing. We will do better, but call us on it if it happens again."

"Of course. Thank you."

"Right, as for clothes or for that matter anything you want, we can order through the logistic supply point. Find what you want on the internet and then fill out the sheet—with links, if possible. All the forms are in the common folders. They will order it and have it delivered to one of five supply points around the country. The supply transports come in weekly. It takes about two weeks to get anything in, but it is untraceable and secure. If you want to go to a city to go shopping, there is a request form in the transportation folder. Fill it out and we will fly you off the ranch on a Guardian transport and make connecting flight reservations so you can do your own shopping. You'll be required to ship anything you can't bring back to one of the supply points, but the inconvenience is worth the security for our location."

"That is..."

Mike chortled, "A lot to go through?"

She shook her head and furrowed her eyebrows. "Well thought out and extremely prudent." There were several portions of the facility she didn't have access to—not that it bothered her, but the secrecy made sense if those areas were classified above her clearance level.

Shae bounced on her toes and snapped a left and then a right hook at the heavy bag. Her exercise regime as prescribed by the twins had toned her neglected muscles and she'd regained her strength and speed. She lobbed a combination of punches at the brown leather and lost herself in the strike and dance she'd performed for over twelve years. A spin and high kick followed by an arm up to block her imaginary opponent, followed by another flurry of punches and several knees and kicks.

"Tuck your left elbow tighter," Joy's command barked out from behind her. Shae tucked it because she'd lost her form. She executed the last flurry again and maintained perfect form as she eviscerated her imaginary foe. She stopped, awash of sweat, and turned, putting her taped fists on her hips. "Nice work." Joy nodded past her to the bag. "You can beat up a bag. Congratulations."

"Is that a challenge?" She hadn't had a workout in the ring in over two years. Damn, almost three. It would feel good to get back to fighting form.

"Soon. You have a couple more months of conditioning. When we hit the ring, I'm not going to hold back on you."

"I never thought you would. What brings you to the gym this late?" Most of the Guardian personnel took part in the early morning PT that the twins led, John included. She preferred the solitude of an almost-empty gym.

"I was at logistics and saw you had some packages. I figured you'd still be here." Joy nodded to the door and the five canvas bags full of items she'd ordered after Mike had told her how to place an order.

"All of those are mine?"

Joy grunted. "No, two are mine. Are you showering here or heading down to the cottage?"

She'd gotten to know and understand this prickly woman over the last two months. That question was obviously an invitation to walk to the other side of the ranch with her. Not that Joy would ever admit it. She chuckled, "Cottage. Give me a minute to wipe down my equipment and take off this tape."

Joy watched her for a moment. "You're good. Why did you stop working for the Mossad?"

Shae blinked and paused from unwinding the tape from her feet. "The Mossad lost confidence in my ability." She wadded the tape into a ball and pitched it into the garbage. "And after my last operation, I'll admit I lost confidence in myself."

"So, you just going to stay here at the ranch for the rest of your life?" Joy picked up a bottle of disinfectant and a clean towel and sprayed the bag and wiped it down.

Shae considered the question while she removed the tape from her hands. "I like what I'm doing with Mike and the twins. Going undercover isn't for me anymore. I was... I was tortured and nearly dead when John and the others found me." She wadded up the tape and tossed it into the garbage can.

Joy tossed the towel she was using to the floor and sprayed the mat under the bag, using her foot to sop up the sweat and disinfectant. "I guess there is a point when we all make the determination not to go back out."

"What was your point?"

Joy snorted. "I'm not there yet. Soon. I want... Well, life has changed. My objectives for my life have changed."

"Undercover operative?"

Joy stopped and looked up at her. "Black door."

"Ah." She nodded and pulled on her socks. Black door could mean any of a wide variety of assignments, but the meaning was clear. As she suspected, the cactus personality kept people away because the woman couldn't have people close and do her job. Interesting that she was married to Dixon, though. The two of them didn't make sense, at least from what she'd seen, although there was no doubt they loved each other. She shoved her feet into her tennis shoes. Opposites attracting and all that. Although she and John were more like mirror reflections. At least now.

"Tell me you bought a coat," Joy asked as they walked out of the gym.

"I did. Amanda recommended a down coat." She glanced down at the bags she was carrying. The largest box was probably the jacket.

"Yeah, they tell you it gets cold, but damn it... their idea of cold is skewed. They plug in their fucking vehicles so the engine block doesn't freeze solid."

Shae stopped and stared at the smaller woman. She wasn't sure if Joy was lying to her or not. "You can't be serious."

"One hundred percent. Last winter I only left the front of the fire to dive under the down comforter in our bedroom. That and a two-week trip to Aruba. I'm thinking about becoming a snowbird and heading south for the winter."

"Would Dixon go with you?"

Joy snorted. "No, which is why I'm only thinking about it. This is his home. Mine too, now." The woman stared out over the land. "A good place to live, to heal."

"It has been for me," Shae agreed as they passed the main house. She nodded to the mansion. "That is an amazing house."

"You mean mansion," Joy corrected her.

"True."

"Frank and Amanda are the best people I've ever met," Joy sighed. "There is a force field or magic around this place. It sucks people in, and they start believing in dreams."

"What's your dream?" Shae asked without really considering the question.

The woman stopped and cast a long look over the buildings, barns, and homes that dotted the other side of the ranch. "This. A home, a husband, maybe a family. Peace, safety, security." The woman shrugged. "Off this ranch, the world continues to spiral, and the dregs of society rise to the top. Here, my faith in humanity is renewed."

Shae adjusted the bags' handles in her grip as she took a breath of crisp, cold air. "Poetic."

"Ah, fuck you," Joy groaned and started walking again.

"Whatever, I meant the ranch, not your words," Shae laughed at Joy's grunt. "Come into the cottage. I have some single malt in one of these bags. I'll grab a quick shower and then we can have a drink."

"Rain check. I have a purple box in my bag, too." Joy wagged her eyes at Shae.

"Oh." She felt her face flush. "Well then, you have fun tonight."

"Oh, believe me, I will. Sooner or later, that man will hit ten."

"What?"

"Nothing. Just have to appreciate tenacity sometimes."

"I have no idea what you're talking about."

"Well, thank God. If you did, we'd have to throw down. Anyway, I'll catch you later. Keep up the rehab. We'll spar."

"I'd enjoy that."

Joy turned and stared at her. "Yeah, I think you would. Maybe that's why I like you." The last part of the comment was said with some kind of wonder. She glanced up at the dark grey sky and sighed, "It's going to rain or maybe snow tonight. Perfect night for the new purchases. Laters."

Shae chuckled as they diverged on the path. She did indeed have some lingerie in her purchases. John was going to come to her cottage for dinner tonight. They alternated spending the evening at his house or her cottage. He seemed to know she needed her independence, at least for a while yet. They'd talked in the last two months about her one day moving into his house. She wasn't quite ready yet. Soon, but there was still a need inside her to have a safe place that was just hers. Jeremiah said it was a coping mechanism and they were working on why she felt she needed it.

She opened the door and set her purchases on the small dining table before she dashed over to the fireplace and lit the fire that John always readied for her during the day. Not because she couldn't do it herself, but because he wanted to do so. He always made sure she had plenty of firewood stacked beside the fireplace so she didn't have to go out to retrieve more. She smiled and watched the kindling catch and grow ravenous. Her life was filled with his small affectionate gestures. He was charming and caring yet never suffocated her or made her feel... less. Her time in the pit had cost her dearly, yet John's attention was filling the empty places, the places that were drained and devoid of anything but horrible memories. The warmth and caring he provided had warmed her as surely as the fire in the old fireplace was warming her now.

He'd warned her the small cottage would turn into an icebox in the next month or so. The first days of October had been unusually warm, but everyone warned her about the cold that would be coming soon and staying. She surveyed her little bungalow. Even though it was a sturdy little structure, there were drafts from the old windows and from under the door. An electric heater to help the fireplace keep the small space warm would be part of her next order. She glanced at the clock. Velvet would be expecting her. The colt wasn't on formula anymore as he'd been weaned at five months, but she still went down to visit and work with gentling him.

She'd been on the ranch for six months, in the hospital for three months before that, but it seemed like yesterday that she'd curled up in the corner of that bed and wanted the world to go away. She stood and stared out the window toward John's house. She'd traveled a twisted trail to get to this place. The cold permeated through her bones, less the chill from outside and more the memories that pushed forward in her thoughts. Even though her hands rubbed her arms, a deep-seated shiver wracked her entire body. If she hadn't been folded into Guardian —and if John hadn't been here—things could have turned out so differently. Thankfully, fate, providence, or perhaps luck had landed her in South Dakota. Whatever guiding hand, she was beyond fortunate. A small smile pulled the corners of her mouth upward. Life *was* worth living.

Before she headed down to the barn, she needed to unpack her purchases. Two jackets and a heavy winter coat, lingerie, a bottle of scotch, three pair of jeans, undergarments, and five sweaters. Now that she knew the process, she'd make small weekly orders to flush out her anemic wardrobe. The lingerie had been a whim purchase, but she wanted to surprise John. She sent another quick look at the clock on the wall. In order to do that she needed to hurry.

Shae smoothed her hair and glanced out the window. The drizzling rain had changed to small snowflakes about an hour ago. John hadn't come home yet; the lights at the house remained dark. She expected him an hour ago. She set the little countertop oven on warm to keep their dinners edible. But she didn't give a spark about the food, she was worried about John. The cell phone she'd been given when Jeremiah first started treating her was on the counter beside her, fully charged and completely silent.

There were a hundred logical reasons for him to be late but, of course, her mind bypassed those and went to the illogical side of the equation immediately. Had he been thrown by his horse? Was there an accident with a piece of equipment? Had he been crushed by a bull? Trampled? The cattle weighed thousands of pounds. Lord, what would she do without him? It was too soon to feel this deeply… wasn't it? She rubbed her arms. Even the thickness of her new sweater couldn't prevent the cold that had nothing to do with the weather. Admitting that she had feelings for John hadn't been hard. Hell, she'd confessed to them back in July when Jeremiah had asked what her intentions were. An amused and misplaced chuckle fell from her lips. God, without realizing it, she'd fallen in love with John, hadn't she? The darkness of the house less than a hundred yards away scared the admission from her soul. He should be here. If he was late, he always called or texted. One of those small courtesies she'd grown accustomed to receiving. Was he okay? God, had his past caught up with him?

She stopped and dropped her head back on her shoulders. *This has to stop.* She was a capable woman who'd been a decorated member of the Mossad. Expanding her lungs to pull a deep breath, she held it for a moment before she blew it out. *You don't work on assumptions. You don't work with fears. All plans are made with known facts.* Yes, it was snowing, but it was an environment that John knew and had worked in before. There were numerous reasons why he hadn't called or texted.

Right, because he'd been bucked off his horse and was in the cold without help. "Stop it!" The loud words split the silence of her little bungalow. She shook her head and walked over to the radio, turning the small box to the only station it received. The warm sound of the music filled the room and gave her something else to concentrate on. The flash of headlights on her back wall spun her. She pulled the curtain to the side and drew a relieved breath. "Finally."

She tossed on her new coat and jogged across the small space that separated them. John was just getting out of his truck and closing the door when she called his name. He spun just in time to catch her as she wrapped him in a hug.

"Hey, what's wrong?" He tried to pull her away, but relief hadn't cast out the fears that had been echoing in her mind. She held on tightly until he wrapped her in his arms. "Shae, what's wrong?"

"You're late. It's snowing. You didn't call or text. I know it is stupid, but I was worried something had happened to you."

He held her tightly and rocked from side to side with her. His chest rumbled under her ear as he spoke, "I'm sorry for scaring you. I dropped my cell into one of the watering troughs. Fried it, it's a paperweight now. I tried to get back before you came home, but Greg called me over when I got in and we had to bring in the vet for one of the bulls. We quarantined him from the other bulls and Doc is doing tests."

Shae leaned back and looked up at him. "I'm sorry."

"For what? Caring about me? Yeah, *so* not going

to reprimand you for that." He leaned down and kissed her as he drew his hands up her arms and cupped her face. She shivered, and this time it was because of the cold. "I need to take a shower; I'll be over shortly." He glanced at his watch. "Damn, I didn't realize it was so late. No wonder you were upset. Should I grab a bite to eat here?"

"I have dinner warming in the oven. It might be a little dry…"

"I could eat an old boot right now. I'm starving. Give me fifteen minutes to chip the day off and wash it down the drain."

"I'll see you then." She lifted up and pressed a quick kiss on his lips. "Don't keep me waiting too long." With a wiggle of her eyebrows, she spun and jogged back to the cottage. Joy was right. Tonight was a great night to test out her new purchases.

The hot water on his back managed to thaw him a bit. The day had been harder than he'd led her to believe. The trough was actually a stock pond, his horse, Dancer, had shied from a branch, and she'd dumped him into the water. He'd worked the rest of the day wet and cold. Dancer had been uptight all day—he should have anticipated her being spooky. It was her first day away from Vader, her colt. Stupid, he was daydreaming instead of paying attention to his horse. Rookie mistake that netted him a wet ass and a broken phone.

He turned and shoved his head under the steaming hot water. The reason he'd been daydreaming met him as soon as he'd pulled the truck in the driveway.

Shae.

She was a constant in his thoughts. The reaction to him being late gave him hope that his love for her wasn't growing in a vacuum. He grabbed a bar of soap and lathered up while his mind hashed over that thought. He'd known for a while now he loved her, but he'd be damned if he'd push her. Everything in their relationship was predicated on her comfort, but he wanted to go to sleep with her in his arms and wake up tangled up in her. A committed long-term relationship, marriage even. Which was... Well, it was unnerving. He barely remembered his mother; his father would never be nominated for Father of the Year, and everything he knew about family was screwed up. Yeah, he and Lori had a good relationship, but toward the end, she was distant. Or hell, who knew, he might have been pulling away from her crazy drive for more. More money, more respect, more of everything.

No, he wasn't going to color the relationship he had with his sister through any kind of filter, even a well-meaning one. They were what they were. Lori had her faults just like he did. Her life was cut short and he'd be damned if he'd allow anything to taint his memories. They weren't a greeting card family, but they were still family, no matter how dysfunctional.

Memories of Lori's death still ached, but maybe now they would no longer dominate his thoughts. Yes, he wanted answers. Damn him, he *needed* answers, but now he had Shae in his life. Perhaps he'd be able to let Lori rest in peace and learn to live with the fact that he might not ever know why things happened as they had.

Five minutes later he was knocking on that little door. It opened the second his fist left the wood. "Come in, it is so cold." Shae pulled him in and shut the door. "Dinner is ready. Go stand by the fire and get warm while I get it on the table."

He chuckled, "It isn't that cold. Yet." He shrugged out of his lined denim jacket. "Smells amazing."

"I tried Miss Amanda's shepherd's pie recipe." She pulled out a flat cast iron pan from the small oven. "Well, actually, I warmed up her recipe." A blush ran across her nose and cheeks.

"I'm sure it is delicious." Hell, he'd eat sawdust and tell her it was the best thing he'd ever eaten if it would make her happy. He hung up his coat and pulled out her chair for her. She smiled and sat down. She served him before she took a serving for herself. They ate and he told her about Dancer's dunking. Her inelegant snort and muffled laughter as he described the shock of landing in a foot of cold water was worth the humiliation of admitting his horse had unseated him.

"You worked in wet pants?"

"All day."

She tried, really tried, but the laughter was stronger. "Hey!" He spread his hands wide. "I'm chafed, you should take pity on me."

"Oh, you poor baby. Do you want me to kiss it better?" Shae lifted up and held out her hand to him.

"Well, if you're offering…" John waggled his eyebrows at her, but the laughter stopped when her sweater came off. "Oh… damn…" She was wearing—hell, what did they call it?—a bustier. Her breasts were held up, full and soft, and the material cinched at her waist. The heavy seams were a darker red than the lighter see-through fabric, but all of it dipped enticingly into her jeans. "Sweet heavens." He reached out and traced the top of the cup that held her breasts. "Beautiful." He lifted his eyes to hers.

"Get naked, there's more." Shae moved away from him and nodded toward the bed. He shucked his shirt, boots, socks, and jeans in record time. As always, he left his boxers on. Shae shook her head and pointed. "Those too."

He took them off and stood, letting her see his need before he sat down on the bed and pushed back so he was leaning against the wall. The cold of the logs barely registered. The only thing he saw was the woman in front of him. She consumed him as surely as the fire in the fireplace consumed the split-cottonwood wedges. The result was heat. Sizzling, mind-boggling heat. No other woman had ever snared his attention to the degree Shae had.

She smiled and turned around. Peeking over her shoulder, she shimmied out of her jeans, pushing them down as she bent over.

"Oh, sweet mercy. Shae, baby, you are slaying me here." She had on a thong, the perfect rounds of her ass split with red lace. The scars that ridged on her shoulders and legs weren't even seen. To him, she was absolutely perfect. She must have finally believed him because this was the first time they'd undressed with the light on. She stood up and turned around to face him. Fuck, he was going to die if he didn't get into her soon. He cupped his shaft in one hand and his balls in the other.

She walked forward. "I know I'm not perfect."

"Babe, you are absolutely perfect. Beautiful."

"The scars—"

He extended a hand to her. "—are part of you. I love all of you. Not just the unblemished parts."

Shae blinked and stopped with one knee on the bed. "What?"

He lifted his eyes, realizing what he'd said. "I said I love you." It was probably premature and damn it, he'd wanted to wait until he was sure she was in the same place as he was, but fuck it. It was the truth. He held her hand and they stayed in that position while he tried to read her expression. Finally, she blinked and came forward onto the bed. She crawled up his legs and straddled his lap. She lifted her hands to his cheeks. He turned and kissed each one, closing his eyes and praying he didn't fuck up the best thing that ever happened to him.

"When did you know?" She whispered the question but he heard it as if a bullhorn had blared an inch away from his ear.

JOHN

"Months ago." He took both of her hands in his. "I didn't want to scare you."

She echoed his words. "Scare me?"

He nodded. "You don't have to say it. I understand if you're not ready." The words sliced him like a fucking knife. He clenched his teeth tightly, waiting for her to pull his heart out and drop it on the floor.

"But I do love you. I don't want to wait to say it." She leaned forward and he launched into action. It took one point three seconds to have her on her back on the bed. Her eyes widened in surprise before a smile split her face.

"Say it again," he demanded before he dropped for a kiss. He plundered her mouth and chased her tongue as her arms wrapped around his neck. He pulled away and repeated his demand. "Say. It. Again." He kissed her between each word.

"How? You keep kissing me!" She shrieked with laughter when his fingers found her ribs. "Stop! Stooooop!" She twisted and laughed under him as he tickled her.

He let up and stared at her; the smile on his face had to be a mile wide. "Say it."

"I love you." He dropped to his elbows at her softly-spoken words. He couldn't pull his gaze away from her eyes. They echoed her words. He could see the honesty. It was a gift he'd cherish until his last breath. He lowered and kissed her. She snaked her legs around him and used those toned muscles to urge him forward. When he encountered her lace thong, he acted on his most basic urges. The fabric lasted a fraction of a second. Shae gasped. He dropped a kiss on her surprised expression. "I'll buy you more just so I can do that again."

"You better." She wiggled under him. "Are you going to do something now that you have access or are we going to talk?"

"No talking, but…" He reached down to the bustier and pushed it down. Freeing her breasts, he leaned down to worship her body. He'd show her exactly what it meant to him to love her. With a reverence he hadn't been able to express before, he led her to the summit and let her crash over it before he entered her. She sighed and with languid arms held him as he found the way to his own peak. Shae's body clutched. Her gasp and nails digging into his biceps pushed him over the edge. He held himself up over her. When she opened her eyes, he pushed her sweaty hair from her face. "I love you."

She smiled and pulled him down for another kiss. When they broke apart to breathe, he rolled to his side and pulled her close. His fingers trailed along the hard wires in the garment she still semi-wore. He smiled as she snuggled closer to him and pulled blankets over them. He was happy. Perfectly, one hundred percent happy for the first time in his life. *"Now watch some bastard louse it up."* His father's words echoed in his mind as he closed his eyes.

CHAPTER 19

Happiness was in the air. Well, actually, there was icy coldness in the air, but for Shae, the day was perfect. John had left the cottage before the sun had peeked over the horizon this morning but not before he rekindled the fire and kissed her goodbye. He was riding north with the hands to start bringing the herd closer to the ranch where they could be managed when the snow prevented them from reaching the other pastures.

Dixon and Drake were in the breakroom, but they only gave a cursory greeting. They were buried in a file and speaking in engineer terms. She'd learned not to ask what they were talking about. One time had been enough. After an hour of meticulously describing the project in fine detail, she had no idea what they were talking about but smiled and caught Mike as he walked by, extracting herself from even more tutelage. She poured a cup of coffee and floated on happy feet to her desk.

The work for the complex wasn't difficult, but it was more than one person could effectively handle, especially the budget and projecting costs for classes. The medical portion of the budget was addressed by Adam and his staff; still, they needed to meld that information into the overall request for resources. Guardian was generous, but the business end of the company had precise reporting requirements and learning the system, how to input the numbers and process the reports, kept her busy for the majority of the day.

A massive man slammed the door open, making her jump. "Dude, who is in our cabin?"

Mike looked up from his work and shook his head. "That is not your cottage, it is Frank's."

"My cabin?" Shae asked, drawing the attention of the man standing in the door.

"Are you in the drover's cottage?" A woman leaned into the office and smiled at her.

"I am." She glanced from Mike to the couple.

"Isaac and Lyric, this is Shae Diamant. She's been

here most of the year and is living in the drover's cottage."

Shae stood up and offered her hand. Isaac and then Lyric shook her hand. "You got a place for us to hang? We're here for the weekend, then we head back to Jacksonville."

The lines in Mike's forehead deepened. "We have other unexpected guests this weekend, probably working on the same thing you are. I have a dorm room."

"A dorm room?" Lyric wrinkled her nose.

"Wait, I have a solution. John is gone. I can stay at his place for the weekend and give you guys the cottage. I'd just need to nip down and grab a few things."

"Are you sure?" Mike and Isaac asked at the same time.

"Yes, of course. He won't mind, but I'll call." She glanced at the time. "He might still have reception." John had been subtly hinting that he'd welcome her to spend more time with him at his house.

She picked up the phone and hit one of the three numbers she had on speed dial. He answered on the fifth ring. "Miss me already?"

"I do, but I have a favor to ask."

"Anything."

"Don't you want to hear what it is?"

"No. Whatever it is, I'll make it happen. That's what people in love do."

Her face flamed and she stared at the floor. "May I stay in your house this weekend? Isaac and Lyric need a place to stay."

"Absolutely. The place is yours." At a sharp, ear-splitting whistle she pulled the phone from her ear, and John's yell could be heard plainly in the room. "She's making a break for it, cut her off!" In a conversational tone he apologized, "Sorry."

"That's okay. I know you're busy."

"We'll be back late Saturday night or early Sunday morning. I'd love to find you in my bed when I get back."

She glanced at the three people across the office; they were talking, ignoring her. Thank goodness. She smiled at the floor again. "I think that can be arranged."

John laughed, "Excellent. I love you."

"I love you, too. Stay warm."

She ended the call and met Mike's eyes. He winked at her. The heat in her cheeks could have melted the snow that had fallen last night. "If you don't mind, I'll take the laptop and the rest of my work. I want to change the sheets and clean up just a bit. I'll see you on Monday?"

"You don't need to take the work; you can finish on Monday."

"I've got nothing else to do this weekend." Except visiting Velvet. She picked up the files and the laptop, shoving them all into the case it came in. "Give me thirty minutes or so?" She looked at Lyric when she spoke.

"Thank you so much, I'm sorry for the inconvenience." Isaac dropped his arm around Lyric's shoulders as she spoke.

"No inconvenience. I'll see you soon. Mike, see you Monday?"

Mike nodded. "Enjoy your weekend."

"You, too." She grabbed her jacket from the back of her chair and hustled out of the office. It took about twenty minutes to wash the coffee cups and random pieces of silverware that were in her sink, change the sheets, and wipe down every surface. Only then did she pack a weekend bag and set it by the door. Just as the knock on the door came, she banked the fireplace. Shae opened it and left moments later.

The ground was frozen under her feet and the brown grass made a crunching noise as she crossed

JOHN

the field. A meow and fluff of fur greeted her at the porch. "Aren't you freezing?" Shae asked the cat as she jogged up the stairs. The animal meowed and headed straight for the door. Of course, the door wasn't locked. Nothing on the ranch was secured, yet the sitting out in the middle of nowhere was monitored by the highest-level security. She'd seen security systems invoices in past budgets. Things that couldn't be observed were in action at the complex. Programs and intranet folders that she couldn't access were greyed out on her laptop. Her clearance was high enough, but she didn't have a need to know. Frankly, she didn't want to know. The work she did for Mike, allowing him to have a more stable home life with Taty, was enjoyable and rewarding. She was used to security measures within the Mossad, but here at Guardian, it appeared that no expense was spared, which spoke volumes on how Guardian valued its people.

The light switch next to the door illuminated the entryway and the hall that split the kitchen from the living room. She'd visited John's house enough to know her way around. Cat headed into the kitchen, meowing like her life depended on it. "You know, I know Drake feeds you. We've got your number."

Cat sat down by the cupboard that held her food

and yowled. "I can tell you don't care. Give me a second to put this in the office and this in the bedroom. You aren't going to starve in two minutes."

The cat disagreed loudly. Shae chuckled and headed back into the bedroom to drop her bag beside her side of the bed. A smile appeared at that thought. She had a side of the bed. They were a couple, and they were in love. Cat padded into the bedroom and meowed loudly. "All right, already. Let me put the computer in John's den and then I'll feed you. Where is your friend? Is she staying inside? Maybe she's smarter than everyone says."

She carried a running conversation with her four-legged companion. She set the laptop on the huge desk and hurried the animal out. After giving Cat her much-demanded meal, she made herself a cup of tea and went into the living room to start a fire. John had left it ready to light. She drew a long match from the holder in the hearth and opened the flue.

Settling back into the couch, she almost jumped out of her skin when her phone rang. There was no number displayed. Frowning, she slid her finger across the face. "Hello."

"Standby for Archangel," a clipped authoritative tone snapped across the connection.

Shae took the phone from her ear and looked at the face. "Who the hell is Archangel?"

"That would be me."

The voice was one she wouldn't forget. "Mr. King. What can I do for you?"

"I need to speak to John, and I can't reach him or Frank."

"He's probably out of cell service by now. He's bringing the herd in with the hands and I believe Frank went with them. Is there... a problem?"

"Perhaps. I need to speak with John before I can confirm that." A huge sigh came through the connection. "All right, I'll take alternate measures to reach him. Do you know where they were going first?"

"They were going to split up. Frank was taking a team and John was leading another. I don't know much more besides that." Damn it, she wished she'd asked more questions. *Why hadn't she?* Gut clenching cold wrapped around her. "Mr. King, is John in danger?"

"What? No, shit, I'm sorry. I need some information about something he was involved with before coming to the ranch." The man's voice softened. "He's fine, I promise."

Shae finally took a breath. "Thank you." What else was she supposed to say?

"Thanks for the information. I've got to go."

Shae looked at the phone until the illumination faded. *Archangel. A code name.* She tucked that information away. There were many things about Guardian she still didn't know, but eventually…

The great whopping of a helicopter firing up split the silence of the ranch. Shae turned to look out the window. It was completely dark. Was the helicopter going out in search of John? She closed her eyes and drew several deep breaths before she called the one person she needed to talk to. A lot had happened recently.

"Hey, Shae, are you all right?" Jeremiah Wheeler's voice was a warm balm against her rattled nerves.

"I am now. Can we talk for a minute?"

"Sure. Give me a second." She heard him speaking to someone before he came back on the line. "What's up?"

"I'm in love."

Her admission met with a low rolling chuckle. "Finally."

"Oh, so you are going to tell me that you knew this? I only just figured it out!" She laughed. God, the man knew how to deflate her anxiety. Only John was better at it.

"I've got to tell you, Shae, sometimes I wonder if

the Mossad let you go because you're not the sharpest stick in the box."

"Oh, you did not just say that!" They both laughed until a soft silence fell between them.

"Congratulations. Have you told John?"

"We have exchanged the words, yes."

"Then what is the problem?"

"I don't know. I guess I'm always waiting for the other shoe to drop."

"Being afraid to trust is something you're working on. You've come a long way." He reminded her of how far she'd come at every opportunity.

"What if it doesn't work out?"

"Then both you and John will face that problem when and if it happens. Don't borrow trouble, Shae."

"I know, but I can't help this feeling that something horrible is going to happen. I've never been this happy." She bit her thumbnail.

"Why do you think you have that feeling? Why do you think something is going to happen?"

Jeremiah's voice coaxed her to look at the question. She thought about it as the helicopter from the Guardian side of the ranch took off and flew directly overhead.

"Something is going on out there?"

"Yeah."

"Is that adding to your feelings?"

"I... yes." God, yes. She was worried about what in John's past was lifting its head and how it would affect their relationship.

"Okay, are you comfortable?"

She leaned back into the corner of the couch. "I am."

Jerimiah's voice took on a professional tone, "Let's start with why you think..."

"Do you hear that?" John's question drew his guys' attention away from the hand of cards they were playing at the line shack's kitchen table. The dull, thudding whomp of the helicopter's rotors grew stronger in the silence. "Fuck." John was up and grabbing his coat before the others had time to react. If a helicopter was coming up here, there was big trouble. Immediately, he thought of Shae. Was she okay? What about his men's families? God, it could be a myriad of things.

The helicopter sat down behind the line shack as far away from the scattering herd as it could get. He glanced at the corral where the horses were being held. Thankfully, they were okay. Antsy, but okay.

He walked toward the helicopter, motioning for his men to watch the horses just in case one of them decided to get stupid.

Dixon met him halfway. "You need to come back. Archangel needs you."

"Shae?"

"She's fine. Guardian Business."

"Give me two minutes."

"Hurry, we went to the other camp first." Dixon nodded and jogged back to the bird.

John jogged back to the line shack. "Gregg, you're in charge. Frank is aware I'm leaving. Bring my kit back. Dancer is acting flighty. If anyone needs to ride her, make sure they stay sharp." There was no doubt Frank knew what was going on. If the bird sat down outside his camp, he damn sure got the scoop from Dixon or Drake.

Gregg grabbed his bicep as he turned to leave. "Everything okay?"

"Yeah, should be."

"Okay, be safe."

"You too. That herd is going to be skittish after this."

"I know. We can handle them." Gregg was a very competent hand who'd been with the Marshalls for almost as long as John had been at the ranch. He gave the man a final nod and jogged back to the waiting helicopter.

The trip back to the ranch took a year, or at least that's what it seemed like. He couldn't talk to Dixon and Drake—there was no comm equipment behind the two men. The second they landed he was out of the bird. Chief was waiting for him with an ATV. He jumped into the small vehicle. "What the fuck is going on?"

"I have no idea. We had orders to find you, get you back, and set you up with a secure video conference connection," Chief spoke over the sound of the engine. Because of the cold, tears formed in his eyes, pushing back toward his ears as they raced toward Mike's office. As soon as Mike shoved the selector level into park, they were both out of the ATV and running up the steps to the main door. "Conference room in the back."

John nodded and slammed down the hallway to the same room where Shae and he had spent hours with Jared King. They both dropped their cell phones in the tray outside the room. Chief hit a code on the door and the lock sprung open. The monitor was active and split into four quadrants. The conversation happening between the participants stopped when he and Mike burst into view.

"What the hell is going on?" He was confused and he needed answers. Now.

Jason King "Sit down, John, we have a lot to go over. Mike, thanks for getting him here."

"I'll wait in my office until you're done," Mike spoke as he closed the door behind him. The sound of the lock activating behind him dropped like a lead balloon from the air.

"Why am I here?"

"Have a seat." Jason tapped on his desk as he spoke. John took off his coat and flipped it onto the back of the seat. He sat down and drew a deep breath.

"Jewell, you can start." Jason once again spoke without looking at the monitor.

"Hi, John. So, Dom Ops has a team of investigators tracking down the leads they were able to garner from several different points."

Jared King interrupted, "One of those points was the information provided by Shae. Actually, it was pursuing the names she gave us, the employees of Amira Raz, the woman who brought Shae to Canada, that gave us a foothold. From information we garnered, we were able to track down what we believe are a pod of mid-level members of Stratus' organization."

John shook his head and stared at the three screens before he looked at the picture of himself in the lower-left corner. "And that involves me how?"

Jared held up a hand. "I'm getting there. The latest takedown was in Chicago. We were able to track and apprehend a person who has been talking. Does the name Edna Barkley sound familiar?"

All the confusion drained from him in less than a second. Edna Barkley was a cover identity he'd constructed. It was one of ten that hadn't been utilized. He'd given the profiles and names to Guardian to utilize should they need it.

John leaned forward. "One of your own people?"

Jason's head snapped up. "No. We haven't touched the identities you've given us. They are locked up tight, paper copies only, and the safe where they are stored hasn't been compromised. Whoever is using the name and cover isn't Guardian. Did the Agency have access to the profiles you were working on?"

John dropped his chin into his hand and sighed. "I didn't think so. Have you checked to make sure this Edna is actually using the life I engineered?"

Jewell nodded. "Down to the last detail."

John shook his head. It wasn't possible. There was no way someone could have found those files.

They were paper, old school, handwritten casefiles with IDs, manufactured school records, letters of recommendation, social security cards. Ten entire lives built in meticulous fashion and they were kept at his apartment in his safe. They were his insurance policy in case he needed a negotiation chip. Thankfully, Guardian stepped up, and they were extraneous. No one at the Agency knew about his excess profiles. No one. "How in the hell did this happen?"

"That's what we need to find out. Walk us through your last couple of days with the Agency." Jared's question pushed him into his past. Again.

CHAPTER 20

Shae paced around John's house after finishing her phone call. The disquiet emanated from a straightforward conversation and hard answers to simple questions. Even Cat had grown tired of her restlessness and meowed at the door to be let out. Her thoughts were a jumble of memories and questions, which was always the case when she finished a conversation with Jeremiah.

She dropped her head back and stared at the ceiling. This mental scramble and rehash were getting her nowhere. But sleep was out of the question, thanks to the noise in her brain. Resigned to a sleepless night, she turned the light on in John's office and padded in. The haphazard way she'd thrown her paperwork into the laptop bag was enough to prompt her into action. She turned on the desk light and pulled out her papers, putting them in proper order before she turned on the computer and lost herself in the details.

The sound of the helicopter coming back registered as she plugged numbers into the budget software. Jeremiah's words echoed in her mind. She wasn't going to borrow trouble. She didn't know why the helicopter left and it didn't concern her. John? Maybe, but when he could, he'd let her know what was going on.

Forcing herself back to the information, she ticked off the line item she left off with and went to the next. "That can't be right." According to the spreadsheet, the expenditure for the last quarter was nearly quadruple what the requested budget was for this quarter. She opened John's top drawer and fished through the items, looking for a highlighter. Nothing. She opened the rest and drew a blank. Her eye caught on the credenza tucked away in an odd-shaped corner of the room.

Shae stood up and stretched, reaching her arms to the ceiling. She was starting to get tired, which was a good thing. There were maybe ten items left on the page she was currently working, and after that she'd go to bed. But first, she needed a highlighter. The pen marks in the columns were too close together and would make finding the error difficult if she didn't mark it in some way. She opened the drawers and smiled at a pack of yellow highlighters. She snapped them up and spun around.

Shae's heart stopped. Slowly, she turned her head to the credenza, and she lowered her gaze to the picture frame on the top of the low hutch. The highlighters slid from her fingers, clattering on the hardwood floor. Gripped in icy cold apprehension, she reached out to the frame and turned it toward her.

"No." *Oh, dear God. No. It couldn't be. But it was... It was her.* The hair was different, but... oh, God, John had a photo of the woman who'd had her tortured. *How? How could he know this woman?* Shae leaned against the wall, her knees gave out, and she slid to the floor while staring at the face of the woman she saw in her nightmares.

There had to be an explanation but... *how*? The woman was smiling into the camera. It was an intimate picture. A picture a close friend... or *lover* would take. Bile rose in her throat. She swiped at tears that rolled down her cheeks, only then realizing she was crying. She pushed up from the floor and lurched toward her cell phone. Her hand shook so badly she had to put the frame down in order to steady herself enough to call John's number. It rang several times as she tried to breathe.

"Hello?"

Shae blinked and glanced at her phone face. She'd dialed right. "Mike? Where's John?"

"Shae, what's wrong? Are you okay?"

"No. No, God, I'm so far away from okay. *Where is John?*"

"He's in the secure conference room here at the office. I answered his phone when I saw your name. Do you need me to come over? You're at his house, right?"

"Don't let him leave. Mike, he knows her."

"Knows who?"

"*Her*! Don't let him leave!" Shae hung up and grabbed the picture frame. She launched out of the house without a coat and ran as if Satan himself was chasing her. Her tears froze against the bitter cold wind as her heart crumbled under the horrid thought pulsing through her thoughts. Did Guardian know they had a link to this woman in their midst?

John shook his head. "After the funds were taken from my local bank, I called them. They told me the funds were withdrawn and the accounts closed by the only authorized person. But I was the only person authorized. It had to be the agency recouping resources. Then shit got crazy when Lori sent me that text saying she thought someone was trying to kill her. I tried to call her. I couldn't reach her, so I ran out of the office. I left everything."

"Could elements of those files have somehow been accessed via your company computer system?" Jewell asked.

"Impossible. They were my projects. I only worked on them at my apartment on my laptop. The laptop was locked in my safe with those folders and the documents. They were all intact when I grabbed them and came to Guardian."

"Who had access to your apartment?" Jared asked the question.

John jumped at a loud banging on the conference room door. "Stand by, something's going on outside."

"Jewell, sanitize the connection," Jason growled.

"Done." All the screens went black.

John opened the door and caught Shae as she fell forward. "Shae, what in the hell?"

She yanked her arm from his grip and screamed, "You! You know her! I trusted you! I love you, you bastard, and you knew her all along! How long have you been lying to Guardian, to me?"

"What are you talking about? I've never lied to you or to Guardian."

"Then explain this!" Shae hissed and shoved his picture of Lori in his face.

"Explain what? That's Lori. It's the only picture I have of her."

"*This* is your sister? Your *dead* sister?" Shae shouted at him. Mike was behind her shaking his head, clearly confused, too.

John nodded. "Yes, why?"

"Because she's *not dead*! She was the one who ordered Maurice to torture me! She was the one that called and told him to kill me! This woman is Stratus!"

The venom in her voice and accusations pushed pieces of the puzzle together in his mind. He staggered back and flopped into the chair he'd been sitting in. "Dear God." He glanced at the screen and noticed Guardian was back up. "My sister had access to my apartment. She knew the combination to the safe."

"Okay. The two of you obviously need to talk. Jewell, start running the other names John gave us. I'll get you the files on the rest of the profiles so you can run a comparison. We need to know if other profiles have been utilized. John, Shae, you've got thirty minutes to talk this out and then we'll dial back in. Archangel out."

The screens went blank and Mike closed the conference room door, leaving them alone. John dropped his head to his hands. Grief, guilt and pain swamped him in a massive wave. "I didn't know, Shae. I swear I didn't know. I saw her car explode."

Shae slid down the door jamb and sat on the floor. "She's your sister."

He nodded. "I never lied to you or to them. Guardian can verify my whereabouts every day since the day I went to them for help."

Shae swallowed hard and nodded. "She's your sister."

He swallowed hard and admitted the truth, "She is."

Shae trembled when she spoke, "She's a monster."

John stared at the picture of his sister. It was one she liked. She'd texted it to him and he'd used it as her contact picture on his phone. He had his phone when Guardian took him in. It was the only reason he had a copy of it. "Are you sure? Absolutely sure?"

"I will never forget her face." The whispered

confirmation stabbed any hope he had of a mistake through the heart.

"I don't want to believe it," John spoke in the same whisper.

"I'm not lying," Shae's hiss reached him.

He snapped his eyes to her. "I know. I don't *want* to believe it, but it makes sense now. Everything Guardian is discovering, what happened in the days before she... died."

"What happened?"

He glanced at the screens and detailed the events that had rocked his world and sent him into hiding from an agency that always affirmed they had no idea who had targeted Shae or John.

Shae sighed and scrubbed her face with her hands. "I thought... When I saw her picture, I thought... I didn't want to believe that you..."

"I can imagine." Hell, she'd flung a hell of a lot of accusations. He knew exactly what she'd been thinking. He was related to the woman who still haunted her dreams. He'd held her several times after she'd wake up from a night terror. Dear God... the woman who tortured her was his sister. He stared at his hands but didn't see anything except memories. Lori's greed, her scheming. She'd used him. Stolen from him and set him up. If he hadn't gone to

Guardian, he would have been killed in one of the two explosions targeting him. He would have died because of her... what... greed? He hated what she was capable of, but even more, he hated what she'd done to innocents. How many more had suffered because of her? Lori's reign of terror was going to end. Guardian was on her trail now, and it was only a matter of time until they tracked her and the rest of Stratus down. He'd be on that team. The one to make sure she couldn't hurt anyone ever again. "She started her actions with me. I'll be the one to end them." He cleared his throat. "I'll sleep in the dormitory after we finish here."

Shae sniffed and turned to look at him. "Why?"

"To give you space. You probably want to talk to Jeremiah, maybe wrap your head around what is going on." He glanced at the clock. They only had a few more minutes.

"Me? What about you?" Shae tossed the question back at him.

"I think it will be a long time before I can understand any of this."

"I don't know if I will ever be able to understand how someone so evil could have you as a brother."

John drew a deep breath. His natural instinct was to defend and protect Lori, but the words Shae spoke were... damn it, they were true. A series of beeps sounded from the monitor. "They are coming back online. Do you want to leave and call Jeremiah?" He mentioned the doctor again.

Shae held his eyes while she shook her head slowly from one side to the other. Her voice held no hesitancy. "No, for once, I don't need him." Shae stood and wiped her cheeks. "We work together to take her down. You want answers, I want justice. We both want her stopped. Right?"

He stood up, coming within inches of her. "If I could take away the pain she caused, I would."

Shae leaned her forehead against his chest and placed her hands on his hips. He wrapped her in his arms and held her against him. All of this, the love he felt for this woman, their future together, Lori would have stripped from him. First with her attempt to kill him because who else could it have been? And then what she allowed—no, directed—to happen to Shae. He pulled her closer. "I love you." He whispered the words against her hair.

"I love you, too."

"I hate to interrupt, but we need to proceed." Jason King's voice jarred them out of the moment.

He let her go and moved a chair over for Shae so they both could sit down. She reached for his hand under the table. He squeezed it and she shot him a sideways look.

"Jewell, tell them what you've found."

"Okay, all ten of your profiles are in use."

His jaw dropped. "Excuse me? What?" The earth-shattering shocks just kept coming, didn't they?

"Yeah, that's what I thought, too, but good news is we have a bearing on all of them. Additionally, the profiles are attached to actual people now, so we have pictures to go with the IDs." A patchwork of faces appeared on the screen.

"She's not there," Shae said after a few seconds examining the females' faces. "No, she's not there."

He nodded, but that didn't mean anything. Lori could make her own profiles. Granted, she wasn't as skilled as he was, but she could have countless IDs and become whoever she wanted to be.

"We are organizing an operation to apprehend all of these people at the same time. Ten teams."

"We're coming to D.C." His tone left no room for argument.

"Figured. We'll have a plane heading your way in the morning. Same protocols are in effect." Jason nodded. "Jared, bring him up to speed."

"We're compiling a list of names. Names of people we couldn't run to ground. I would like you to dissect them and see if they are fake profiles. Hopefully, we'll have the people using your profiles in custody and be able to extract more information from them at that time."

"Oh boy," Jewell muttered in the background.

"What?" Jason's head snapped up and everyone stopped talking. Shae squeezed John's hand, but he didn't think she knew she had a death grip on it.

"Just for shits and giggles I threw up the faces associated with the profiles and I'm running them through all the facial recognition databases we have. The man here, using the Collin Sower's ID? He's wanted by MI6."

"He didn't change his facial features?" John leaned in. "Everyone knows manipulation of the nose or jaw can throw the facial recognition off. Less than an eighty percent match won't trigger the facial recognition software."

"Nope. He's a one hundred percent match." Jewell tapped on the keyboard. "I'm just getting started. Give me twenty-four hours. I'll get you everything I can on who he was and who he is now."

"Shae, I need to know where you stand before I pull you into an active op. I'm calling Jeremiah. You won't be going on any missions unless he clears you." Jason leaned back in his chair as he spoke.

"He'll clear me."

The determination in her voice left little doubt she was right, but John agreed with Jason, they needed to know for sure that she could handle the adrenaline hype of a mission.

"We'll see. The plane will be there in the morning. I'll get Jeremiah there before the sun comes up. If you are cleared, you're part of the team. If not, you'll remain at the ranch."

Shae nodded. "Understood."

"Oh, bingo. Another hit." Jewell's voice was damn near a shout. "We are scratching the top of the mother lode. She's wanted by the FBI, money laundering, drugs, and get this, three counts of murder. Seventy-three percent match, variations noted in the jawline and nose. I'm applying those parameters to all the other searches. Thank you for that little hint, John."

"You two try to get some rest. Things are moving rapidly. We'll bring you in for a briefing before you get on the plane. Archangel out." His screen went black. Jewell waved and Jared turned away from the screen as they went black, too.

"Rest." Shae snorted. "I don't think I'm going to be able to follow that order."

"Let's go back to the house." He looked around. "Where is your coat?"

"Oh…" Shae looked around. "I don't think I wore one." She shrugged. "It wasn't important at the time."

"Here." He lifted his coat from the back of his chair and dropped it over her shoulders before he opened the conference room door.

Mike looked up from his desk and stood. "Anything I can do to help?"

"No, thank you. We'll be heading out in the morning." He looked down at Shae. He couldn't imagine leaving her behind.

"I just got a notification of an inbound bird. Projected arrival time is 0800 hours." He turned his attention to Shae. "I got a notice to have the conference room ready for Dr. Wheeler at 0700 for your Go/No Go evaluation."

"My what?" Shae cocked her head.

"Sorry, it is what we call the determination any of the doctors make that allow someone back into the field. It is either a go or a no go." Mike turned off the light in his office. "It's been a long day even though it's only ten-thirty. I'm ready to call it a night." He tossed the keys to the ATV to John. "Take this, it will get you home sooner."

He caught the keys and put his arm over Shae's shoulders. "Let's go."

CHAPTER 21

Shae poured them each a shot of bourbon. John was taking a shower. He smelled of cattle and horses, or so he said. She didn't dispute the fact, and honestly, she was thankful for a few moments alone. She leaned against the counter and stared sightlessly into the night. Earlier this evening her mind had been whirring about minutia. How had she let such minor things worry her? She was in love with John. Moving in with him was, as Jeremiah called it, a no-brainer. Funny how meteoric impacts made all the noise of life fall into place immediately.

The thought that John had betrayed her, that he was somehow involved with that woman, had cemented into her thoughts immediately. She hadn't given him the benefit of the doubt. She'd accused and lashed out, and John, in his steady way, had absorbed her accusations. How did she deserve the love of a man like him? Well, after months of counseling with Jeremiah, she knew the answer to that question. One didn't deserve love, they either received it like the gift it was or they didn't. John had given her his love. She'd accepted it and had given him her love. To think that woman had placed their precious connection in jeopardy was right on course for her.

That damn woman needed to be stopped. Shae drew her hand through her hair. Stopped. *Ha.* She had ideas of how to stop the bitch. But how could she wish death for John's sister? Dear God, she couldn't let that woman come between them again, but after what she'd done, that was next to impossible. There would always be a divide between her and John now. He loved the woman he knew as his sister and she understood that. But at this very moment, if Shae could put a bullet between the woman's eyes, she would.

How did a man of John's character have a sister like her? She heard him as he padded down the hallway and closed her eyes. Communication. They needed to talk. Hard, direct words that could separate them forever.

"One of those for me?"

She smiled and handed him one. "Salud." They both downed the drinks and she poured them one more. "We need to talk."

"We do." John took his glass and then her hand. They walked into the living room where he stoked the fire before he sat down on the couch with her.

"I want you to know I love you. This situation with your sister has the potential of driving a wedge between us and I don't want that, but I can't help what I feel." Shae took a sip of the bourbon, keeping the glass in her hands, giving her something to concentrate on.

John took the glass from her and set it beside his on the coffee table. He held both her hands and waited until she looked up at him. "The girl that grew up with me is not the woman who did this to you. I don't know what happened to make her change. I will always cherish my memories of her. That young woman is who I remember, who I will continue to love. The woman who was involved in your torture, in providing profiles for criminals, well, she isn't a person I recognize. I don't know when or how she took the wrong road. It could have been while I was in the military or after.

"I've lived with the guilt of her death for years. It

nearly destroyed me. I thought that maybe if I paid more attention, if I could have gotten to her sooner… I asked myself what I missed. My car and my apartment were targeted. If Guardian hadn't stepped in, I would have been in the car. The apartment explosion was only an hour after I'd cleared out. Guardian used the vehicle explosion to stage my exit. To the world, I was dead. At that time, we believed the Agency was trying to eliminate me. But now…"

"She tried to kill you and then to hide anything you had in your apartment."

He nodded. "What would she gain?"

"Money." The word popped out of her mouth before she could stop it.

John nodded. "Those profiles would be worth millions. She was good but lacked the patience to learn the new software, the new safety measures that governments were including. She didn't work with me as I learned them."

"So, she needs money?"

John shook his head. "I don't know. If she's Stratus, why would she need money?"

"Good question." She fell back into the cushions with him. He tucked her into his side, and she let herself relax against him.

"I won't let her come between us." His chest rumbled as he spoke.

Shae sighed. "She already has."

"True, but no more. No matter what happens past this moment, we make the decision to not let her come between what we have. We are stronger together." His thumb caressed her arm, running up and down.

She lifted away from him and stood. She wrapped her arms around herself and stared at the fire. "I need to know that she won't take you away from me."

John rose and closed the space between them. "I'm here. With you. Always." He dropped his hands to her hips and tugged her closer. "Always." His lips dropped to hers. The warmth of his tongue opened her. She wrapped her arms around his neck and pulled him closer until there was no space between them.

John picked her up without releasing her from the blistering kiss. Finally, he broke away and carried her through the house to the bedroom. He lifted a knee onto the bed and laid her down, immediately covering her with his body.

Once again the kiss possessed her, lifted her worries, and firmly shoved them away from them as a couple. John was assuring her with his body that he was there with her and it was exactly what she needed. She returned his kiss with just as much need and passion. She pulled the hem of his shirt and he lifted away to rip the damn thing off. She pulled her shirt over her head. To hell with the buttons. She sat up as he straddled her and unhooked her bra, flinging it to the floor. John smiled in a wickedly delicious way and moved to the foot of the bed. He tugged on her jeans and she unfastened them. He slid them down her legs. "Damn." He pressed his hand against his cock, which was still confined by denim. "You're going to make me cum in my pants. You are so damn beautiful."

Shae lifted a leg and let her body fall open. John's eyes riveted on her sex. "You have too many clothes on." The thong she wore wouldn't last. She'd lost most of the new ones she'd purchased, but it was so worth it to see John lose his mind.

He dropped his jeans and stared at her. "All of it." The groan he let loose was almost wounded. He removed his boxers and crawled onto the bed. She gasped when he lowered and licked the inside of her ankle. He lifted his eyes and smiled. Oh, God, this was going to be... "Ah!" A small bite along the inside of her knee followed by a lick and a kiss. John reached the apex and she arched toward him only to have him drop to her other ankle and start the divine torture again.

Her hands fisted the bedcovers as she propped herself on her elbows and watched as he worked his way up her leg. By the time he reached the V of her leg she was shaking, her hips undulating of their own accord. She wanted his mouth on her, wanted to feel that friction and the... "Oh, yes!" She hissed the word and dropped onto her back, her hands threaded through his hair, and as he divided her with his tongue she hung on. John's shoulders settled between her legs and the feel of his chin, nose, and tongue as he added friction and pressure to her clit was unbelievable. He entered her with two fingers and curved them as he sucked her clit into his mouth. She exploded. There was no other word for what happened. Her body drew tight and then with rhythmic thrashes, she orgasmed, not once but twice.

She opened her eyes sometime afterward. John was above her and a devilish grin lingered. "You liked that." He leaned down and kissed her.

"I think you made me pass out," Shae laughed as she wrapped her arms around his neck. The taste of both of them on his lips was erotic and so intimate. "Perhaps it is my turn to make you pass out?"

He scooped her up and rolled them. Shae laughed as the world righted itself. She straddled him and leaned down, her breasts flattening against the hair on his chest. "Hello, cowboy. Oh… I heard a song on the radio."

"You did?" He lifted up to kiss her, but she moved back, teasing him.

"I did. Something about saving a horse?"

He laughed, "I may have heard that song. Are you going to ride this cowboy?"

"Until he passes out." She lifted and centered his heavy shaft under her. Her body accepted him, but she was going to tease him like he teased her. She lifted and lowered until finally, he was deep inside her. His hands gripped her thighs and she smiled down at him. She cupped her breasts in her hands and started a slow dance on his cock, up and down with a figure eight when they were joined deeply. His hiss and the way his fingers tightened on her thighs told her what she needed to know. She dropped and braced her hands on his shoulders before she sped up and used more of her weight to bring them together. His chin kicked back and the cords of his throat convulsed as he swallowed hard.

She leaned down and licked his neck before she doubled her efforts and speed. He felt amazing inside her but what she was doing to him was heady and emboldened her farther. She stopped and lifted off him.

"No!" His eyes popped open.

"Shh…" She turned around and took him inside her again.

"Oh, fuck." His hands found her ass and she moved her hips forward and back as she lifted and sank down. "Shae… God, Shae…"

She reached down and rubbed her clit as she moved, making sure he could feel what she was doing. His hands cupped her hips and he brought her down hard on his cock. His barked shout as he came set her off and she climaxed again while rubbing her clit. The sensation of coming in this position with John buried so deep inside of her drew out the orgasm.

Finally, with one hand braced against his thigh, she tipped to the side and fell onto the bed. His hand landed on her hip. "You kill me." He panted the words, which pulled a smile from her. A completely-sated, in-love, God-that-was-great-sex type of smile.

"You're still talking. Not dead."

"Oh… right."

The comment struck her as funny and she started to laugh. He moved, spooning her from behind, putting them crosswise on the bed. "Shae?"

She twisted in his arms so they were face-to-face. "John?"

"I want to marry you." John pushed her hair out of her eyes. "I love you and I'm willing to wait, but I want you to marry me. I need you to know that."

She lifted her hand to his face. The love in his eyes was all she could see, and she knew that love was mirrored in hers. "I love you." She leaned forward and kissed him. "I want to marry you, too. One day, in the future, I want to have a family with you. But we need to finish what she started. When it's over, we will have our time."

"When it's over." John smiled and pulled her into his chest. "Guardian has a saying. Whatever it takes, for as long as it takes."

"It's a good saying." Shae closed her eyes, exhausted, content, and in love. She had a good idea what it would take to rid themselves of that woman. Tomorrow she'd worry about how long it would take.

CHAPTER 22

Shae sat across from Jeremiah. They'd been talking for a half-hour. Her eyes kept sliding to the digital clock mounted on the wall by the huge video screen.

"In a rush to get somewhere?" Jeremiah moved his eyes to the display and back to her.

"We have a transport due in at eight. To take us to..." She paused and then looked at Jeremiah. "Where is Guardian's headquarters?"

"D.C.," he supplied.

"Oh. To D.C., then." She folded her hands around her empty coffee cup. "I'm fine. I can do this."

"I know you want to do this, but what happens when you come face to face with John's sister?"

"I won't know that until it happens. In reality, I could be on a different team and not be within a hundred miles of her. I've worked missions before. I know what a sweep entails. She could run and we'll never find her, or she could die trying to evade apprehension." She leaned forward. "But I need closure. I need to know that I did something to help."

"But you decided you didn't want to do missions again. That's why you are pushing paper here at the ranch."

"And I love what I do here. It keeps me productive and I provide a service, even if it is only allowing Mike to go home at a decent hour. I have every intention of settling here with John. He's asked me to marry him."

"Congratulations. When's the date?"

"After."

"After?"

Shae snorted. "Stop. You know exactly what I mean."

"So, you are postponing your happiness until this situation is resolved."

"Yes."

"What if it is never resolved?"

"We will cross that bridge when we come to it. The immediacy of the situation would suggest it will be resolved." She glanced at the clock again. "Are you going to prevent me from going?"

Jeremiah stared at her long enough to make it an uncomfortable exchange, but she didn't glance away. She held his stare.

"Why should I let you go?"

"That woman almost took my life from me. I went through some pretty low times and I don't want to go on missions as a routine. But I am strong enough to maintain discipline and manage not to shoot the bitch between the eyes at the first opportunity I get. If only for John's sake."

"You want her dead?"

"I want justice, but I would only take her life when use of deadly force would be authorized."

"And when is that?"

"To save my life or the life of another."

"You haven't qualified on a weapon."

Shae chuckled, "I'm an expert marksman. If Guardian wants me to qualify it would take moments to show them my skills."

"And what happens when she's captured or killed?"

"Then John and I come back, and we live our lives."

"That simple?"

Shae dropped her eyes to the table. Was it that simple? She searched her heart and her mind before she nodded. "It is that simple. Events like this put minutia into perspective, don't they?"

A twitch of a smile lifted the corner of her doctor's mouth. "Indeed." He leaned back in the chair. "I'm going to give you a go under one condition."

"A condition?"

"Yes. If you can't agree to it, you're staying here at the ranch."

"What is it?"

"Any flashbacks whatsoever and you pull yourself from the mission."

"I haven't had any in months. Even when I found the photograph, I was angry, confused, and very emotional, but I didn't have a flashback."

"You haven't been under the stress you're going to place on yourself with this mission. I have your word on it, or you don't go."

"I will pull myself from the mission if I have an episode." Shae extended her hand.

Jeremiah took it and held it. "Be smart, Shae. You have a lifetime to look forward to with John. She is not worth losing that future."

Shae released his grip. "Believe me, I know that. And that is what is keeping her safe."

Jeremiah chuckled, "You must have been a kick-ass operative."

"I still am." Shae lifted an eyebrow at him. "But now I have a reason to be careful."

"So, you do. Be safe, Shae. I'm here if you need me."

She watched him leave. Resolve, determination, and confidence coalesced as she considered the broken, damaged path that led her to this moment. She'd survived. She was strong and whole. She was ready. It had taken almost a year, but the woman that had emerged from that mission was different yet the same. Stronger and yet permanently wounded. Determined but apprehensive. Her strengths were bound to her weaknesses and through the melding, she was whole again. Changed, true, but ready nonetheless.

John stood beside Shae as they waited for yet another entrapment area to clear them through to Guardian's offices. She glanced at him and lifted an eyebrow. He smiled at her and put his hand at the small of her back when the buzzer releasing the locks sounded. Shae breathed a sigh of relief when they exited into a hallway. "Rather security conscious, aren't they? Four checkpoints?"

"Actually, you got the abbreviated entry," Jacob King spoke as he walked toward them. "Sucks for pizza delivery, but it keeps us alive and in business." He extended his hand and John grabbed it. "Let's head in or we are going to miss the sweep."

John snapped his head to the right, looking at Jacob. "It's happening now?"

Jacob nodded. "We've determined the location for all ten. All of them are CONUS and we were able to deploy teams to take them down. From what we've ascertained, these people are mainly white-collar criminals with one murderer thrown in. Rich people who could afford to buy a cover. Jewell is tracing money now. The coffers under the assumed names are overflowing. She's backtracking to see where it is coming from and if it is connected to Stratus or if she can track it back to incidents they were involved with under their previous names. Various agencies around the world would be interested in evidence to substantiate their cases and have these people extradited to the appropriate country and entity once we are through with them."

"Any ties to her yet?" Shae asked as they turned and twisted through a myriad of hallways.

"Other than Lori having access to the profiles? Not that I'm aware of, but I haven't had a follow-up briefing yet this morning. I was working an overseas situation while the others worked this op."

They turned down a hallway that John recognized. The door at the end of the hall was where he'd received his briefing on Lori's name and the set of numbers. The light outside was a solid red. Jacob stopped at one of the briefing theaters and opened the door. "Ladies first."

Shae gave him a quick smile and entered the darkened theater. There were LED lights illuminating the stairs. The theater was ablaze with screens and two consoles of computers with three operators at each console. Jared King was at the floor of the screens facing the ones on the right. He had headphones and a mic on. A man John had met once or twice on the ranch, Nic, was facing the monitors on the left. He was similarly equipped.

"Jared is running the op with these five teams and Nicolas DeMarco has the other five." Jacob motioned to the seats at the front of the stadium seating. John sat down and leaned forward, his elbows on his knees as he flicked his eyes over the computer systems the techs were operating. Damn, tech had really passed him by in the years he'd been gone from the game.

He blinked and leaned back in his chair, watching the men in front of him. Shae reached for his hand and he slid his together with hers. He'd learned how to live on the ranch. Not the daily chores, the cattle, horses, and ever-present repairs, but how to live. Through the ebb and flow of the days and months, he'd tapped into the undercurrent of quality time spent by himself, and yes, with others. He stared at the equipment. Years ago, he would have given anything to explore the operating systems, learn the new software, and figure out how to make it do things for his 'profession' that the developers hadn't intended. He'd used a child's holographic story software to manufacture holographs that he could imprint on IDs. The simplicity was astounding. But that accomplishment fell flat compared to what they had now.

After this... 'situation' with Lori was done, he was going back to South Dakota. He was going back to living a simpler life. Simpler—but not easier. The challenges he faced every day mattered to the

Marshalls. They mattered to the hands that he oversaw, and the achievements and hurdles he conquered mattered to him. He glanced down at the floor. It would be a good life, a perfect place to settle down with Shae and raise a family. Once the shadow of his sister's treachery was past them. If it ever moved past them. A ghost of a feeling tickled across his skin leaving goose flesh.

"Final drill down." Jared King's voice boomed over his thoughts. "Team leaders, confirm go."

The leaders popped off answers in order and the screens populated with similar but different pictures. Helmet cameras. Shae leaned forward but didn't release his hand. He followed suit.

"On my count, we go on one." Jared glanced at his partner up front who nodded at him. "Three, two, one!"

The audio and video noise quadrupled as the teams rushed forward. Different terrains, different abodes, and two were outdoors, but the teams all moved with the precision he'd become accustomed to when he worked with Sierra Team.

"Get me a better shot on Team Four," Jared commanded, and the camera switched to another helmet view.

"Breaching," one of the team leaders spoke. The

door opened and they moved forward. John glanced from camera to camera and listened as a jumble of voices marked the progress of the sweep.

"Get down! Federal officers!" The words echoed over and over in one form or another. One woman took off but had no chance of outrunning the team in the five-inch heels she was wearing.

"Gun!" The word spun every head in the theater.

"Shots fired." The team in question filled the middle screen suddenly.

"Tango Four is down."

"Tango Three, watch it, he went to the right."

Jared snapped his fingers. "Nic, take the other teams."

"Roger that, comms transferred to my headset." Nic directed the command to one of the computer technicians on his side of the room. A head bobbed up and down. "You have comms with the exception of Tango Team."

"Tango Leader, status."

"Barricaded suspect. Tango Four is hit in the leg. We'll need medical."

"Does the perp have an exit out a window?"

"Negative--"

Shots rang out and the camera dropped to damn

near floor level—the team leader taking cover. "Fucker is shooting through the door."

"What type of weapon does he have?"

"Looked like a nine mil." The team leader looked over at his downed man. "Did you see what he had, Scooter?"

"A fucking nine mil. Thank God, three inches higher or a larger caliber and I'd be singing soprano."

John and Shae chuckled along with everyone else in the room.

"How many shots have been fired?" Jared directed the question to his computer operators.

"Standby. Four the first exchange. Six... no, seven during the second exchange."

"If he has a standard fifteen-round clip, he has four left," Jared spoke into the headset.

"Yeah, unless the bastard had one in the chamber," Shae whispered.

"Possibility of one in the chamber," Tango Team leader replied. John squeezed Shae's hand and winked. He'd bet anything the woman was one hell of an operative.

"Do you have sufficient cover?" Jared asked.

John glanced over to the right. Nic was speaking low and working with the other nine teams. He didn't see any teams hustling; it appeared the others didn't encounter resistance.

"We do."

"Knock nicely and see what kind of answer you get."

Tango Team Leader laughed, "Hold on." Through the helmet camera, they watched the man low-crawl over to a table and reach up. He reversed course with a vase in his hand. "Knock, knock, motherfucker." The team leader pitched the vase at the bathroom door and took cover. It shattered into a thousand pieces and the person who'd barricaded himself inside fired over and over in rapid succession.

"Did you get a count?"

"Four. That's fifteen," the computer operator responded.

"Tango One. Your call. Fifteen expended."

"Roger that. Tango Two?"

"Ready."

"Three?"

"Affirmative. In place."

"Four, you tucked away?"

"Roger that, Skipper."

"Five?"

"I'm here and I'm getting bored."

"Guardian, we are going through the door. Two, I'll take out the door and go high. You are low in case that bastard caps me. If he does, you take him out or I'll come back and haunt your ass. Three and Five, once we breach you have apprehension."

Acknowledgements rang out and the team leader counted down, "Three, two… one!" They watched as the team leader sprang up and raced to the door. He kicked the door and it flung open.

"Don't shoot! Don't shoot!"

"Where the fuck?" The video showed two team members running in and pulling the shower curtain back. A mousey looking man stood in the shower, his hands shaking so badly he could hardly hold the gun. "Tell them I'll pay! I swear, I'll pay!"

One of the men grabbed the empty weapon from the little man. "Who the fuck do you think we are, man?"

"Stratus?" The little guy swallowed hard and looked down.

"Oh, dude. You just pissed yourself." The team member looked straight at the team leader. "Not my turn. I'm no longer bored. I'll call dibs on taking care of Scooter's leaky leg."

"Thanks, man, good to know I rank above some asshole pissing himself."

Jared King shook his head. "Tango Leader, are you clear?"

"Affirm, sir. Just need to mop up. Literally."

"Ambulance is on scene, sir," the computer operator interjected.

"Medical on scene. Tango One, I want your apprehension here. Get you and your team on the bird we have waiting. No questions, no talking to him, nothing. We clear?"

"Absolutely clear, sir. We'll be on the first thing flying."

"Affirmative." Jared turned to Nic. "Everyone good?"

"Seamless. All primaries have been apprehended and are being expedited here."

"Perfect. We'll start with Mr. Pissy Pants."

"He definitely looks like the weakest link," Nic chuckled. "I take it we are going to play dominoes. Drop one, spin them on the others, and then work the entire haul."

"That's the plan."

John looked over at Jacob. "What are you holding them on?"

"Take your pick. Stratus is a recognized terrorist organization. We have reason to believe they purchased these fake identities from Stratus for the intent of alluding apprehension."

"Throw in proceeds of foreign crimes and material support for terrorism and they will be going to jail for a long time. We pretty much live in the confines of the Patriot Act," Jewell King spoke from behind them. The woman cocked her head. "Hi, I'm Jewell."

"Shae Diamant." Shae smiled at the woman then looked between her and Jacob. "Is everyone who works here a King? You two are definitely related"

Jewell laughed, "Nah, but there are a lot of us." The woman gave a short whistle, and all heads turned her way. "Once we have the video backed up and teams taken care of, Collen, Durbin, Richard, and Amal, you're needed in Theater Four. We have forty-five minutes until go-time. Let's get it cleared up."

The operators spun and picked up the speed of their furious typing. Jared King walked over, his headset and mic still draped from his shoulders. "Give me five minutes and we'll head to the conference room."

Jacob stood and stretched. "I'm in that op. Going to grab a bite to eat with my wife before it starts. You two good here?"

John nodded and they settled back down in the chairs.

"Impressive operation." Shae motioned to the monitors.

"Do you miss it? Being in on the action?" John tried to look interested in what was happening ahead of him, but he had to know if this was something that ran in her blood like it coursed through the Kings and the people who worked here at Guardian.

"No. There is an adrenaline rush, sure, but my time doing this type of thing is over. With this one exception. And you know what? I'm okay with that. I was carried on a wave, out of the Army, into the Mossad. I had nothing or no one to entice me to settle down."

"Until now."

She smiled and bumped his shoulder. "I know this guy."

"You do?"

"I do. He's pretty amazing, although sometimes he smells of horses and cows."

"Ah, that is a detriment to any relationship."

"Nah, he's worth it."

"Good to know." He dropped his arm over her

shoulders and soaked in the warmth of her by his side.

"Do you want anything to drink or eat?" Jared King asked as they walked into a huge conference room.

"Your brother insinuated that getting pizza into this place is next to impossible." Shae lifted an eyebrow and Jared laughed.

"My brother didn't mention that we have other ways to get food. He likes to mess with people. It is his favorite pastime. I can get you whatever you'd like."

Shae laughed and waved him off. "I'm not hungry." She turned to John. "Are you?"

John sighed. "More anxious to get this done than hungry."

"Well then, let's get to it." Jared closed the door behind them and picked up a remote. The walls, which were glass, obscured so no one could see in. He hit another button and a large screen dropped from the ceiling. Powering it up, he tapped on his tablet for a few moments and slid his finger, casting the document on his device to the screen. "This is a graph of the people we tracked from input received through interviews, yours included, Shae."

She nodded. There were names she recognized on the graph. Following the crosshatch of lines from person to person, they didn't seem to tie back to anyone. Dead ends abounded.

"Shit." John's words sounded like he'd been gut-punched. She turned to look at him, and he'd lost all the color in his face.

"What?" Jared asked at the same time she did.

"That's her." He nodded toward the name that seemed to intersect with all the others. "Lorelei Wilde."

Shae tried to catch up with him. "Wait? What? How do you know?"

He swallowed hard. "It's her actual name."

"Her name isn't Lori Baker?" Jared's confusion was obvious.

"No, that is an alias she worked under at the Agency."

"Baker? Not Smith?" Shae asked.

"Family ties weren't to be advertised. They can be used against you."

"So, your real name isn't John Smith?"

"No, I took the most common name in the country when I took Guardian up on their offer."

Shae dropped into a chair and stared at the chart. She jerked her head from the screen to him. "What's your legal name?"

"John Smith is my legal name now. I was born Johnathan Wilde."

"Jewell, could you come to my conference room, please? We need your assistance." Jared put the phone back down in the cradle. "She'll be here in a minute and we'll pull the information we have on Lorelei Wilde. We did a cursory check as she was mentioned by..." Jared slid his finger across his tablet. "Here. She was mentioned as a possible acquaintance of one Shamus O'Brian, who was connected loosely through business with Brittlyn Meyers. Ms. Meyers is Stratus. We've been monitoring her telephone, office, apartment, and travels for almost a month. Intelligence that we've gathered has doubled our knowledge of this bubble of Stratus. Since the Fates have been taken out of the picture, Stratus has splintered. We believe that the organization has withdrawn into secluded nodes and is trying to reorganize."

At a knock at the door, Jared cleared the screen and opened it. "Hey, you guys. Whatcha need?"

"Lorelei Wilde." Jared nodded to the screen. "How far did you dig on her?"

"Um, let's see." Jewell sat down and started tapping on the tablet she'd brought with her. "Ms. Wilde, where are you? Ah, here we go. We did a level-three data mine. Basic background search, financials, schools, arrest history. Why?"

"That's my sister."

"Ah, no." Jewell shook her head. She tapped her screen several times. "This is Lorelei Wilde." A picture appeared.

John and Shae spoke in unison, "That's her." The woman who'd had her tortured still made her gut churn. She pulled her eyes away from the screen.

"What?" Jewell squeaked. "No, *this* is your sister." She tapped furiously and another picture appeared.

John swore under his breath and scrubbed his face. "That's not Lorelei. That's a woman who Lorelei hired on several occasions to double for her in our father's scams. Paula McCann." She did bear a striking resemblance. *Shit.*

"You think Paula McCann died in that car explosion, not Lorelei?" Shae asked.

He shot a look at Shae. Why the hell hadn't he thought of that? "Damn it. It could have been. I was a long way away." John turned to Jared and Jewell. "Where is Lorelei now?"

Both dropped their attention to their tablets.

"New York. Tribeca. Recent credit card usage," Jewell chirped and continued tapping.

"We need to get eyes on her," Jared spoke to Jewell and grabbed the door handle.

Jewell acknowledged him, "I'm on it."

John arrested Jared's movement with a hand on his arm. "Shae and I are going to be on the team that takes her down. Get us to New York. Now."

Exiting the facility was straightforward and expedited by Jared King. He opened the door to the parking facility and a black SUV pulled up. "This is your ride to the airport. We have Sierra Team flying into New York. They were diverted in air, but you've worked with them so we're rearranging missions. They will land thirty minutes before you and meet you at the private terminal. We'll have the op configured and brief you and Sierra Team when you arrive."

They piled into the SUV. Privacy glass kept them separated from the driver. Shae grabbed John's hand. "I'm sorry."

John's head snapped in her direction. "Why?"

Shae shrugged. "Even though she ordered my…"

She cleared her throat and continued, "... and she sold those profiles to criminals, she's your sister."

John was silent for a moment. "I appreciate it, but Lori is alive. Which means the woman who I thought was her died in her place. Murder. She sold covers to criminals. She ordered your torture, and she is part of Stratus. How high up in the organization is yet to be determined. Speculation aside, she stole years of my life from me." He turned and stared at her. The anger in his eyes surprised her. "Don't worry, I plan on making sure that my sister pays for everything she's done. Everything."

CHAPTER 23

John felt resolve click into place when he saw his sister's name on that board. Resolve and another emotion—anger. She'd been living her life when he'd been grieving her loss. The hours, days... hell, months he'd spent wondering if there was something he should have seen, something he should have done in those first few moments. It was sickening the hours he mourned her, mourned her loss when she was alive and thriving in the layers of Stratus.

"Why wouldn't the Agency where you both worked not know she's alive?" Shae asked him as they were deplaning in New York. The bitter cold sliced down the runway as they huddled into their coats and trotted to the small terminal building.

"Why would they look for a dead person?" John asked as he pulled open the door.

"Well, there is that," Shae answered as they stomped snow off their shoes.

"About time you decided to get your ass in here." Luke walked forward and extended his hand.

"Luke, good to see you. I'm not sure if you remember her, but this is Shae Diamant, we met her in Canada about a year ago."

The man's head snapped back on his shoulders. "No way."

Shae laughed, "Way. Nice to meet you, Luke, and thank you for your part in liberating me from that pit."

"Man, I never wanted to kill someone as bad as I wanted to kill that bastard that worked you over. Lucky for his fat ass that I don't do that for a living." Luke winked at John. He chuckled and nodded as Travis, Sierra Team's skipper, walked up.

"John, been a hot minute."

"It has indeed. Travis, this is Shae Diamant. We met her in Canada about a year ago."

The man blinked and swung his gaze from John to Luke back to Shae. "Ma'am, I must say you look much better today."

"I'm sure I do." Shae nodded to the men standing behind Travis.

"Sorry, this is the rest of us. Ricco, Scuba, Harley, and that guy over there is Coach, our medic."

"Ma'am." Coach smiled. He turned to John. "I see you're still holding her hand. Good job, my man."

John glanced down to their intertwined fingers and remembered Coach telling him to hold her hand and talk to her. "Don't figure on stopping."

Coach smacked Travis on the back. "Score one for the Coach."

"Whatever. We've got a van waiting and a secure connection at the other end of the ride."

John settled into the vehicle beside Shae and dropped his arm around her shoulders. Travis drove and the team settled into seats with Ricco in shotgun. "So, I'm sure the question on everyone's mind is why were you where you were?" Luke twisted in his seat to ask the question.

She glanced at John. He shrugged. "You can tell him to mind his own business, but everyone here has the clearance to hear."

Shae drew a breath and glanced at the men who were all twisted to look at her. "I was a Mossad agent tracking Stratus." She stopped and shrugged. "I found them."

"No shit," Scuba snorted.

"Did a damn good job of it, too," Ricco laughed.

"Well, if you're going to do something…" Harley chuckled.

Shae laughed with them, but when they quieted, she leaned forward. "Thank you for everything. I wouldn't have survived much longer."

The somberness of the Canadian mission returned in full force. "Well, I'm glad we were able to reach you in time," Luke spoke, and the men nodded.

"So am I." John tucked her under his shoulder and the rest of the ride was made in silence, although John watched Shae react to the drive into the city. Her eyes were glued to the cityscape and the awe in her eyes as they drove deep into the belly of New York City was akin to a child's wonder at Christmastime. Subtle gasps when landmarks came into view were heard only by him. He moved slightly so she could see out the window. She glanced at him and smiled. "I've always wanted to go to Times Square and a Broadway show."

"I'll take you." And he would, damn it. If his sister could live her life in the open, Guardian could make sure he could live his. Granted, he was going to live in South Dakota, but he would take Shae to Times

Square and to a Broadway show and anything else she wanted.

Her smile widened and she squeezed his hand as they walked into the downtown office building. The New York offices for Guardian Security were unsuspecting, but the professionalism he'd always encountered with Guardian echoed down the tight halls of this portion of the company, too. A gentleman with grey hair at his temples extended his hand to Travis. "I'm Ross Stapleton, Chief of Guardian's branch here in New York. Follow me."

The team of seven walked down the corridor single file and into a conference room. Stapleton closed the door and motioned for them all to take a seat. He clicked on the screen and nodded to them. "This briefing is classified and Jared King has provided all of your clearance levels to me. Skipper, can you attest to the identity of your team and that these are the passengers you picked up from the arriving aircraft?"

Travis nodded. "I can."

"Authenticate pitch."

"Screwball."

"Good, now that the pleasantries are over, here is the latest we have from HQ. The woman in question is Lorelei Wilde. Guardian's computer folks are still digging, but there is nothing on her to indicate any connection to Stratus."

"How can that be? She was the one who gave the order." Shae leaned forward.

"Guardian backtracked her financials to the dates you were located in Canada. They show she was in New York City the entire month, credit card usage throughout the city. Taxis, shopping, meals."

"That can't be right. John, I know I'm not wrong." Shae twisted grabbing his arm.

"What about the sale of the deep covers?" John threw out the question.

"Dom Ops is interviewing the people who had assumed the covers. We'll have more on who and how later."

"We have to bring her in." John leaned forward. He drew a breath and laid it all out. "She's a dead woman who isn't dead, the only person with access to my work other than myself. We have an eyewitness placing her in Canada in charge of a kidnapping, assault, and attempted murder."

"Oh, she's going to be brought in. That's why you're here. What we need to do is figure out how to extract her without creating a small war zone in Tribeca." Stapleton pointed his remote at the screen. A street view flashed up on the screen. "The area she lives in is residential and populated with upper-middle-class families." He hit the remote again. "This is a drive-by photo of the building where she lives. This is her floor."

"Is that a garden terrace?" Luke spoke as he squinted at the screen

Ross Stapleton nodded. "It is. She's one of two apartments on that floor. We have no information on the second tenant. Guardian is digging."

"Do both apartments have access to the terrace?"

Stapleton nodded. "From the blueprints we were able to pull from the city, yes."

"Think we could do it?" Luke asked Travis.

The team leader leaned forward. "We could, the wall has limited windows. We could gain access from the rooftop."

"Rappel down?" John asked.

"Yeah." Travis nodded. "Not a tactic we like to employ, especially in a highly visible environment like this. What is the lighting at night? We could be caught on video by a thousand phones."

Shae turned from the photo and asked, "Why not cut the power?"

Ross rubbed the back of his neck. "To the building? That's doable"

Shae shook her head. "No, to the entire block."

"Oh, I like her," Luke chuckled.

"The entire block?"

John smiled and nodded in agreement. "It would put the entire block into darkness. As soon as the power is cut, we'd move."

"We?" Travis laughed, "Oh, no. Not happening."

"It's a fifty-foot rappel. We'll sign a waiver." Shae threw up her hand dismissing the team leader's concern.

Travis crossed his arms over his chest and leaned back in the chair staring at both Shae and John. "And if you drop to your death?"

Shae snorted. "A waiver, you know what this is, yes? It means you aren't responsible."

"I'm not worried about the rappel, I'm saying no because of the way we're going to get on top of that building." Travis leaned forward.

"And how is that?"

"Zipline." Travis nodded to the taller building to the right. "From that rooftop to this one."

John leaned forward and stared at Travis. "I'd freefall jump from that rooftop to this one if it meant finding out what the fuck is going on. This is my life, our life, not just a mission. We are going and I don't care what gymnastics we have to go through to be there. You've worked with me; you know I'm not rash or stupid. Neither is Shae."

"Didn't say you were, but I don't know her skillset and I don't want to jeopardize my team because you need closure. You can wait until we take her down and bring her out."

"That's not going to happen." John leaned forward. "Call Archangel if you doubt my word." He tossed that trump card out and slapped it on Travis' desk.

He glared at Travis until the man sighed, "Your funeral." He looked over at Ricco. "Dude, Google how to write up a waiver." The rest of the team chuckled at the request.

"Guardian will still have to approve the tactic and get the city to black out a full city block," Ross spoke as he stared at the photograph.

"If I know Guardian, they won't ask for permission." Luke leaned forward. "Tonight, then?"

Ross turned off the screen. "I have men trying to get eyes on her now. Once we make contact, we can verify location and set up the takedown."

"Then we wait," John said. He'd hold until the boiling rivers of Hell froze over to get answers.

Waiting had never been her strong suit. Shae walked the ninety-seven strides down the long hallway of Guardian's offices in New York. There were electronic locks on a few of the doors and lights that were illuminated indicating people were working inside the secure areas. She pivoted at the end of the hall and started the journey back to the other end of the passageway.

"Guardian's going to have to replace the tile."

Shae spun at the comment. Luke leaned against a door jamb. "Restless." She moved so one of the New York Guardians could pass.

"Are you ready for what's going to happen tonight?"

She leaned against another door jamb out of the way of those who wanted to pass by. "I believe I am."

Luke cleared his throat and glanced both ways down the hall before he spoke, "You and I have similar experiences. I don't know how long you were held. They had me for three years."

She froze at the admission. "My God." The words whooshed out of her escaping breath.

He nodded. "It isn't as easy as you'd think... going back out into the field. There could be triggers. Anger. Rage." He shrugged.

"Yet here you are." Shae nodded. "Proof it can be done."

"True. If you need to talk or if you want to stop at any point, let me know. I get it. No questions, no hassle, just tell me."

Shae nodded. "Thank you. I hope it doesn't come to that."

The man shrugged. "I've known John for a few years in passing. Got to know him better last year. He thought she was dead."

"There are a lot of unanswered questions." She had no idea where this conversation was going or for that matter why she was talking about John with a stranger.

"Finding out a member of your family has turned against you, transgressed on that relationship, can be difficult to deal with emotionally. Some people find it hard to believe that family could be… treacherous."

Shae narrowed her eyes at him. "John has no such doubts. He's well aware of what she's done."

Luke nodded. "But when it comes time, if we aren't there, if shit turns south…"

Realization of what he was saying landed on her shoulders with the weight of a tombstone. She held the man's eyes and vowed, "I have his back."

Luke dipped his chin. "Stapleton wants us back in the conference room in five." He turned on his heel and headed back down the small hall to the conference room.

She took a deep breath and released it, counting to ten. Tonight wasn't going to be easy for her, and frankly, that *was* what she'd been focusing on. Luke shifted her thoughts from herself to the man she loved. How hard was it going to be for John to confront his sister? What damage were her actions doing to him? What explanation could justify what she'd done? Rolling her shoulders, she lifted away from the door jamb and followed Luke. Only time would tell.

CHAPTER 24

John checked his rigging one more time before he moved to where Shae was standing. "Secure?"

She nodded. "You?"

He tugged on his shoulder harness. "Good to go."

They stood in the darkness watching Sierra Team do a dance they appeared to have done countless times. Travis called them all over and sank to a knee when everyone was around him. He spoke to everyone, making eye contact with each of them as he spoke, "One more time with the game plan. Two lines. Ricco and Scuba will deploy the cable. The stairwell entrance on the target building is made of cinderblock. That's where you'll sink the cables. Once you secure the line on both sides, you're over the wall first. Then Shae and John. Luke and I will be behind them. Coach and Harley are bringing up the rear and will make sure that cable is released so we can pull it up from this rooftop after the mission is over. Luke, you man the inside stairwell once we are over there. We don't want any unexpected guests." He glanced around. "We aren't going into this looking for a lady. This woman is Stratus, and from the sound of things, she's high up in that organization. Comms are on as soon as we are at the garden terrace. Guardian will be able to hear everything but communicate only with me." He focused on John. "We take no chances."

John nodded. He got why Travis was zeroing in on him. He was a weak link in the chain. *His* sister, *his* emotions, *his* problem, not theirs. "I'm solid. No chances."

Travis nodded. "All right, we have one minute. We wait for the power outage and then we move in. We all go in alive, we all come out alive."

"Whatever it takes," the team said in unison.

"As long as it takes," Travis finished for them.

Shae and he took their places to the side of Ricco and Scuba. He leaned over and whispered, "I love you."

Shae turned to him just as the lights went out.

Her words, if they were said, were wiped away by the sound of rocket-propelled cables being fired.

Ricco and Scuba secured the lines and clipped their safety gear onto the cable. In unison, they swung their legs over the wall, clipped a zipline handle to the cable and their rigs, and with a nod to each other, were screaming across the darkness to the rooftop below.

When they saw the signal, John and Shae assumed the same position. He attached the handle to the cable and his harness. He glanced over as Shae completed fastening her handle to her rig. He nodded and they moved as one, sliding from the wall into the cradle of the harness as they flew across the darkened street below. It took only seconds to land with a jolt on the roof of the building across the way. They unhooked and moved out of the way. Travis, Luke, Harley, and Coach sped across the cable in the same way. Harley and Coach worked to release the cables from the cinderblocks as Ricco and Scuba anchored rappelling lines into the roof of the building.

Luke hissed from the stairwell door. "Incoming. You have a minute, maybe less."

Travis cussed and motioned for John and Shae. "There must be an alarm with a generator backup on this rooftop. You two down the side and take cover in the garden. Do not engage. Copy?"

John nodded and hooked his harness into the rappel line in perfect synchronization with Shae. They stepped over the wall and lowered into the darkness.

Several breathless seconds later, he landed on his toes and unclipped from the harness, pulling his nine mil out to cover as Shae unhooked. "Let's go."

Shae snapped her head up. He could barely see her in the darkness when she hissed, "What part of *don't* engage didn't you understand?"

John moved into the darkest area of the garden, not to hide but to move closer. He could feel Shae following him. He stopped and waited for her to get closer. "We've both got plenty of missions under our belt. Don't tell me you want to hide in the dark."

She withdrew her weapon and flicked the safety off and whispered, "Not in the slightest."

The sounds of a muffled shout and the muted scuffling from above paused their advance for a moment. The distinct whap of a long-range bullet hitting the rooftop fifty feet above them caught and held his attention, but there was nothing he could do if the men were pinned down. John crouched down and moved quietly toward the plate glass doors that they'd seen in the photographs and on the blueprints of the building.

There were a few candles lit, casting a warm yellow glow about three feet into the garden. Shae put a hand on his shoulder. "Look." She motioned to the frame of the door.

"What?" He didn't know what she was looking at.

"Laminated polycarbonate. Bulletproof glass. If it is locked, we can't get in, not without an army." Another rifle shot echoed into the night, causing someone to stir in the apartment.

"We left our army upstairs." John watched from the darkness as Lori walked up to the plate glass door. "Then we need to have her ask us in."

"How?"

John nodded to the room and Shae stilled. "I'll walk up to the door. She'll open it."

"She could kill you," Shae whisper-hissed at him.

"She won't get the chance."

"How do you know?"

"Because if she tries, I'll kill her, or you will. Turn on comms so Guardian can hear everything." John switched on his comms, pulled Shae in for a quick kiss, and then stood, stepping out into the light.

The surprise he expected to see flashed across his sister's face. Her hands flew to her mouth and she scrambled forward to unlock the door. "John! Oh, thank God! I thought you were dead."

He lifted his nine mil, stopping his sister's forward movement. "Stay right there."

"John, what are you doing?"

"Protecting myself."

"Against whom?" Lorelei opened her arms, the folds of her silk robe swaying with the motion.

"You. Why did you fake your own death?" He knew Shae was watching from the darkness. A shadow moved in the apartment and John stepped to the side, putting his sister directly between where the shadow had been and where he was.

"The Agency wanted me to go undercover. It was a hard decision, but they convinced me it would be safer for you if you thought I was gone. Then the reports of your apartment and car exploding…" Her voice caught. "John, you're all I have in this world. I thought you were dead."

"Funny. I thought the same thing about you. Why did you sell them?"

Lori shifted and he followed suit. She blinked and a small tick of a smile tilted her lips. "You found out about that? The Agency sold them."

"No, they didn't."

She frowned. "How would you assume to know that? I work for them. I know they did."

"The deputy director of the CIA conferred with all black door operations today. The Agency had no knowledge of them or their use by criminals."

A man emerged from his left with a weapon trained on him. "Oh, look. We have a draw," Lorelei murmured. "Why couldn't you have stayed dead?"

He smiled at his sister. "Because you made too many mistakes, Lori. You never should have stolen Guardian's property."

"Guardian?"

"My employers." He thumbed the trigger back on his weapon; the action made a deafening click in the quiet of the power outage now that the fighting had quieted. "You stole my work. Work I gave to them." The man on his left moved slightly. "If he shoots me, you're dead. Again."

"I'm not too worried. I've found death isn't anything like they portray in movies. You'll jerk around when his bullet hits you, your aim will be off, I'll live."

"It's not my aim you need to worry about," John chuckled, his focus staying on his sister.

"Really? What, you have someone hiding in the

shadows with you? My men have taken care of whomever was on the rooftop."

"I'm hard to kill, too." Shae stepped from the shadows, her aim on the man who had drawn on John.

Lori's eyes narrowed. "I know you."

"You introduced me to Maurice." From his peripheral vision, he could see Shae. Her arm was rock solid as she held her weapon.

"Oh, yes, Amira's little mole." Lorelei moved her hand toward the pocket of her robe.

A wicked smile flashed across Shae's face. "Move any further and you'll be dead, but no… I'm so much more than Amira's mole. I'm a survivor, I'm your brother's lover, and I'm going to ensure you spend the rest of your life in prison for who you are and what you've done."

Floodlights blinded him as the power turned back on. He dove to his left and shouted, "Shae, get Lori!"

He lifted from his roll and charged the bodyguard. The percussion of the man's weapon's discharge deafened him, but he was under the man's arm and the bullet went high. He tackled Lorelei's minion with a shoulder into the guy's gut. They went down hard and rolled in a fight to control the weapon.

They wrestled in an ugly display of brute strength. There was no opportunity to pull away and punch, but John threw elbows, bit, and kneed in a deathmatch for control of the weapon. John's shoulders and arms burned with the effort to keep the weapon trained away from him. The man beneath him grunted with the same strain. John heard more gunshots. Adrenaline coursed through him and clarity sharpened his efforts. He lifted his head and brought it down hard on the nose of the man under him. A spray of warm wetness hit his face. Shouts from somewhere near him registered briefly. He lifted and hammered away at the son of a bitch again.

A sudden slack in the man's grip fueled him. He lifted and slammed his forehead down as hard as he could against the other man's face. Another spray of blood covered them both. He blindly grabbed for the weapon and twisted it from the bastard's hand. Three sharp shots riddled the downed bastard. John lunged to the right and rolled behind the planter.

He wiped the blood from his eyes and stared at the dead man. Where had the shots come from? Friend or foe? He held still, silent and searching the area across from the building exactly one hundred and eighty degrees from the building they'd ziplined from.

He jerked his weapon to the right to cover a slight rustling. Travis held his hand up. John wiped more blood away from his eyes and noticed the Skipper had blood on his shoulder and wasn't using that arm. "Sniper." He nodded to the left, the same building John had been searching before Travis surfaced.

John nodded his understanding.

"The team is trapped. Power is going out again. Can you take him out?"

"Not without a rifle." And a fuckton of luck locating a sniper on higher ground in the dark.

Travis reached down and slid a compact M-24 case along the ground. "Archangel and Alpha told us to bring one. Just in case. Shae?"

He pointed toward the apartment. "She went after Lori." He hadn't seen either woman and he prayed Shae was all right, but he had to trust her to do her job. That was what she was trusting him to do.

"I'll go in when the power cuts. The team is holding. If you want them to move to try to draw him out, talk to Guardian on your comms. They can hear

JOHN

you. HQ is trying to get someone up to that rooftop, but right now, you're our only play."

"Anyone else injured?"

"Nothing serious. You?"

"Not my blood. When?" John wiped his face again.

Travis cocked his head as if he was listening. "Ten seconds."

John nodded. "He'll have to change scopes or use a handheld infrared to target us. As soon as the lights go out, get inside. I'll grab the weapon on the way to the northeast corner."

"The scope isn't infrared."

"I won't need it." He had a plan. Maybe.

The block went dark and they moved. John grabbed the weapon and used the back wall as a guide to get to the small protrusion at the northeast corner. "Guardian, I'm going to need that power back on, but right before you do, I need someone on the roof to move something. I'll take my shot then. I'll count it down; you repeat to the team." John put together the M-24 in the dark from muscle memory. He'd fired for proficiency at least once every three or four months while he was at the ranch. The action of the weapon was as familiar as breathing. He shouldered it, revealing only the barrel over the lip of the decorative wall surrounding the garden.

"Guardian, on my count. When I say three, have someone on the roof move something and light the block up when I say one. I want to blind that son of a bitch. It should give me a couple seconds to find him." He drew a breath and exhaled slowly. "Ten." He closed his eyes and rested them until he said five. At four he opened his eyes and the ambient light seemed much brighter thanks to his eyes adjusting. At three, he prayed someone on the roof got the word. Two, he drew a breath filling his lungs halfway before he stopped breathing and whispered, "One." The lights snapped on and he searched the edge of the building for… there! He centered the hash lines on the scope and squeezed the trigger. The weapon kicked in his hands, but he focused on the target and watched as the shooter went down. "Guardian, move the team to the stairwell now, now!"

He kept his eyes trained on the edge of the building, but the shooter never reappeared. He heard the team enter the apartment. It sounded like someone kicked the door in. He'd watched the team clear rooms before. Harley and Ricco entered first, then Scuba and Luke, then Coach had the tail. He'd been with them as they cleared so many spaces last year. He kept his rifle at shoulder level, scanning the skyline of the building across from them.

"John?" Ricco hissed a whisper from the other side of the sliding glass door. "I'll cover."

He dropped his rifle and hustled his ass into the apartment. "Shut the doors, ballistic glass."

Ricco slammed the door shut. "This way."

"Where's Shae?"

"Through here." Ricco jogged down a long hallway and John was on his six.

Ricco stopped suddenly and nodded for him to enter a room to their right.

Shae sprinted after John's sister. The woman had the advantage of knowing the apartment and had a head start. Instinct and training stopped her at the corner to the hall. If the woman had access to a weapon, centering herself in a corridor would paint a bullseye on her. She peeked around the corner and ducked back. With the hall clear, it was a matter of finding the woman and taking her down. The blueprints they'd studied of the apartment flicked through her mind. Bathroom first door to the right.

Guest bedroom to the left and a den that had a connecting door to the master suite.

Shae positioned herself and took one more look down the hall. Nothing and no noise. She'd seen the woman flee down this corridor, so now it was a matter of search and destroy. *Destroy, damn, don't you wish*. She slid around the corner with her weapon ready. The bathroom door was ajar. She pushed it back as far as it would go and did a quick visual sweep before she lifted onto her toes to look into the swimming pool-sized tub.

Cleared, she moved on to the guest bedroom. She entered the room and cleared the closet while still listening intently in case John's sister tried to trap her in the smaller room. Empty. She repeated the process of entering the hall. Gunfire from outside paused her forward movement. She cocked her head and listened. That sounded like a high-powered rifle. She crossed her leg in front of her other and side-stepped down to the office. The door was shut. She looked farther to the master bedroom. That door was ajar.

If she owned this apartment, where would she keep her weapons? In the bedroom, yes, but also in the office. The low sound of whirring from the office caught her attention. She lifted to her toes and soundlessly made her way into the bedroom. Cautiously and too damn slow because she hadn't cleared the room, she made her way to where the office door joined the bedroom. She turned the knob just as the power went out. A muffled curse was her invitation in. There was moonlight from the windows in the bedroom. Shae closed her eyes tightly for a count of ten and then squared on the door and kicked it open, hoping to startle the woman.

Only she didn't startle Lorelei. No, it was just her damn luck the door slammed into the woman's face and planted her flat on her back. Out cold. Shae rolled the stunned woman and yanked a set of zip tie cuffs from her tactical pants and snagged her wrists. With a sharp tug, she neutralized any threat Lorelei could have presented. A small Glock 43 scraped across the hardwood floor when she lifted the woman to her side so she wouldn't choke on the blood flowing from her nose. Shae shoved her hand under Lorelei and snatched it up. She cleared the weapon, which didn't even have a round in the chamber, and then pocketed it. She toed Lorelei's hip to make sure she was still breathing, although she'd rather drop kick the useless witch into next month. When the woman groaned, Shae snapped, "Next time, try bringing a big person weapon to the fight, bitch."

The lights flickered back on a mere second before the report of a high-powered rifle slammed through the apartment. It took every shred of self-control not to rush back out to the terrace, but she had to trust John could handle himself. Her job was dealing with this… the 'c' word rattled around in her brain, but Shae had never uttered the most offensive word she'd ever heard, let alone thought about it applying to anyone.

Well, for Lorelei, she'd make an exception.

She rolled her eyes at the sound of the front door crashing in and the men on Sierra Team shouting, "Clear!" as they moved through the apartment. Lorelei moved, rolling slightly. Shae glanced down at John's sister now that the lights were on. "Oh, damn, I think you broke your nose." The woman moaned something that sounded like a cuss word. Shae snorted and glanced around the room. "What were you doing in here?" A paper shredder sat beside the desk with a half-shredded piece of paper sticking out of it. "What do we have here?"

She heard the team advancing. She wiggled the paper out of the machine and yelled out, "Office on your right, clear. One in custody." The door swung open. Travis leaned against the door. His right arm was dangling from his side, but in his left hand he held a forty-five and it was aimed at her. He dropped it after he noticed Lorelei prostrate. "What happened to her?"

Shae looked over her shoulder at the woman on the floor. "Her face met the door when I kicked it. Breakable little thing, isn't she? Where is John?"

"He'll be here in a minute. What do you have there?" Travis nodded to the paper.

"Don't know, but she was trying to get rid of it. I heard the machine running when I circled back through the bedroom."

"Is it a cross-cut shredder?"

Shae lifted her foot and pushed the front door of the shredder in. It released with a click. She pulled out the bin and chuckled, "Oh, yeah. It's paper dust."

"We'll take all of this in as evidence. Maybe the tech folks like puzzles?"

Shae glanced up as Ricco stopped at the door. John rounded the corner. "Are you okay?"

"I'm fine. She's not doing so good." Shae nodded to his sister. "Can you believe she ran into the door?"

John glanced at his sister and then laughed. Shae blinked at him—the response wasn't at all what she'd expected. "The door or your fist?"

Shae sighed. "It was actually the door when I kicked it open. I have to admit, I'm really pissed she didn't put up a fight." She looked up at the man she loved. "I wanted to hit her. More than once. I should probably talk to Jeremiah about that when we get back. I might have anger issues that I wasn't aware of."

"Nah," Coach disagreed. "We've all wanted to hit her more than once. No offense, John. Skipper, I need to take a look at that shoulder."

"None taken." John glanced at the paper Travis held in his hand. "What's that?"

"Something she was trying to get rid of." Travis held it out to him and then held up his hand. Every member of the team stilled. Travis dropped his hand to his ear cradling the comm device. He nodded. "Roger, copy all, Guardian. Ricco and Scuba, we're taking everything as evidence. Harley, get over to the other building and pull our cables. There should be a couple of New York guys downstairs to help gather all the equipment and they've found the shooter. You dropped him, John. One shot through the heart. Paramedics on scene downstairs. Coach, coordinate treatment for her." Travis pointed toward Lorelei.

Coach shook his head. "After I look at that damn

shoulder, Skipper. She's breathing and cussing. You're still bleeding. Priorities."

Shae glanced back at Lorelei. The woman's eyes pinned her with a stare. "You should be *dead*." The woman hissed the words.

All conversation in the room stopped. Shae walked over and lowered into a squat in front of the woman who'd ordered her torture and death. "Did you tell Maurice to kill me?"

Lorelei smiled and the drying blood from her nose bleed cracked under the stretch of her lips. "I have no idea why you think I would have done that."

"Did you kill Joshua or just order it done, not wanting to get your hands dirty?"

"I know my rights. I want a lawyer," the woman spat at her.

Shae wiped the spittle off her cheek using every iota of willpower not to draw back a fist and bust a few teeth from the woman's skull.

John's combat boots came into view as she stared at the abomination zip tied next to her. "You don't get a lawyer, Lori."

Lorelei's eyes whipped over to him. She rolled onto her back so she could see him better. "I'm untouchable. You can't prove anything."

John held out a hand and helped Shae to her feet.

"See, that's where you're wrong." He held up the half-sheet of paper. "Stratus is a terrorist organization. Normal procedures don't apply. Plus, now I have these names. I'm assuming you engineered covers using them. I'm better than you ever were. I'll find where you cut corners, where you got sloppy. I know your signature, where you let little things slide. You were never patient enough to follow the entire process. I'll find these people and Guardian will bring them in and turn them against each other. Stratus is dying, and finding these people is nothing but another move in a game of dominoes that Guardian is winning. You're only one in a vast number of people who are never going to hurt anyone ever again."

The woman spat at him and kicked out, flailing her legs in an effort to cause some damage. Shae stepped out of the way and shook her head. This pathetic woman wasn't the monster of her nightmares. She stepped back and found the desk with her hands, still watching Lorelei as she screamed obscenities. John stood in front of her. She lifted her eyes to his. "You were the one with the rifle?"

"There were two of us. He had the high ground."

"And you still were able to make the shot?" She reached out and placed her hand on his chest.

"Guardian turned on the lights. I knew it was coming. He didn't. That was my only tactical advantage." John pulled her into his chest, and she closed her eyes. She sighed deeply and let herself lean against him. "We should help."

"Let the team do what they've trained to do. We're done with this."

"I miss Velvet and the smell of cows. And Cat. Sasha, too."

John laughed; his chest vibrated under her ear. "Then we should go home."

Shae leaned back and smiled up at him. "Home sounds wonderful."

CHAPTER 25

The snowbanks were a pain in the ass to bust through first thing in the morning. John stopped short and cussed under his breath when a clump of snow snaked down the back of his leg and melted at his ankle. He reached down and yanked his jeans back down over the top of his boot and worked his way to the barn door. The hands would be starting the snow blower soon to clear a path, but as ranch manager, he prided himself at being the first to work, even though it meant pulling himself away from Shae's warm body. In the weeks since they'd returned to South Dakota, all the debris of his past and hers settled into manageable rubbish that they, along with the occasional talk with Jeremiah, could handle.

Shae had moved into his house immediately after they'd returned, which made Isaac and Lyric extremely happy since Isaac's plans had changed and he needed to stay at the complex for whatever he did for Guardian.

John stomped his feet and turned on the barn lights. One by one, horses dropped their heads over the half-doors of their stalls. He stopped by each to stroke and praise the animals. Velvet was in the stall closest to his office. The little cream-colored lineback dun had grown into a majestic animal, albeit a bit spoiled. He stopped and scratched behind the colt's ears. "Today's the day, bud. Let's hope I don't mess it up."

The colt bounced his head and puffed out a sound that could have been, 'don't worry you did,' to 'you've got this.' Damn, he hoped so. He had to do a ton of research, and hopefully, he got it right. If not, well, then maybe he'd get an 'A' for effort.

Within thirty minutes, the sounds of snowblowers firing up and the tractor they'd installed the snow blade on turning over made him smile. His men knew what to do and did it. There wasn't a slacker in the lot. He finished feeding the horses and turned them out for the day. The weather forecast was for clearing skies and sunshine, which would help to clear the massive dump of snow.

Nine hours later, he made his last check of the horses that had been brought back into the stalls and headed to the small corner of the tack room that he'd claimed. He had forty-five minutes to make it back to the house. He pulled the wooden crate out and opened the lid, examining the inside. The silver menorah he'd ordered from a specialty shop in New York sat cushioned on a royal blue and silver pillow. The candles, nine in total, were hand-dipped tapers that fit perfectly in the base of the menorah. He smiled at the gelt he'd purchased for her—traditional, but he couldn't pass up the chocolate coins—and finally, he removed the small wooden box with the first night's blessing—inscribed in Hebrew—on the top. He opened it and picked up her copy of the Torah, the one she had as a child. He'd contacted her mother via Guardian and asked if she still had it. The woman provided it but never asked about her daughter. Fitted along the side of the old, tattered Torah was a smaller box of the same wood. He lifted the lid and smiled. An oval diamond solitaire.

"Starts tonight, huh?"

John spun at Frank's voice. "Hey. Yeah. First night of Hanukkah."

JOHN

"Got to admit, I don't know much about the holiday."

"I didn't either, but I researched it. I'm sure I probably messed up things, but I kept it basic. I'm hoping for extra credit for intent versus execution if I bugger it up." He placed the Torah and ring back into the box and replaced the cover.

"Got word today that your sister has been formally charged." Frank walked over to the bridles on the wall and trailed his finger along the reins of one of the fancier setups that had a hand-tooled headband and silver-heart conchos.

John pushed the anger he harbored against his sister down. "Yeah? All the charges stick?"

"They did. I hear a few more counts were added based on all the work you did."

He shrugged and hefted the crate into his arms. "She made her bed."

"That she did." Frank turned out the light after him and walked silently with him through the barn and held the door open for him when they exited. The brilliant blue sky and crisp, cold air took his breath away both literally and figuratively.

"The beauty of this land is addictive." Frank shoved his hands in his pockets and stared at the horizon.

John stopped and propped the wooden crate on his hip. He cocked his head and then nodded. "This land is amazing. Figure it would just be dirt if you weren't around, though."

"Family is an important thing, son."

"That it is." He smiled as his mind went to the ring inside the box he was holding.

"You should get yourself one." Frank winked at him and headed up to the big house.

John chuckled. The man was either a mind reader or he'd rummaged through the box John had just retrieved from the tack room. He didn't figure Frank would ever invade anyone's privacy, so... mind reader it was.

He loaded the box into his truck and headed back to the house. He pulled up and darted into the house because he could see Shae and Joy talking at the fork in the path. He placed the box on the coffee table and started the fire.

"John? Is everything okay?" Shae called out as she entered the house. Cat darted in with her and jogged over to him where he was sitting on the floor by the box. "Oh. What are you doing?" She glanced from the box to him sitting cross-legged on the floor.

"Come here. I have something for you." John

picked up the loud rumble and squeak-making cat and let her settle in his lap.

Shae slipped out of her gloves, hat, and coat and came to sit down beside him. She leaned over and he took the kiss she offered. "Why are we on the floor?"

"Well, I did a thing."

She rolled her eyes and nudged him with her shoulder. "The last time you did a thing I was learning how to drive my new truck. Please, tell me you didn't buy me another truck."

He chuckled, "No. Not a truck."

"Well, that's good. So, what *thing* did you do this time?"

He rubbed his hands against his jeans; even though it was cool in the house, he was sweating bullets. He reached for the crate and set it in front of them. Cat leaned forward and sniffed the wood and meowed. "Well, I know what tonight signifies." He lifted the lid and she gasped. He removed the silver menorah and placed it on the coffee table. "I also got these." He lifted out the velvet pouch that held the hand-dipped candles.

"Oh, John. It's beautiful. What a thoughtful gift." Shae lifted the menorah and examined it. "Exquisite."

"Remember that little shop we went through off

Broadway when we were in New York? I called them."

Her eyes glittered when she lifted them to his. He could see the happiness and he prayed that the next set of gifts would be as well received. He dipped his hand back into the crate and retrieved the small box. "I did some research and I found out that two nightly scriptures are read each night of Hanukkah but on the first night a third is read. This blessing."

He handed her the box. Her hand shook as she took it. He caught a small sniffle as her finger traced the words inscribed on the box. "It is perfect." She leaned onto his shoulder and his arm went around her, cradling her to his side.

"Open it." She shot him a quick questioning glance. He nodded to the box. "Please."

Her hands shook as she lifted the hinged lid. She gasped and nearly dropped the box. They both reached for it at the same time and righted it before the contents spilled. She pulled out the Torah and opened it to the front. A child's writing had filled in the dedication page. He assumed she'd done it when she received it.

"How did you get this?" She carefully turned the book over and lifted the back cover. "It's mine."

"I was able to locate your mother. She still had it."

JOHN

He carefully picked it up and handed it to her. "There's one more." He tapped the little wooden lid at the side of the box.

She glanced at him again. "More?"

"Just one more, I promise."

Her fingers shook as she reached into the little box and lifted the small lid. Her hands flew to her face, and the sudden move and gasp she gave startled Cat, sending her skittering into the kitchen.

John lifted the ring and held it between his thumb and forefinger. "Shae, I know we already agreed we'd do this after everything was settled."

She held out her left hand. "Yes! A thousand times, yes!"

John threw back his head and laughed, "You're supposed to let me ask."

"You're too slow. Yes, I'll marry you!" She lifted onto her knees and tackled him, sending them both to the floor. She covered his face in small kisses before he captured her and brought her mouth to his. The connection could have morphed into wonderful sex, but he was going to make sure her night was perfect. He stopped the kiss and glanced at his watch. He slid the ring on her finger. "We only have a few minutes until sunset."

Shae popped off his chest and grabbed the menorah. "Bring the candles. We need to do this by the…" She skidded to a stop and smiled at the table he'd placed in front of the window last night. "You knew."

"I read everything I could find. I tried to get it right."

"You did. Thank you." She lifted on her toes and placed the silver menorah in the middle of the table. He handed her the candles and watched as she celebrated the first night of Hanukkah. Perhaps next year he'd be able to participate with her as her husband. He smiled at the thought of learning her religion and traditions, perhaps blending his into hers and raising children together so they knew and respected both.

She leaned back into his chest and he dropped his arms over her shoulders, crossing them to hug her. "Happy Hanukkah."

"I haven't celebrated it properly in years." She whispered the words and shook her head. "You take away my ability to breathe."

He chuckled, "I like to make you breathless."

She turned in his arms and lifted onto her toes. "When are we getting married?"

"When do you want to?"

"Ummm…" She pulled her bottom lip into her

mouth and worried it. "Can we do something small here on the ranch?"

He narrowed his gaze at her. "From what I've seen, it would be difficult. We could manage if you don't tell a soul. Once Frank and Amanda find out, or the twins, or even Mike, well, things tend to snowball."

"Well then, how about we arrange everything and have them down for a dinner party, only they get a wedding instead? We can do it in the spring. Set up something outside."

"We'll need to find a Rabbi and a priest."

"It couldn't be that hard, could it?"

"I have no idea, but we can figure it out. Together."

"Together. I like that. Perhaps we should practice this togetherness you speak of?" She leaned up and kissed him. This time he lingered in her sweet taste. She pulled away and smiled. "You smell like horses and cattle."

"True. But I thought you liked horses and cattle."

"I do, very much, but I don't want to sleep with them. You go shower, I'll make dinner and open a bottle of wine, then we'll lay in front of the fire and make love."

John closed his eyes and groaned. "If I told you I'm not hungry could we skip the food?"

Shae laughed and he opened one eye to glare at her. She smiled and stepped away from him. "Shower. Come back and find me over there." She looked at the fireplace. "I'll feed Cat for the second or third time today and send her home."

"Deal." He dropped for another long, slow, tantalizing kiss. "Are you sure about that shower?"

She sighed and shook her head. "Yes. I have something I want to slip into for you."

His head kicked back sharply, and he asked, "A purple box delivery?"

She nodded, laughter dancing around in her eyes.

"Be right back." He dropped a fast, hard peck to her lips and jogged down the hall to the bedroom, her laughter following him as he went.

Singing wasn't one of his strong suits—actually, he couldn't carry a tune in a five-gallon bucket, so he whistled through his lightspeed suds and rinse routine. He forewent the boxers and pulled on a clean pair of jeans, commando, leaving the top button undone. The towel he used to dry his hair was still hanging around his neck as he padded his way out to the front room.

The lights were out and Shae had added several

logs to the fire. The room was hot, or at least he thought it was until she walked into the room from the hall bathroom. Then the ambient temperature went into the nuclear zone.

"I couldn't resist." She lifted the see-through, gauzy red material. The bottom trimmed in white fur and the cuffs of the robe were treated the same way, but that only framed the beautiful package inside. A frilly red nightgown made of lace and something that made the tiny skirt flare out hugged her toned, lithe body. The thigh-high white leather boots were what did him in. On anyone else, he'd have rolled his eyes, but on Shae, the spike heels looked like an invitation to a feast of epic desires.

"I want to get you out of that, but I don't want to forget how beautiful you look." He reached for her and pushed the fur collar off her shoulder, leaning down to kiss the skin that covered her shoulder.

"You like it?" Her husky voice rolled to him through a lust-filled haze.

"Love it. Love you." He murmured as he lowered them both to the bearskin rug that he rolled out each year at the first snowfall. With her underneath him, he feasted on her and memorized her body again as if each taste and touch were the first time. He made love to his fiancée, but she was so much more than that. Their bodies combusted in the consuming heat of their shared passion. The sensation of being consumed by her body was too strong to ignore and it required every trick he knew to push back his release and wait for her. Shae's long arms wrapped around him when her body clenched him in wonderous, rippling waves. He followed her into his climax, unable to do anything except luxuriate in her warmth.

Shae pushed his hair away from his sweaty face and traced his eyebrows with her fingers. "I love you, Johnathan. You were my salvation and my destiny. Your strength and kindness gave me the courage to reach out for your hand."

He smiled at her and rolled onto his side, bringing her with him so they were face-to-face on the rug. He extended his hand. "Take my hand, Shae. Walk with me into the best part of our lives."

She laced her fingers through his. "Only with you. Forever, with you."

EPILOGUE

Jeremiah picked up the phone without looking at the caller ID. "Doctor Wheeler."

"Jeremiah, how have you been?"

Gabriel's voice was a pleasant surprise. He cast a glance at the display and smiled. Unknown caller. Like all his calls from Guardian. It was why he didn't bother to look at the display anymore. "Doing well, thank you. To what do I owe this call?" Gabriel didn't just pick up the phone to pass the time of day.

"Just the way I like it, straight to business," Gabriel chuckled.

"I'm not one to let moss grow under my rocks." They both laughed at his corny-ass joke.

"I have a special situation I'm monitoring. I

needed to know what your schedule looks like. The Guardian I'm watching is…"

Jeremiah leaned forward at the silence and asked, "Is he working with Joseph?"

"No. He's a regular operative, although we had him paired up with one of the operatives from Joseph's location, that is until recently. He's offered to tender his resignation, but we haven't accepted it and put him on administrative leave. He's right back in the mess he barely escaped from when he joined the service."

"What is your primary concern?"

"He's a damn good operative. He has a past that makes most of our day-to-day dealings seem like a walk in the park. While in the service he was too close to an IED and sustained some brain damage. He is smart and resourceful, but he has a bad stutter which we overcame with the use of sign language."

"All right." Jeremiah picked up his pen and carded it through his fingers.

"I have a feeling when he comes back to us, he's going to need help."

"Is there anything we can do to help him while he's there?"

"I'm working on that," Gabriel admitted.

"Do we have a timeframe?"

JOHN

"Any day or maybe next year. It depends on a myriad of factors. None that I can manipulate."

"Excuse me, can you repeat that? The all-powerful Gabriel is admitting defeat?"

"Har, har, smart ass. Even I can't cure incurable diseases."

"Damn, someone close to him?"

"Yes and no. He's caring for his mother with cancer and his father, who has dementia. His father was abusive to him and his mother."

"Siblings?"

"Not any relation that would lift a hand to help."

"And he caught your attention how?"

"He's a friend of a friend who has helped us in several situations. Homeland."

"Ah. I can make room. Want me to talk to Doc about a place for this guy to stay?"

"Not yet. Not just yet. I'll let you know if or when he'll be coming up."

"There is doubt?"

"Personal choices are in play. If he is pushed into a situation and makes the wrong decisions, it could be very difficult for anyone to help him."

"Damn. Well, you have my attention. I'll be ready when you call, that is assuming you'll send me his jacket so I can understand everything."

"Of course." Gabriel cleared his throat and added, "I'm glad you said yes when I offered you the position. You've been an integral part of keeping my people safe. Thank you."

"I think we both know I wasn't going back to Lompoc."

"True, but you didn't have to stay in Hollister, either."

Jeremiah smiled. "Yeah, I kinda did."

Gabriel laughed outright. "Okay, you did. You have quite the story to tell your children one day."

"No. They'll never know about what happened."

"There was nothing you could have done differently."

"Still."

"Take care of yourself, my friend."

"I will. Say hi to Anna for me."

"Consider it done." Jeremiah hung up the phone and smiled. The profession he'd chosen had led him down some very dark and twisted roads. He leaned back and stared out of the window and watched the local inhabitants of Hollister, South Dakota, go about their daily business. If someone had told him all those years ago he'd be practicing here in a town of three hundred and forty people while working for one of the most respected federal entities in the country, he'd have committed them for a forty-eight-hour hold, just to make sure they weren't a danger to themselves or others.

Jeremiah stared out the window again. It seemed like only yesterday...

To read more about Doctor Jeremiah Wheeler's story, click here!

ALSO BY KRIS MICHAELS

Kings of the Guardian Series

Jacob: Kings of the Guardian Book 1
Joseph: Kings of the Guardian Book 2
Adam: Kings of the Guardian Book 3
Jason: Kings of the Guardian Book 4
Jared: Kings of the Guardian Book 5
Jasmine: Kings of the Guardian Book 6
Chief: The Kings of Guardian Book 7
Jewell: Kings of the Guardian Book 8
Jade: Kings of the Guardian Book 9
Justin: Kings of the Guardian Book 10
Christmas with the Kings
Drake: Kings of the Guardian Book 11
Dixon: Kings of the Guardian Book 12
Passages: The Kings of Guardian Book 13
Promises: The Kings of Guardian Book 14
The Siege: Book One, The Kings of Guardian Book 15
The Siege: Book Two, The Kings of Guardian Book 16

A Backwater Blessing: A Kings of Guardian Crossover Novella

Montana Guardian: A Kings of Guardian Novella

Guardian Defenders Series

Gabriel

Maliki

John

Jeremiah

Frank

Creed

Sage

Bear

Billy

Elliot

Guardian Security Shadow World

Anubis (Guardian Shadow World Book 1)

Asp (Guardian Shadow World Book 2)

Lycos (Guardian Shadow World Book 3)

Thanatos (Guardian Shadow World Book 4)

Tempest (Guardian Shadow World Book 5)

Smoke (Guardian Shadow World Book 6)

Reaper (Guardian Shadow World Book 7)

Phoenix (Guardian Shadow World Book 8)

Valkyrie (Guardian Shadow World Book 9)

Flack (Guardian Shadow World Book 10)

Ice (Guardian Shadow World Book 11)

Malice (Guardian Shadow World Book 12)

Harbinger (Guardian Shadow World Book 13)

Centurion (Guardian Shadow World Book 14)

Maximus (Guardian Shadow World Book 15)

Hollister (A Guardian Crossover Series)

Andrew (Hollister-Book 1)

Searching for Home (A Hollister-Guardian Crossover Novel)

Zeke (Hollister-Book 2)

Declan (Hollister- Book 3)

A Home for Love (A Hollister Crossover Novel)

Ken (Hollister - Book 4)

Finally Home (A Hollister Crossover Novel)

Barry (Hollister - Book 5)

Hope City

Hope City - Brock

HOPE CITY - Brody- Book 3

Hope City - Ryker - Book 5

Hope City - Killian - Book 8

Hope City - Blayze - Book 10

The Long Road Home

Season One:

My Heart's Home

Season Two:

Searching for Home (A Hollister-Guardian Crossover Novel)

Season Three:

A Home for Love (A Hollister Crossover Novel)

Season Four:

Finally Home (A Hollister Crossover Novel)

STAND-ALONE NOVELS

A Heart's Desire - Stand Alone

Hot SEAL, Single Malt (SEALs in Paradise)

Hot SEAL, Savannah Nights (SEALs in Paradise)

Hot SEAL, Silent Knight (SEALs in Paradise)

Join my newsletter for fun updates and release information!

>>>Kris' Newsletter<<<

ABOUT THE AUTHOR

USA Today and Amazon Bestselling Author, Kris Michaels is the alter ego of a happily married wife and mother. She writes romance, usually with characters from military and law enforcement backgrounds.

Made in United States
Cleveland, OH
27 August 2025